THIS HEART WILL LOVE AGAIN

A Novel

By Dhani Ewing

SOUTH BEACH PUBLISHING

Copyright

Dedication

To Lisa.

This one is for you, and your little girl.

DHANI

x

 Early Winter

Winter is my least favourite season of the four, and to my dismay, it seems to have bypassed autumn earlier than usual but with a biting vengeance for those like me, who dread its arrival.

"Crikey, it's freezing," I mutter to myself, as I rush up the stairs toward the spacious master bedroom, yearning to lose myself under the goose-feather eiderdown.

It's early October and this time last week, I was sat at my favourite seafood restaurant at Sutton Harbour, as the sun's rays dusted my face in its welcoming glow. Now, leaves cling desperately to the trees but soon enough, gnarled branches will battle biting winds and frost until the first flourish of spring returns colour and vibrancy to the world once more, many months from now.

With a shiver, I step into my bedroom and realise I'm a contradiction because although I hate the cold, a warm bedroom is often the cause of a restless sleep and worse, a prickly mood the following day. Usually, I'll turn the thermostat down until I wake at six am, then crank it back up, so the room is warm and toasty for when my husband, Jamie, slides out of bed thirty minutes after I do.

Settling down on the comfy mattress, my mind is taken away to my spiritual home. *Ten weeks*, I tell myself, daydreaming about our annual Christmas vacation to Antigua, part of the Leeward Islands in the Caribbean. I think of crystal clear waters, sun drenched white sandy beaches, coconuts in the palm trees, and the chance to wear a two-piece bikini, but most of all, the chance to relax and recharge my batteries. A smile finds its way to my lips as I wish for the swifter passage of time.

It's the polar opposite to my current predicament of late.

When leaving my house, I'm forced to cover up like I'm about to embark upon an expedition to the Arctic Circle, and that's just getting to the car. Plus, the nights draw in far too early at this time of the year, plunging me into what seems like perpetual darkness, and a mild case of Seasonal Affective Disorder, treated with a therapy lamp that sits on my dressing table.

Spring seems an eternity away, and although I've a lot to be thankful for, it's during these long, drab months of reduced sunlight, I look forward to the solace of my bed, and tonight is no different.

Despite the fact it's only ten pm I slide under eiderdown and release a long sigh, preparing to consign today's shenanigans working at a busy hospital to history.

Instantly, I feel the weight of the world slip from my shoulders. I could easily drift off to sleep, but I won't because there's somebody missing.

My husband, Jamie, isn't home yet, so I point the remote control and switch on the TV. As I snuggle down to watch the latest episode of Virgin River on Netflix my phone vibrates on the bedside cabinet. I pick it up and smile, the same thing I do whenever I think of him. Then there is the familiar fluttering of butterflies in my tummy. *He's still the one.* When our eyes first met across a crowded Concert Square bar in Liverpool twenty years ago, I knew he was the man I would marry. At the time, we were first year students at John Moores University, and what many thought would be a typical teenage romance, destined to fizzle out, turned into our fairy tale.

I push myself up into a sitting position and answer. "Hey, handsome man."

"Hey, angel face." I still get tingles hearing his deep, manly voice.

"How was your day?"

"Boring, tedious, uneventful, pick any one you like," he groans, which tells me he's had enough and just wants to be home and back in comfortable surroundings. "I've missed you, but I'll be home in about an hour."

"I've missed you too."

"What are you doing?"

"I just climbed into bed but won't go to sleep until you're home."

"It's late, so don't wait up if you're too tired. I'll try not to disturb you when I get home."

"I don't mind." There hasn't been a time since our wedding night eighteen years ago that I hadn't kissed him goodnight and told him I loved him—it wasn't a habit I was about to change now. "Have you eaten?" I know what he's going to say before he says it.

"Yeah," he replies. "I bought a sandwich from Subway earlier on."

He can't see my eye roll, and although I'm not the type to nag, junk food has never sustained or satisfied my big bear of a man who has the biggest appetite and annoyingly, never gains weight, no matter how much food he shovels in. Me on the other hand; I only have to look at a chocolate eclair and gain ten pounds, not that he'd care because regardless of my size, as long as I'm healthy, I know he still fancies me. "There's some leftover stew in the fridge from last night. I'll re-heat it and warm some fresh rolls up in the oven too."

"You don't have to fuss, Serena." It's his way of saying, yes please.

"It's no bother, Jamie, and I have some freshly made pickled red cabbage if you want that too?" Whatever he says, I know he appreciates me taking care of him. Not that he isn't independent and can't look after himself, he can and better than most. He's old-fashioned in a lot of ways and likes simple food; nothing spicy, or too adventurous, so the less faffing in the kitchen the better as far as he's concerned. I often suggest something out of the ordinary, a Thai Green Curry, Enchiladas, perhaps, but he repeats the same mini-speech every time. It used to irritate me, but now it's part and parcel of who he is, and I wouldn't change that for the world. "Meat and veg was good enough for me growing up, so it's good enough for me now."

He's only just turned thirty-eight, but his past is never far from his present. His modest childhood forged the man he is today. Coming from a loving, supportive family, but one that had little in the way of money or food, every meal counted. He ate whatever was put in front of him and remained grateful for it because he knew the alternative would be little else.

Despite struggling, as many did back then, my wonderful in-laws raised the perfect gentleman. Jamie is unfailingly kind and considerate, adorable, selfless and makes me feel beautiful every single day. Yes, he has what many would see as strange ways, but I accept every facet of his personality. His simplicity keeps us grounded and whatever I can do to ensure he feels special, I'll do, even down to something simple like re-heating his favourite meal. After a hard day in meetings with company accountants, it's the least I can do.

"You're too good to me." He is always appreciative of my efforts, no matter how miniscule they may seem. "I must have been good in my previous life to deserve a wife like you."

His words touch me because they come from a place of truth. "I know and you can thank me for being so wonderful later on."

"Oh, yeah," he replies, his voice dropping a few octaves to a throaty growl. "And how do you suppose I do that?"

"I can think of about ten different ways."

"Absolute filth," he jokes. I can picture his lop-sided smirk as naughty thoughts invade his mind.

"You love it."

"Just being next to you is enough for me, Serena. I love you."

"And I love you too, Jamie, more than life itself." I swing my legs out of bed. "I'll go and sort the food so it's ready for when you get here."

"Shall I stop off somewhere for a few bottles of wine?"

"Yes, that would be lovely." I don't often drink during the week but a crappy day like today on shift at the local hospital has dimmed my spark somewhat, so when the mood takes me, I enjoy a nice glass or two of Rosé.

"Once I've eaten, we can take the wine up to the bedroom and try out some of those things you've got me thinking about."

"You have it all planned, don't you?"

"Well, yes, but first things first…"

"Go on…"

"Can you put four of those bread rolls in the oven, I'm starving?"

I chuckle and shake my head, unsurprised by his request. "Typical man, always thinking of your stomach."

"I'm recharging my batteries for the night ahead, so I need all the fuel I can get."

"I'll put eight in then," I joke, knowing he could still scoff the lot and go back for another helping.

"Cheeky! Look, I'm about to come off the motorway, so I'll call you from the shop and tell you what they have—though I don't think they're going to have anything spectacular on offer."

"It's okay, darling, you choose for us. Just get home as fast as you can, so I can give you a big kiss."

"Will do. See you soon, angel face." In all the years we've known one another, his pet-name for me has never changed. "I love you," he tells me once more.

"Love you too. Drive safely." I end the call, slip into my fluffy dressing gown, step into what he calls old-lady slippers, and make my way down the winding staircase to our newly-fitted kitchen.

Glancing about, I realise how blessed I am because we live in the most spectacular of properties. We're not saddled with a mortgage, nor do we have to deal with noisy or nosey neighbours. The grounds around our home are beautifully landscaped and maintained. We have everything we want, well nearly—the only thing missing in our lives is children. Sadly, it wasn't meant to be.

Suffering from Endometriosis, conceiving a child of our own proved too difficult for me, and while our marriage went from strength to strength despite this particular setback in our lives, I know we both ask ourselves that same question—what if?

We could have adopted, in fact, we discussed it for many years, but our lives took another turn. With Jamie's successful yet demanding business profile on the rise, I continued my training to become a nurse, eventually climbing to the position of Matron. Life took over, and as the years passed by, we relished the time we got to spend together, and gradually, talks of children became infrequent and the stuff of pipe dreams.

What if? I ask myself again, knowing we're still young enough to raise a family of our own. Then I realise there's little point dwelling on things I cannot change and shift my focus to the task at hand.

I open the larder-style fridge and reach for the Tupperware container then empty the stew into a pan, setting it on a low heat.

The aroma of comfort food soon fills the cavernous kitchen. I'm a little peckish too, but I've eaten already and won't indulge. Still, it doesn't stop me sampling a small taste as I stir it slowly. It's not long before I want more and dunk a lump of fresh bread into warming food. When I'm finished, I turn on the fan oven to pre-heat.

While I wait, I tend to the fire in the living room and make sure the room is toasty for Jamie's return. Glancing at the clock, time has flown. He'll be close by.

"Bread," I remind myself, as I rush back into the kitchen and place eight bread rolls on a greaseproof paper-lined baking tray and slide it into the oven.

Ten minutes later, the stew is ready, and I take the rolls out of the oven.

Glancing at the clock again, it's ten forty pm. The doorbell sounds. "Good timing," I shout as I rush to the door. He's forgotten his keys again. "You'd forget your own head if it wasn't attached..." Pulling the door open, I'm confronted by two uniformed police officers. "Oh..." My heartbeat picks up a pace as my stomach lurches. "Can I help you?"

"Are you Mrs Serena Tate?"

"Yes, that's me." Glancing past them, I note the patrol car outside my gate. "I'm Serena." Terror swells deep within me. "Is anything wrong?"

They hold up their identification, but I barely offer a glance whereas I should be more cautious.

"I'm PC. George Luck, and this is my colleague, PC. Alistair O'Donnell." After scrutinising their badges to confirm they are who he says they are, I hold my breath, not ready for whatever is coming next. "Are you married to a Mr Jamie Tate?"

"Yes, I am." I detect the tremor in my voice.

"Could we come in for a moment?"

"Erm, yes." I stand aside and gesture for them to step inside. "First door on the left, please make yourself comfortable."

"Thank you," PC. Luck says as both walk past me and into the living room.

"Just give me one moment to turn the food off." I know I've already done it, but I dash into the kitchen anyway and take the opportunity to grab my phone from the table. Hitting redial, I'm relieved when the call connects. "Come on, Jamie," I urge, my voice barely a whisper. "Answer the bloody phone." Panic rises as I hear his familiar voicemail greeting. But it's only a recording and not him. I wait impatiently for the beep and speak. "Hiya, love, it's only me, just checking in to see if you're okay? Call me as soon as you get this message, please."

"Mrs Tate." I turn to find both officers standing at the door.

"I'm just calling my husband to see how long it will be before he gets home."

PC. O'Donnell takes the lead. "Could we sit down at the table for a moment? There's something we need to discuss with you."

I switch to hostess mode and take the pan off the halogen hob and rest it on the draining board. My actions make no sense, but the little things are stopping me from absorbing bigger issues. I don't want to sit down. "I've made a lovely pan of stew, would you both care for a bowl?"

"No, thank you," PC. O'Donnell replies with a smile.

"Mrs Tate, please." PC. Luck speaks up. His voice is soft and melodic with an Irish lilt to it.

I turn and lock eyes with him. Blinking rapidly, tears suddenly cascade down my cheeks. "I don't want you to say it."

"I'm sorry to–"

I hold my hand up and interrupt before he can finish. "I told you I don't want you to say it." My tone is harsh. "Not that, not now, not ever." I hold my head in my hands, knowing in seconds my blissful existence is about to come crashing down around me.

"Your husband was involved in an incident earlier on and–"

I turn to look out of the window but can see nothing in the darkness. I lean on the countertop, allowing it to take every ounce of my weight. Then I hear a terrible strangulated sound followed by a feeling of searing pain in my chest. "NO, NO, NO, NO, NO!" I scream, frightening myself into the realisation I am that noise. "He's not..." I bring the palms of my hands crashing down onto the cold marble. A pool of blood tells me I've hurt myself, but I only feel numb.

PC. Luck rushes over to inspect the deep cut to the palm of my hand. "Mrs Tate, are you okay?"

"I'm fine." I wrench my hand away and wrap a tea towel around the wound. "My husband will patch me up when he– when he..." My voice trails into nothingness.

"Mrs Tate, your husband is still alive, but we need to get you to the hospital right away."

Suddenly there is a glimmer of hope in the whirlwind of misery I've been thrust into. "I spoke to him earlier and he was fine. In fact, he'll be home soon, he's just stopping off for wine." I can't reconcile what I know should be happening and what I am being told.

"Your husband was badly injured following a raid on the off-licence on Wallis Street, and while Paramedics attended the scene fairly quickly, they were unable to revive him."

"Oh, God!" I raise my eyes and send a silent prayer. *Please, Lord, don't take him away from me.* "You said he was alive."

"He is, but it doesn't look good. The doctors can tell you more once we get you to the hospital."

Denial fights its way to the surface. If I tell myself it's not him, it won't be. "No, no, you've definitely got the wrong person," I say, almost excitedly. "Jamie never goes to that place on Wallis Street—ever."

"There is no question as to Mr Tate's identity," PC. O'Donnell adds. "It is your husband. We are certain of it."

"Where is he?"

"The Royal, it's not too far from here."

"I'm a Matron there. If Jamie had been brought in, somebody would have called me already. You've got the wrong man."

PC. Luck speaks up. "I wish that were the case, but sadly we identified your husband at the scene using his credit cards and driving licence."

"Oh, God." The room spins but I can't lose it, not now.

"We would like to get you there as soon as possible, Mrs Tate."

"I have to get dressed and call his parents."

"Okay, we'll wait down here for you."

I dash out of the kitchen and up the stairs into our bedroom. "Where's my phone?" It's in my hand. Scrolling, I find my father-in-law's number and press dial. It rings for a few seconds then he answers. "Hello, Jimmy, is that you?"

"Serena, it's late for you to be calling. Are you okay?"

"Jamie has been in an accident." I hadn't meant to blurt it out so tactlessly, but I can't seem to think straight.

I hear him gasp and Miriam, my mother-in-law, in the background asking what is wrong. "Is he okay?"

"What's going on Jimmy?" Her shaky tone conveys worry.

"Miriam, please, let me talk to Serena and find out. Go on…"

"All I know is, there was some sort of accident, and he was taken to the Royal—will you meet me there?"

"Yes, yes, get dressed, Miriam, our Jamie has been hurt."

"Oh, my God," I hear her cry out in the background.

"The police are here now and waiting to drive me there."

"Keep your phone with you and I'll call you as soon as we get there."

"I'll see you there, and Jimmy…"

"Yes?"

"Jamie is going to be fine."

"Course he will, poppet."

I end the call and pull a clean pair of jeans and a turtleneck jumper out of the wardrobe, then make my way back down to the kitchen.

Chapter Two

Reality Bites

In silence, I sit in the back of the patrol car. Lost in a loop of what ifs and utter disbelief, it feels like the longest journey I've ever taken, and while there are questions I want to ask, there are no words, only thoughts of Jamie holding me tightly and reassuring me that he is okay.

"We're here," PC. O'Donnell announces, turning in his seat as PC. Luck slows the car to a stop outside the Accident and Emergency Department I've walked in and out of thousands of times over the years.

Suddenly I'm overwhelmed with a feeling of dread. "Thank you for bringing me."

It isn't like this on TV shows, or maybe it is, and I've never paid that much attention before now.

PC. Luck opens the rear door then holds out his hand. "Please, allow me to help you."

I take hold knowing I can't do it alone. One mis-step and I'll fall flat on my face. "You are very kind."

"PC. O'Donnell and I are going to take you straight through to your husband, and just so you know, a doctor is there and waiting to talk to you."

"Thank you." What else am I supposed to say? I briefly wonder who it will be. I know most of the staff in the place. "Your parents must be proud to have raised such lovely boys."

Both nod their thanks.

"Follow me." PC. O'Donnell closes the driver side door and walks ahead of us.

I'm whisked straight through the accident and emergency department but take nothing and nobody in as I'm guided past faces that are only a blur. That smell all hospitals have, and one that I deal with daily, churns my stomach and I want to throw up. Suddenly, I feel weak and unable to go any further. "I can't…"

"We've got you." PC. Luck holds me at the elbow while PC. O'Donnell holds the other.

I've never been good at small talk, so why start now? I just need to see Jamie, to tell him I love him. He will know I'm there. "What if he's dead?" I don't want to allow doubts to creep in, but what if it's too late to say goodbye? "Is it too late?" Every fear seems ready to come to pass.

"Just around this corner and you can speak to the doctor, then your hand needs looking at."

I know exactly where he is taking me. I could navigate this hospital with my eyes closed. "I'll be fine, it's just a little cut." The double doors ahead of us open automatically and I step into a world of hurried activity and endless beeping from machines ventilating patients. I struggle to focus, then remember Jimmy and Miriam are on their way. "Gosh, my in-laws, I need to let them know where I am, but I can't use my phone in here."

"Give me their number. I'll call them for you." I offer a weak smile at PC. O'Donnell, grateful for his help.

Another police officer approaches. I note the pitiful expression on his face, and the fact he doesn't want to look directly at me.

"Mrs Tate, this is my colleague, PC. Miller."

He acknowledges me. "Ma'am."

"Is the doctor waiting?" I ask.

"Yes, but he is speaking with his team right now." He turns to me and takes my elbow. "Mrs Tate, if it is okay with you, I can take you through to your husband while you wait for the Doctor."

I turn to look at the two officers who brought me here and mouth the words, *thank you*.

With a nod of their heads, they turn away.

I'm guided through another set of doors. "Where is he?"

"Just through here."

I step into a familiar world where machines breathe for those who can no longer do it for themselves and look at the person lying on the bed to the left of me. Professional mode kicks in and I look at what is displayed on the screen. I'm sad because there is no hope for the poor soul. *What a mess*, I think to myself. His face is bloodied, but I spot the swelling and purple mottled skin underneath the heavy gauze. The top of his head is covered by a thick bandage, but blood has seeped through already.

"Mrs Tate?" An older man in a white coat approaches.

"Yes," I reply, wondering where Jamie is.

"My name is Doctor Latchford, and I am treating your husband."

I know him by reputation though it's my first time meeting him. "Where is my husband?" I ask.

A confused expression sits on his face. "Your husband is right there, Mrs Tate." He points to the man in the bed behind me.

I shake my head in disbelief. "That's not my husband." My voice cracks. "No, that's not him, you've got the wrong person."

"Mr Tate has suffered severe facial injuries, and trauma to the top and back of his head." He speaks matter of fact, like most doctors do when delivering bad news.

I turn slowly, but I don't see the man I married. Then, I spot something I recognise; the band of gold I slipped onto his finger on our wedding day. "Jamie..." My words are hitched in my throat.

"Mrs Tate, would you like to sit next to your husband, and I can discuss what is happening."

"Why is he hooked up to all these machines?"

"Your husband is still alive but is no longer breathing of his own volition."

"He's on life support?"

"That is correct."

"Why?"

"Because your husband is unable to breathe unaided, so the machines are doing it for him."

As a trained nurse, I know the answers before he speaks and hope for something different. I'm on auto-pilot and it's not lost on me that I'm behaving like a machine too. "How long before he wakes up?" I'm ushered toward a brown plastic chair and take a seat though I don't realise another nurse is inspecting the wound to my hand until the tea towel it is wrapped in is caught on skin as they try to remove it. I flinch but whatever pain I feel is not important. "Tomorrow? The day after, when?"

"We have more tests to complete before a definitive prognosis is provided, but I believe your husband has suffered brain stem death and will not regain consciousness." He takes a moment as my world collapses around me. "Without advanced life support, Mr Tate would slip away peacefully."

I hear his words but don't take in their full meaning. Clinging onto hope, or lost in a river of denial, I speak. "So maybe tomorrow he'll open his eyes?"

Doctor Latchford kneels next to the chair I'm sitting in and takes my other hand. "Mrs Tate, I know this is hard for you to hear but Jamie's injuries are severe and if he were to wake, he wouldn't be the man he was before the accident."

"But you can help him, right?"

"I don't believe that is the case, and as much as I want to give you hope, if Jamie were to survive the removal of life support, he would require care for the rest of his natural life, and that would include you bathing him, seeing to his toilet needs, feeding him through a tube..."

"People have recovered from worse than this before."

"Jamie's head injuries are severe and extensive, and it is my belief he suffered catastrophic brain damage—I need you to understand what that means."

"I do understand." Snapping, my words come out as a growl. Admitting to the possibility of losing him crushes me like a ten ton weight. As a trained nurse I've stood by helplessly while family members have hope ripped from them. This situation is not something I ever envisioned for myself.

"There is something I need to discuss with you, Mrs Tate."

"What?"

"When your husband was brought in a little earlier, we found his donor card."

I hold my hand up to silence him. I don't want to hear what he needs to say. "No, I'm not having this conversation with you, not now, not ever."

"It is your husband's wish to donate his organs to others who are in need of them."

"*He* needs them." I fight to hold onto my temper because Jamie is still alive and already, vultures are circling, wanting to take parts of him away and dish them out like treats at a Halloween party.

"Mrs Tate..."

"My name is Serena."

"Okay, then, if you wish, Serena, you are one of our most experienced nurses and know his prognosis as well as I do— the chances of your husband regaining consciousness are virtually nil, and if by some small miracle he does wake up, the man left behind would rely on you for everything."

"In sickness and in health, Doctor, and if that means I care for him until his dying breath, I'll gladly do it."

"Your husband has suffered extensive injuries he can never recover from and there is no way back from that."

"With respect, you don't know everything."

"I agree, and I wish there was another way that we could bring him back, but the man you married is gone and deep down you know that."

The beeping from the machine is incessant. Every beep and my eyes seem to flicker. While I've become so accustomed to them as part of my working life, on the other side of the fence, it means one thing; that Jamie is still alive. "Then why is he still breathing?" Again, I'm asking questions I know the answers to because I'm not ready to admit I've lost him.

"The machines are doing that for him."

"Jamie would never leave me." I close my eyes and send a silent prayer to God. "He promised I would get to go first. That's always been the deal and he never lied to me."

"I am so sorry, Serena. I wish things were different, truly I do."

"It's not his time."

"Talk to Jamie, let him know you're here, you know as well as I do, he can still hear you."

This time, I allow his words to sink in and know exactly what they mean. Jamie isn't in a coma as such because his brain is already dead. His vital organs are only working through artificial means. "Can you leave us alone, but dim the lights before you go?"

"Of course." I find pity in his kind eyes. He nods to his team, and they exit the room one by one.

The room is cleared, and the lights are dimmed. Jamie preferred lamplight, or candles and though his eyes are closed I want to make him as comfortable as possible. When things are as I know he would like it, I take a seat next to him and hold my hand in his.

"Well, what are we going to do about this mess?" I ask, waiting and willing for him to speak. "You promised you would never leave me behind, and now look, you're lying there in that bed without a care in the world, and the one time I need an answer from you, you can't give it." I kiss the top of his hand. "I don't even know if you're still in there or if you can hear me, but I need to say this to you…" Tears fall that I cannot stop, and I'm robbed of words I so desperately want to speak. Taking a moment, I find the strength to carry on. "I love you, always have, and always will." I look up to see the screen monitoring his bodily functions and know what every reading means. "And though it breaks my heart to let you go, I promise to honour your last wish." For some reason I shake my head and chuckle because he always puts the needs of others first. "Why am I not surprised you want to do this?" I kiss his hand once more then hold it close to my cheek, treasuring his touch and knowing it will all too soon become a distant memory. "You are the kindest man I know, Jamie, and while I have to face a world without you in it, knowing your selflessness will give others the chance to live, how can I be sad?" I try to remain positive, but I can't and sob as his parents, Jimmy, and Miriam, enter the room.

I use what strength I have left to stand and fall into my mother-in-law's arms. I feel Jimmy's hand resting on my back.

"I'm so sorry, my darling girl," Miriam says bravely through her own anguish. She's losing her son and still comforts me. I cling to her for support and hold my hand out to my father-in-law, but his bloodshot eyes are fixated on his stricken son.

"What happened, Serena?" There is anger behind his words. "We've spoken to Doctor Latchford, but we still don't know how he's in here like this."

I look into his eyes. I don't know the intricacies either but tell him what I can. "Somebody hurt him is all I know, but he's not suffering."

"Who would want to hurt my boy?" At my urging, Miriam takes the seat next to Jamie's bed and holds his hand.

"The police will tell us what we need to know when we're ready to speak with them."

"Latchford said he won't wake up." Jimmy appears cold in his response but it's his way of coping. I've seen it before with patients' families, like emotional shutters coming down to protect them from further heartbreak.

"I should give you both time with him alone."

"You don't have to do that, darling." Miriam reaches out for me. "There are things we need to talk about."

"He's your son, Miriam, and you're both entitled to say your goodbyes."

"Stay," Jimmy orders. "He needs us all together right now."

"Have you spoken to Helena and Ben?" I ask, thinking of Jamie's beloved siblings.

"Yes," Jimmy answers. "I called them on the drive over here."

"Both on their way, so whatever decision you make, please allow them the chance to get here and say their goodbyes too."

"Of course, but while we wait, I'll go and get us all a coffee."

"That sounds nice, love." Miriam is holding herself together, but I know it's an act.

"Yes, why don't you do that, Serena," Jimmy snaps. "A nice strong cup of coffee is just the thing that will bring our son back to us."

Miriam's expression speaks for itself. She's angry with him, but he's entitled to speak his mind, no matter how skewed his thoughts are right now. "That is quite enough from you, Alexander." Born Alexander James, she only uses his given name when he's stepped too far out of line.

"I'm sorry, Serena, I didn't mean to upset you, either of you." I reach out for him, but he turns away. "No…"

"I'm holding on by a thread here, and if I'm honest, I don't know what to say or do."

"He's hurting and doesn't mean it, Serena."

"I'm losing the love of my life…" I don't want to cry in front of them and press my hands against my mouth, desperate to stop grief from exploding from me like molten lava. I turn to leave the room, but Jimmy reaches forward and pulls me back.

"Serena, wait, please."

"What?"

"I'm so sorry."

He holds me tight.

I know there is more he wants to say but words fail him.

Instead, a harrowing sound fills the room as father prepares to say farewell to the son he adores.

Chapter Three

Say Goodbye

I've spent the last few hours with Jimmy, Miriam, Helena, and Ben, just talking out loud to Jamie, sharing memories, telling him how much he means, everything he already knows of course. But this is as much for us as for him though it doesn't lessen the dark void creeping into my existence.

"Do you remember our first dance? You tried everything to get out of it, but you still did it, just for me." Casting my mind back to the white wedding dress I had no business wearing. But I felt so beautiful in it along with all the finery, I didn't care that I wasn't a virgin. It's still hanging in my walk-in-wardrobe.

Helena's mouth turns up at the sides. She's replaying happier times and memories of that special day that now seems so far away. "Oh, he hated having to dance in front of all those people." There is happiness laced with loss in her tone, everything the look in her eyes conveys without the spoken word. "But Dad told him it was your day, and he would regret it if he didn't." She looks to her father crying next to her.

"Jamie never let me down, not ever."

"It's not fair." Ben chokes on his words. He can't take that same trip to better days. Usually, he's the joker in the room and now, he's a shadow of the man who has treated me like a beloved sister since the day we first met. He's eight years younger than Jamie and is single with no kids of his own but one day he will make the most fantastic husband and father. "We had so many plans, a trip to Yosemite and the Grand Canyon, canoeing down the Amazon, and now, because of that bastard..." His words trail off because he doesn't want to engulf himself with anger though every single person gathered would understand. "…sorry…"

"You can still go, son." Miriam holds onto his hand that little bit tighter, but he barely registers a mother's touch. "Visit all the places you spoke about. Your Dad and I would love to see the pictures."

His eyes find hers and in a touching gesture he leans in to kiss her cheek. "Without him, it wouldn't be the same."

"I'll go with you," Helena volunteers. "If you want me to."

"You, camping?" Ben's shocked expression makes us all, except Jimmy, laugh. "That I'd pay good money to see."

She feigns offense because she knows of all the people assembled in the room, she is least likely to canoe up the Amazon, though something tells me she would do it with aplomb. "I can slum it with the best of 'em, you know."

"I'll believe that when I see it," Ben teases, but still reaches out to hold onto her hand. "Princess Helena sleeping amongst spiders and other creepy crawlies, behave yourself."

"Just you wait and see, smart arse. I'll show you—"

Jimmy bangs his hand against the door, startling us all back to reality. Usually a quiet man, his raised voice is totally out of place. "Why are you all carrying on as though life will ever be normal again, huh? What's the point in any of it?"

"Jimmy, don't do this now," Miriam urges. "We all deal with things differently, and this is their way."

He doesn't listen and carries on with his rant. "*My* son is lying right there…" he points, "…brain dead, a fucking vegetable, and nothing will ever be the same again, so keep laughing and joking but no matter what plans you make, my kind, remarkable, precious boy is gone."

Miriam crosses the room and holds her arms out to him. "That's enough, Jimmy."

He turns down her offer of an embrace. "No, Miriam…"

"Now is not the time. You know he might hear you."

"Jamie is gone for Christ's sake, so why should I keep my mouth shut?" She grips the top of his arms, but any reasoning he usually has is diminished by pain and loss.

It shatters me to see him in so much agony.

"Don't do this to yourself," she pleads.

"It should be me lying there, not him. It's not right—"

Helena wipes her eyes with the sleeve of her jacket and speaks up. "Dad, please...Mum is right..."

"I should be the one to go first, not any of my children."

"Jimmy, please..." I can't bear to witness him torture himself like this but there is nothing right when a parent outlives a child.

He's too far gone to stop now, and while I don't blame him, Miriam is right, and the timing is off.

"In a few minutes, those, those..." He gathers himself to say what needs to be said, "...whatever you want to call them, will come to harvest his organs and then what? What are we left with aside from—"

Helena interrupts him, and for the first time I see inner strength shining through. "Dad, it's what Jamie would have wanted."

"And what about what I want, Helena, huh? What about the fact I don't want to lose my oldest child, that I don't want him lying there with his head caved in. Do I get what I want?" His outburst seems to rob him of all energy, and he falls silent.

"This isn't Helena's fault," Miriam warns as chinks in her armour appear. "Nobody in this room is to blame for what happened."

Ben seems worried by the turn in events but there isn't a right or wrong way to behave when all is said and done. Emotions are at breaking point, there is no soundtrack to life because without Jamie we're left with an endless winter. "Mum's right, Dad."

"I don't want to hear it right now, Ben, okay."

"I'm allowed to have my say—"

"Not right now, Benjamin," Jimmy hisses unfairly.

"Yes, Dad—"

We're all on edge but my anger spills over at this despicable mess on display. "Show some bloody respect, all of you." I've never spoken this way to the nearest and dearest people in my life and it shows in their shocked expressions. The room is suddenly quiet aside from the background noise of the machines and ventilator working tirelessly. I turn to look at my stricken husband and speak my truth. "Do you think the last thing Jamie wants to hear is his family at war with one another?" I direct my question to Jimmy because he instigated this. "Well, Jimmy, do you?"

He's rendered speechless for a moment then shakes his head, while biting his lip. After a few seconds he finds the words he needs to say. "I'm sorry...all of you. Please forgive me, I don't mean to be—"

"I don't want any apologies, just some well-earned dignity for my husband."

"We're sorry." Miriam takes Jimmy's hand. "Come on, love, we need to keep it together, just for a little while longer, okay." She has the strength of a Trojan warrior. It inspires me and for a moment I wish I could remain as stoic as she. "Let's just get through this, for Jamie, okay."

I've spoken my mind but need them to hear my words while I still have the strength to speak them. "We all love Jamie, and not one of us wants to be in this position, but we have two choices here, fight amongst ourselves, or stay strong for one another because what comes next is going to be the hardest for us all to bear."

"I don't think I can do it," Ben adds, and suddenly I'm reminded how much he looks like his older brother. "I don't want to be in here when they take him away."

"I can't either." Helena holds onto Ben for support.

"There is no written rule." I've said these same words to so many families, and now I'm saying it to my own. "Do what feels right for you."

"I want to say goodbye to him, in private, if you don't mind, Serena."

"He's your brother, Ben, and if that's what you want, you have my blessing." Being an only child, I don't know how it feels for him to have to see whatever is coming. I'm just thankful he has the chance to say what he needs to say before it's too late. "I can stall the team for a bit to give you and Helena time with Jamie."

"Would you mind..." Helena's eyes are red-ringed from crying. "...if I stay too?"

"You don't have to ask because he adored both of you."

Miriam takes the lead in uncharted waters. "Come on, Jimmy, we'll go and get some fresh air with Serena and leave these two with their brother." She opens her arms and holds them both for a moment then turns toward the door.

Silently, Jimmy and I follow, and with another look at Jamie, we close the door behind us.

"Will they be okay alone?" I ask.

"No," Jimmy adds, abruptly, "but it's what they want."

My question was purely out of concern and no way was it meant to come across as though I objected to them spending time with Jamie.

Wanting to avoid being caught in another storm, Miriam cuts in. "I need a drink."

Silently, I thank her for stepping in. "This way then."

Walking along the corridor, life carries on as various medical professionals dart from room to room. I feel empty inside and while I don't say anything, there is relief I'm not in the room with Ben and Helena because dealing with my own broken heart is testing my resolve.

Standing outside Jamie's room as Jimmy and Miriam say their goodbyes, Doctor Langford approaches. "Are you ready, Serena?" He holds the clipboard with the relevant paperwork attached. *No, I'm not bloody ready, you twat.* It's a stupid question to ask because when would anyone ever be ready to sign the document that brings the curtain down on somebody that is precious to them?

"No but give them to me anyway." Taking them from him, I scrawl my signature then close my eyes and pray, hoping somehow God will allow him to hear my words. *Please don't hate me because I did it out of love.* Langford has my permission. It's done, just the way Jamie wanted it.

The door opens and the first people I see are Miriam and Jimmy. Tears fall, and for a second or two, I wonder if they will ever dry. Nothing is said.

Earlier on, they decided it would be too hard to escort Jamie on his final journey and I had to respect that, even if I worried it would be something both would come to regret somewhere along life's highway.

For me, leaving him now is unthinkable. These will be the last steps I shall ever take with him. I'll take them willingly, and alone.

"The team will be here shortly, Serena." His job is not one I would ever want, and while I wish there was more he could do for my husband, I am thankful he is overseeing these final moments and affording Jamie the dignity he deserves.

"I understand, Doctor."

"I'll be back soon." Uncharacteristically for any senior medical professional on duty, and maybe because I am one of them, he envelops me in his arms. It's a magical moment I will never forget. "If you need me before then, please have one of the nurses come and find me."

"Thank you."

I turn and am surprised to see Ben and Helena approach.

Their heads are bowed and neither seem to want to look inside the room.

"Do you need more time with Jamie?"

"No thanks, we've only come for Mum and Dad," Helena replies while Ben remains silent. Her voice wavers because she thought she'd done the hard part, and now she's faced with that terrible moment again, turning her back and walking away knowing it is the last time she will be close to him while he still breathes, albeit artificially.

"Okay."

She looks into my eyes, and I see the depth of sorrow. "There's so much I want to say and do, to help you, but I-I..."

"He's your brother and loves you both..." I take a few moments to focus on taking my next breath. "Jamie was and is immensely proud of the wonderful people you are, remember that."

This time, it's me that opens my arms. We embrace. I need their strength though they have none to share.

"Kiss him goodbye for us," Jimmy requests as he leads Miriam out of the room. "He knows we love him, but tell him again, please."

"I will." Without warning, he pulls me close as his chest heaves with a sob I know he's tried and failed to hold in check. I squeeze him tight, wanting to reassure him in any way that I can but this is uncharted territory for us all. "Jamie's not in pain, nor is he suffering, and we have to be at peace with that." I speak brave words when all I want to do is run away, hide, and shut the world out. Like a child, if I can't see it, it isn't happening. But it is. "I'll come and find you in a while, but if you need to go on ahead, I can get a taxi home."

"Nonsense," Miriam adds clutching onto Jimmy for support. "Besides, where would we go?"

"We'll be waiting in the chapel if that's okay?" Ben adds. They are the first words he's spoken since his own goodbye to Jamie. Helena nods then lowers her head again. "Then, if you don't mind, could we all come back to yours with you?"

"You are always welcome at our house." It's a slip up because Jamie will never return. "I love you all, never forget that. We are *still* family and *always* will be." I turn away before I lose the courage I've somehow held onto. What I wouldn't give for just one more day, to hear Jamie say something, anything, to tell me he loves me. Instead, an empty silence fills the space.

I watch with sorrow as the four of them walk away.

Briefly, Miriam stops and turns back. Her eyes are wide, her skin pale, but it's the quivering lip that almost pushes me over the edge into the abyss. "Look after my baby, please."

"I will."

The transplant team are standing at the far end of the corridor but remain courteous and wait for Jamie's family to enter the lift before they approach.

Doctor Latchford re-appears and places a hand on my shoulder, his gentle voice and touch reassuring. "It's time, Serena."

I look down at Jamie, hoping and praying I'm doing the right thing. "Okay."

"Are you ready?"

"No, I will never be ready, but I have to do what is right for him."

"I'll be with you every single step of the way, Serena."

I nervously observe proceedings as Jamie is prepared for the journey to the ground floor operating theatres. The members of the team are methodical, and everything is done quickly, respectfully and with minimal fuss.

"Let's go," Doctor Langford decrees.

Walking behind Jamie as he is wheeled toward the lift, I focus on the swathe of bandages wrapped around his head, then I pinch myself, desperate to wake from what I want to believe is a terrible nightmare.

The lift doors close. After thirty seconds and with a small ding, they open once more into the brightly lit corridor that leads to the numerous operating theatres.

Doctor Latchford steps out first, then Jamie is wheeled out after. Seconds later, Betty, a colleague and friend, approaches. My feet don't seem to want to move.

She takes my hands in hers. We've both been here before with patients' families but this time it's personal. "I wanted to come, Serena." She's an older nurse I've worked with many times before. "I couldn't bear the thought of you doing this last part alone."

"I-I..." I try to speak but nothing I say will make a difference anyway. The wheels are in motion, and when we reach the end of this corridor the man I know, and love, will be gone forever. "I'm not ready to say goodbye to him."

She presses her finger on the button that holds the doors open. "Nobody ever is, darling, but this is what Jamie wants, focus on that for now."

I think of the few times Jamie and I discussed what would happen if one of us was to go before the other and know I'm doing the right thing. "Go, now," I whisper. "Before I change my mind."

She nods her approval and with a gentle push, the gurney moves into the light. I follow close behind but am stopped in my tracks as Betty slows down to acknowledge what is happening. It takes a moment for me to realise, then a lump forms in my throat as I see the white-walled corridor lined on both sides with colleagues, most I know from my years of service within the National Health Service, some I don't, but all have come to pay respects to a man who will help countless others in death. It means more to me than I can ever say, but once again, words fail me.

"Oh, Jamie, they're all here for you." I choke out my words and while what I say is mostly true, I know their attendance is for me too, to show they stand in solidarity with one of their own. I wipe my eyes as I pass the faces I recognise, and the others I don't. Some reach out to take my hand briefly. I see sympathy in their eyes and know I'm not alone. It's a tender and touching moment, and one I hadn't expected. But as well-meaning as it is, the moment is too raw for me to express any gratitude verbally. Physical pain kicks my arse and I feel like I'm being ripped in two–a part of me is screaming to stop the madness while it fights against the other part to let him go. *Let it be Serena.* To keep him alive by machine is cruel. Freeing his soul from torment is the last kindness I can give him. "Thank you, all," I finally whisper as we glide past.

We've reached the doors to the operating theatre.

The transplant team are inside and waiting.

It's time.

Betty steps aside and holds my hand in hers. "We're here for you, luvvy, every one of us."

And with one last glance back I notice all present have turned their backs, wanting to give Jamie and I one last moment together. I lean down to kiss his cheek as my tears drop onto his face. Gently wiping them away, I remember Jimmy's request and whisper into his ear. "Your dad wanted me to tell you that he loves you, that they all do, okay." I deliver their kiss as promised.

Leaning my head on his shoulder, a lifetime of memories flutter in and out of my mind. But there is one that surpasses them all—the unconditional love I felt the moment we met. I kiss his lips, lingering a touch longer than I should, then speak. "Fly now, my darling, you're free."

Chapter Four

One Last Kiss

Jamie was pronounced dead at ten am this morning.

I can't help but think that only hours ago, he was still alive and looking forward to coming home.

Now, I'm back home, but shock has rendered me speechless and no matter how I try, I can't find my voice. Instead, my mind clashes viciously with my own will, and with no clear winner I'm still trying to make sense of how, and why, my husband was taken from me.

One of my well-meaning colleagues stopped me as I was leaving the hospital last night. "So sorry for your loss," she said, and while my immediate response should have been thank you, my mind spun off into another direction.

"I haven't lost anything. I know where Jamie is. He died." It was a blunt response but as simple as that, and no matter how people choose to articulate it, that's the cold, hard truth. But looking back, of course her words were meant to soothe me in some small way–they didn't. Still, I've since made a mental note to write to her and apologise.

Wandering aimlessly around a house that was too large for two people let alone just me, I find myself in the kitchen and stare at the Le Creuset casserole pan still on the stove. The stew will be past its best by now and needs to be thrown down the waste disposal unit. But that's a job for another time.

I can't remember the last thing I ate and wonder what to cook for tonight's dinner. *He'll be home soon*, I tell myself dreaming up something simple I know he will devour, and seconds later my subconscious corrects me. *He's gone,*

Serena. And I feel that sudden whoosh as my body absorbs the shock all over again.

The house is cold and I'm shivering because I haven't bothered to turn the central heating on. But what's the point of making myself comfortable without Jamie here? I'm an empty shell existing inside an empty shell, a place that was once our home, but no longer.

My mobile phone vibrates, but rather than answer, I stare at it. I don't want to talk to anyone, not right now, perhaps ever again. All I want is to wake up, turn over and smile as he snoozes gently beside me. Yet this isn't a nightmare, but my new reality. The rattling sound stops, but seconds later it begins again. I finally turn my phone off, deciding to deal with missed calls, voicemails, text messages and emails another time.

Closing my eyes and cradling my aching head in my hands, the landline rings and while anger tempts me to rip it from the wall, I realise it must be important if somebody is that desperate to get hold of me.

Rushing to the hallway, I pick it up and hold it to my ear.

"Hello," a voice I don't recognise on the other ends says. "May I please speak with Mrs Tate?"

"Speaking," I reply, my throat is dry and my voice hoarse.

"Ah, this is Archibald Wilson from Goddard and Sons Funeral Home."

"Oh, yes, what can I do for you?"

"I apologise for calling so late in the day, but I wanted to inform you that your husband will be ready for you to see from nine am in the morning."

"So soon?"

"Yes, but if you do not wish to see Mr Tate I quite understand."

"No, no, I want to see him, nine am, you say?"

"Yes, please ask for me when you arrive, and I shall take you through."

"Thank you, Mr Wilson, but before you go, may I ask you one question?"

"Of course, anything."

"How does Jamie look?" I know it's probably a morbid question to ask but my overriding memory is a head swathed in bandages with gauze covering lacerations to his perfect face.

"Just as he does in the picture you kindly supplied to us."

"That's a relief. I will see you at nine."

"I shall see you then. Good evening, Mrs Tate."

I end the call and sit on the chair next to the telephone table. Devoid of energy, I look at the antique grandfather clock Jamie bought for me on our fifteenth wedding anniversary–it's just gone five pm. Every tick will feel like an eternity until I see my beloved again.

Trying to think of something to occupy my mind, I decide to call Miriam. Turning my mobile phone back on, I find her number and press dial.

"Hi, Miriam," I say, trying not to sound as bad as I feel.

"Hello, darling," she replies. "I've been thinking about you all day."

"How are you?" Then I admonish myself for the stupid question. "Sorry…"

"Don't apologise. I'm just trying to make sense of everything."

"Is Jimmy okay?"

"He's gone off into his garden shed."

"Should I drive over?"

"You're always welcome but don't make the journey just for him. He won't come out of there for a while anyway."

"Mr Goddard from the funeral home called and said we can see Jamie from nine am in the morning."

The line is suddenly muffled, and I hear her strangulated sobs in the background. "Hi, Serena, it's Ben, sorry about that, but Mum had to go."

"Look after her for me, Ben, I can call back later."

"No, it's fine. Can I help with anything?"

"I was calling to say we can see Jamie in the morning–would you like to?"

"Right now, I don't know."

"That's understandable."

"Look, Serena, I'm so sorry, but I need to go and sort Mum, can I call you later?"

"Yes, of course." I'm about to hang up when he speaks.

"Serena, are you there?"

"Still here," I reply.

"We all love you."

His kindness reduces me to a gibbering wreck, and I can't reply. Instead, I end the call and find myself staring into space.

Sometime later I'm drinking a large glass of Scotch when Miriam returns my call.

"Hiya." I try to sound less gloomy.

"Please forgive me for going off the phone like that before."

"There is nothing to forgive."

"Everything just came at me, right at that moment. And I've tried so hard to be strong for everyone else."

"Jamie was your son." I'm torn because I don't know what tense to speak of him in any longer so correct myself. "Is your son."

"And your husband."

"We'll say goodbye together if you'd like?"

"I want to, but I'd rather you had time on your own with him before we get there."

"That's not necessary, Miriam, we're family."

"I know, but I think it's important you get that time. Jimmy, Ben and Helena think so too."

"Are they all coming?"

"Ben and Helena, yes, but Jimmy can't bear it and wants to remember Jamie as he was. I'm hoping he will change his mind..."

"He has to do what's right for him."

"Yes, he does, but I'll try again later because I don't want him to have any regrets."

"If Jimmy would prefer, I have no objections to him going in first, or on his own."

"You're a good girl, Serena."

"We've all lost him." Speaking the words feel like a sledgehammer to my gut and for a moment I struggle to breathe.

"Serena, what's wrong?"

"Nothing, I promise."

"You don't have to hide anything from me."

"I swear, I'm okay, just worried about tomorrow."

"Tell you what, we'll swing by in the morning and then we can all go together, how does that sound?"

"Better."

"Then that's what we'll do, now you get some sleep."

"I miss him already, Miriam."

"So do I, love, and tomorrow we'll tell him that, okay."

"Call me if you need me."

"Same to you. Love you lots."

"Love you too. Give Jimmy, Ben and Helena a hug from me."

"Goodnight, my darling. Try and get some rest."

"I will. You too."

No matter our intentions, I doubt either of us will sleep.

I don't know how long I sat at the kitchen table for, nor do I remember going to bed, but I woke up at seven am, terrified I'd slept too long. Glancing at the clock tells me I've cut it fine.

Knowing I need to get ready in an hour, anxiety rips through me. I hadn't expected to drift off so sleeping as long as I have has thrown me out of whack.

Swinging my legs out of the bed, I dash into the bathroom, desperate for a wee, then turn the bath taps on, intent on looking my absolute best for Jamie.

Thirty minutes later and in record time, I step back into the bedroom washed, waxed, plucked and ready to face the mirror. Jamie always preferred me looking au natural and I won't disappoint him on today of all days.

Even in my drunken state, I must have had my mind set on what needed to be done because my outfit hangs on the back of the bedroom door; a fitted dark grey trouser suit I'd often wear for training sessions at the hospital but instead of the tight, clingy top he liked, only because it showed too much cleavage, I decide to opt for a more restrained silver silk blouse.

Sitting at the dressing table, what I see looking back at me in the mirror is a woman looking years older than her actual age. Do I care? Not at all but making a silk purse from a sow's ear is going to be quite the task.

Dark circles under bloodshot eyes make me look tired yet I'm remarkably alert considering how much Scotch I think I drank last night. Though awake, I'm probably still drunk.

Thankfully Ben is driving us to the funeral home because I have a feeling I'd be over the limit.

I do my best and look presentable, but better than that, respectable.

Time is against me now, so I fly down the stairs and flip the kettle on. I need coffee, and if I'm quick, I might be able to manage two cups before my ride arrives.

Just as I'm finishing my third cup, my bladder forces me into red alert. I dash to the downstairs toilet as the doorbell rings.

I leave the door open and call out, "Hang on," then wipe my undercarriage, pull my knickers and pants up then tuck myself in.

Opening the front door, I'm surprised to see Jimmy.

"You came."

"I didn't think I would, but..."

"I'm glad."

"Are you ready to go?"

"Just let me grab my bag."

"I'll wait in the car."

"Is Miriam here too?"

"Yes, but Ben and Helena decided at the last minute they didn't want to see him."

"That's fine."

"If truth be told, I'm terrified."

"Come here." I pull him into a hug.

He pats my back and edges away. "I'll wait in the car, take your time."

The journey to Goddard and Sons Funeral Home is a silent one, but small talk isn't the answer. Instead, I'm left to sift through my thoughts, knowing I've got to be strong. Later, I can fall apart, but Jimmy and Miriam need my strength more than ever.

Stepping into the renovated Victorian building, I'm impressed with the classic yet understated interior, *Jamie would approve*. Approaching the desk, the receptionist if that's the right description for her, looks up and smiles. "Hello, my name is Serena Tate, and these are Jamie's parents, Mr and Mrs Tate. Could we please speak with Archibald Wilson?"

"Of course." She gestures to a sitting area. "Please take a seat and I shall fetch Mr Wilson for you."

A few minutes later, a short, rotund bespectacled man of about forty, dressed in a formal black suit and wearing the shiniest shoes I've ever seen steps toward us. "Mrs Tate, I am Archibald Wilson." He offers his hand.

"Hello." I shake his clammy hand and wonder where it's been. "This is Jamie's mother and father, Jimmy and Miriam."

He shakes their hands too, paying them the respect they deserve. "Jamie is ready if you would like to see him now."

Suddenly I'm without voice again. I turn to Jimmy for help.

"Would you mind if we all went in together?"

Jimmy takes over while I clutch Miriam's hand in mine for support.

"Of course not, Mr Tate, please, follow me."

We are guided through another waiting room and stop at a set of double doors.

"Jamie is just through there." Mr Wilson opens the door with ease.

My feet don't want to move. I catch sight of the coffin and freeze. "I can't go in."

Jimmy turns and looks at me with caring eyes. "You don't have to do anything you don't want to, Serena." He is calm, despite his son's coffin being only a few feet away. "Miriam, would you like to go in?"

She nods. I look into her eyes, desperate to feel the strength I need to propel me through the doors. But I know she has none to give. "Hold onto me, Serena," Miriam says, "and we'll get through it, okay, sweetie?"

"Yes," I reply, casting my eyes down toward the polished wooden floors.

"This way," Mr Wilson says quietly.

A few steps and I know what lies before me, but I don't have the courage to look until I hear Jimmy's laboured breathing. "My beautiful boy," he cries when speaking the words. I finally look at him, and he's trembling from head to toe. "It should be me lying in there."

Miriam cries out her sorrow next to me. She's looking at Jamie too. "Oh, my darling…"

Look at him. Slowly, I allow my eyes to wander but fear has me in thrall. *It's Jamie*, I remind myself. Taking a deep breath, I finally look and for a moment it's not him, but a crude waxwork dummy carved to look exactly like him. The white shroud I insisted he be dressed in lends a biblical look.

I can't see the top of his head, where most of his trauma was, because it's covered too, but his face looks just as it should.

Releasing Miriam's hand, I need to touch him once more, and though I've worked as a nurse for years, he's colder than I expect him to be. "Jamie…" I whisper his name as I gently stroke his cheek. Cuts and bruises are still there underneath heavy makeup, but to me, he looks perfect, and as he should. I lean over and place my lips on his, one last kiss. "My love, what am I going to do without you?"

He won't answer.

He can't because he's not in there any longer.

His soul has departed and gone on to a better place.

Chapter Five

Into the Arms of Our Lord

It's early November and winter arrived with a vengeance. But for once, my focus isn't on the weather or escaping to warmer climes.

Today is the day I say goodbye to the only man I have ever loved.

But lost in my own world, others are still at the forefront of my mind.

I had lost my reason for living, but I knew what Jamie would say to me if he could. *Get off your backside and stop moping.*

And he'd be right because I had to find a way to live again, to honour his memory, to do the things we planned, go to the places we hoped to visit, even if it means I do it alone. I couldn't wither and die like a neglected house plant starved of water and sunlight.

But, right now, standing outside the church, it's too hard to put one foot in front of the other, let alone map out a future I can't and don't want to envision without him.

"One step at a time, sweetie." Despite Jamie's wishes for mourners to wear something colourful and fun, Miriam is dressed entirely in black. It's her right as his mother so I don't question her choice. Instead, I find myself trying to pierce the veil that hides so much of the anguish I know she's pushing down. I hear it in her voice even if I don't see it in her eyes.

"I can't, Miriam." I know I'm holding the service up, but I can't help the way I feel. "If I go through those doors, I'm just a widow, the woman who used to be married to Jamie Alexander Tate. I don't want that, I never did." We promised one another a happy ever after. But the scumbag Jamie tried to stop robbed me of a future I thought was set in stone. The same question whirls around inside my head. *Why didn't you just let him go instead of playing the hero?*

Jamie had witnessed the robbery, and after confronting the thief, gave chase, resulting in a passing car driving into him. He was thrown into the air, banging his head on the corner of the pavement. Another driver who hadn't seen anything then drove his car over Jamie as he lay dying on the roadside.

Both drivers stopped their cars and tried to help. I know it will haunt them forever.

The guy who held up the shop is still on the run, but karma is a bitch.

One day he will be forced to pay for his involvement in the death of my husband.

Did he realise what was happening? It's another question that haunts me because I don't have the answer.

"I'm right here with you," she says quietly.

I don't vocalise how I imagine Jamie's demise to have played out because I don't want to hurt her any more than she already is. What I do know is the entire thing was caught on CCTV. I never want to see that footage, but it will be used in any criminal trial, at which point I shall excuse myself from the proceedings. "Thank you."

"My boy loved you, Serena. You have to do this now, for him, just like we discussed."

"I want him back." I crumble and hit the hard, cold ground covered in a light dusting of first snow. And whoosh, in four simple words, eighteen years of marriage to the man I vowed to spend the rest of my life with, reveals my one wish.

"Oh, darling." Miriam kneels next to me, though in her early sixties, she is in no shape to be on the hard asphalt. Holding me close, I rest my head on her shoulder. "We all do, but it doesn't work that way."

I'm numb throughout the service and focus anywhere but the mahogany coffin that sits before me covered in floral tributes. *He's in there*, I tell myself. Only *a few feet away, but cold and dead.* I focus on the picture of him, pulling tongues at the camera, on an easel set to the side.

Empty words are spoken eloquently by Father McClelland. "The Lord is my shepherd; I shall not want. He maketh me to lie down in green pastures: he leadeth me beside the still waters. He restoreth my soul: he leadeth me in the paths of righteousness for his name's sake. Yea, though I walk through the valley of the shadow of death, I will fear no evil: for thou art with me; thy rod and thy staff they comfort me. Thou preparest a table before me in the presence of mine enemies: thou anointest my head with oil; my cup runneth over. Surely goodness and mercy shall follow me all the days of my life: and I will dwell in the house of the Lord for ever."

They bring me no comfort but were chosen specifically by Jamie as detailed in the instructions left in his last Will and Testament. I have no idea why this particular psalm because he was not the religious type, although he believed in God. *That's another question I will never get an answer for.* It doesn't matter so much anyway because it's what he wanted.

Miriam squeezes my hand as the purple velvet curtains close around the coffin.

"Into the arms of our Lord safely you go," Father McClelland adds. "Take comfort in his light."

A chorus of amen rings out from the oddly dressed, packed congregation of mourners.

Suddenly, the opening bars of the song wrench me back to reality.

I think of Jamie walking into any given room and saying, *"Alexa, play In Dreams by Roy Orbison."*

I'd roll my eyes at his taste in music before we'd begin a waltz around the kitchen, or the bedroom, the dining room, wherever the mood took us really. But I'd give anything to hear Jamie serenading me along with the music one last time. Even with his two left feet, I'd welcome the dance once more.

Closing my eyes, memories taunt me of what once was. I don't want to relive them, not right now anyway. But I'm told it's a part of grief, of the brain registering loss, though in my present state of mind, it's a load of codswallop dreamed up by psychiatrists rather than regurgitate the same old platitudes.

"He loved this song," Helena says, sitting to the right of me. She's wearing a lurid orange dress, and lime green heels with a matching fascinator and veil. I'm reminded of a rainbow-coloured version of Cruella De Vil, and while she looks ridiculous, honouring one of Jamie's last wishes is paramount and more importantly, he would find her outfit hysterical.

Ben is in a more sombre attire and wears a grey suit, and a matching shirt with a bright pink tie with yellow polka dots. It's as far as he can go on the road to crazy, but I respect him for trying.

"He did." And I smile because somewhere in the cosmos, he will be cutting up the dancefloor just like Fred Astaire.

The closing bars bring silence and a sense of finality. But I don't move.

Instead, the congregation stand and shuffle quietly out of the church, leaving me and Jamie's immediate family together. We're not ready to leave and I'm sure they feel as I do–the service was moving and planned meticulously by him but only left us longing for his touch.

I push myself to my feet and look into the eyes of the other four people, devastated by his passing. "It's exactly how he wanted it."

"It was a lovely service," Miriam added. "Everything was just right and typically him."

I cast my eyes downward at a still seated Jimmy, his aura as black as his suit, bereft and left without direction. "Jimmy..." He's hollow inside, and without a path forward.

Ben hooks his arm through his dad's and helps him to his feet. "Come on, old man, let's go."

I step into the aisle and allow them to pass. The hard part is now out of the way. Now, it's time to return to Jamie's favourite hotel for a wake I desperately want to miss. "I'm going to hang back for a few minutes if you don't mind?"

Ben and Jimmy are already halfway up the aisle, the same one I had walked down on my journey to become Jamie's bride. Neither stop.

Miriam and Helena turn.

"Shall I wait with you," Helena offers.

"There's no need, you go, just give me a few minutes and I'll follow you out."

"Okay." I wait for them to turn and grip onto the pew in front of me. It takes every ounce of strength not to fall, but with ironclad will, I stay upright and look up at the stained glass window depicting angels in a fierce battle with one another. The image reflects my lack of inner peace.

Then, in the silence of this holy place, I weep openly, allowing myself a few minutes then pull myself together.

Soon enough the car pulls up outside the venue. A wake full of mourners and well-wishers I have little energy to deal with. But it's how things have always been done. Still, after an hour, I have nothing left to give and make my excuses to leave.

Once back home, I open the curtains, having already observed a custom thrust upon me by Miriam that has no significance as far as I can tell, but I went along with it anyway. Now, in the silence, I've become mistress of all I survey. One word teases me, *alone*.

All around there are reminders of him, of us, snap shots of two decades of happiness, loving and living. Now they only serve to taunt me of what I've lost.

I cross the room and pick up my favourite picture of Jamie, on the beach in Antigua. It was there he'd first made me promise never to bury his body.

"Why?" I'd asked, never imagining the day would actually come.

"I'm terrified of waking up in my coffin." An irrational fear of scratching to get out. For him, it was the stuff of horror movies, but I had respected every single wish I knew of, and today was no different, no matter how it tore me to shreds inside. "Please cremate me and sprinkle my ashes right away."

It was a morbid but practical conversation and one most couples probably have sometime during their marriage, little realising reality would one day come knocking in the form of the Grim Reaper.

Rather than being confined to a wooden box or an urn on the mantelpiece, I'd spoken with his parents and siblings. It was difficult but we all agreed to honour Jamie's wishes and sprinkle his ashes. Nobody was to keep any, instead they would be released on top of the cliff above his favourite spot—Lulworth Cove, close to a picturesque village of West Lulworth on the Jurassic Cove in Dorset on the southern coast of England.

We'd spent many happy times there and it seemed only right it should be his final resting place although letting go of him would be hard. There was some consolation because I knew I'd have somewhere to visit where I could feel near to him.

So, a few days later, we all made the journey. I felt apprehensive, that my life roared ahead on full throttle. But I wasn't in control.

"It is very beautiful here, Serena." Miriam links her arm through mine and stares up at the grey winter sky peppered with clouds.

"He loved it here, we both did."

"And you will again," Jimmy adds. He hasn't said much since the funeral and I'm thankful he's finally found his voice. "I've never been here before but can see why it means so much."

"It feels wrong leaving him behind, but where else would he want to be? Stuck on top of the fireplace, or on my bedside cabinet? It'd make me feel better having him near, for a while anyway, then I'd hear his voice telling me he felt claustrophobic."

Standing in this once magical place, I hold a secret I'm not ready to reveal yet. *Will they hate me for it?* It was done with the best of intentions, and I will tell them all at an appropriate time. It's not the time to dwell so carefully, I put my hand in my coat pocket and feel at peace, certain I'd made the right decision.

"You knew him better than anyone, love."

Jimmy nods his agreement. "Miriam is right, you did, so it has to be your choice at the end of the day, no matter what was discussed."

"But what do you both want?"

"Jamie back," Miriam's voice cracks, and her eyes shine with unshed tears. "Nothing more."

"If I had one wish..." My thoughts trail off to never-never land.

Jimmy is the practical one, he always was. "Wishes are for fairy tales. He's gone but it doesn't mean we will ever forget the light he brought into our lives. Releasing his ashes in a place he treasured is the right thing to do."

I glance over to Ben and Helena. Both are crying, and while I want to comfort them, I must remain strong if I'm to get through these next few minutes.

We're stood at the right spot as memories fade in and out. Each one brings a stab of longing. *Stay strong*, I urge myself. *Just a little while longer.* Carefully, I unscrew the lid. "You were, are and will always be the love of my life and no matter where you go, I hope you know that."

Miriam slips her hand into mine and sobs beside me whilst Jimmy grieves quietly, and with dignity. Ben and Helena cry too.

"With you I always felt beautiful, that my life was blessed with magic, and I could conquer anything, but now you're gone, I'm lost and tied to a world I no longer want to be a part of." I fall to my knees and tug my hand from Miriam's. Then I do what I don't want to and lift the lid from the copper urn. Sliding my fingers into the ashes, it feels wrong, too invasive, too final. "But I can't go with you, not yet, because to do so would be a sin, and I don't want anything to keep us apart when my time comes."

Miriam kneels beside me with Jimmy next to her, his hand resting on her shoulder. Ben and Helena hold hands and take comfort in one another.

"So, for now, my love, I say farewell, until we meet again." I hold a handful of his ashes, then push myself to my feet and reluctantly set him free. "Fly…" I watch as the air catches hold and carries him toward the blue water below. I turn to Jimmy. "Help me, please. I can't do it alone."

Jimmy steps forward, sadness etched into every line of his face. And without word, he bends to take a handful too. He holds onto them for a moment but waits for a gust of wind. When one comes, he opens his hand. "I love you, son." He turns to Miriam, a few steps behind us. "Come on, you'll feel better if you do it. You too, Helena, Ben…"

"Scattering my son's ashes won't ease the pain I feel in here, Jimmy…" She clutches her chest. "…nothing will."

Ben and Helena shake their heads and fall into line with Miriam.

"I'm so sorry," I say to them all.

"It's not your fault, Serena," Helena adds. "None of this is, but it's harder than I imagined it was going to be."

Deep down, I sympathise with her though I can't help feeling she is selfish. I can't let it go. "I think it's important we all do this."

"Why?" Helena pulls out a handkerchief and blows her nose.

"We are his family," is all I can manage to croak before I crumble. "He worshipped you all. Just like I did him, and now he's gone, forever, and nothing I say or do will ever bring him back." My eyes sting with tears and I wonder if they will ever dry.

Nothing surprises me where Miriam is concerned. She finds hidden strength to do what I know is anathema to her. "Let's do it together, the five of us, just like he'd have wanted. What do you think?"

Though I know casting what is left of her beloved son to the four winds is killing her inside, she does it. "I can do that," I reply.

"We'll do it too." Ben answers for both him and Helena.

"So will I," Jimmy adds. "This is the last thing we can do for him, so let's do it right."

We watch, united in sorrow, as Jamie's ashes billow across the bay. Closing my eyes, I offer silent words I pray he will hear. *Send me a sign so I know you're okay.*

Suddenly I feel unseasonal warmth on my face.

Opening my eyes, I see the rays of the sun blazing through the clouds.

I can almost hear his voice telling me... *Serena, I'm okay.*

Chapter Six

Without You

Spring is finally here but with none of the vibrancy as times past because life in whatever form it comes has no meaning anymore. There is no rhyme or reason for existing and make no mistake, I'm left with only that, an existence.

Without joy or hope, my world is shadowed by grief and mired with memories that torture me.

I'm stuck in my own personal hell. It's an empty room, a hall of mirrors where every shred of bitterness is reflected back at me.

Two months ago, I officially resigned from my job though my resignation was refused by Andrew Barnes, the Administrator of the hospital. Instead, and against my better judgement, I agreed to be placed on long-term leave but insisted it be without pay.

I didn't fight his refusal to allow me to resign because I had no fight left in me. I had nothing to offer those who might need me, nor did I want to give false hope to my bosses; that one day I would feel enough like my old self to return.

"You'll be welcomed back with open arms when you're ready," Andrew had said. *"Take as much time as you need and call me if you need anything."*

"It feels nice to be wanted," I'd replied, grateful.

"You are one of us and that won't ever change and if you need me to reinstate your pay, I'll do it without question."

Money isn't an issue. I have more than I ever dreamed of because Jamie left me well provided for. I was also the beneficiary of enormous sums of money from various life insurance policies but even without that, his company, Tate Technology, turns over a fortune every year.

I do worry how long it will last without him at the helm, so the offer from an interested party in Washington DC, America, to buy it, leaves me torn.

In reality, I need to talk to Jimmy and Miriam, but it's been some months since we last spoke and not from their lack of trying. Now, I fear it's too late for me to invade their world and ask for guidance.

Rolling over in bed, I stare at the letter leaning against my bedside lamp. I've been determined since the reading of the will not to open it, but right then, a voice pushes me. *Do it, Serena*. Did I just imagine it? I don't know but it's enough for me to pick up the envelope. I stare at his perfect penmanship and read what is written on the front, My Darling Wife, and realise I can't sidestep the moment any longer. His words scream at me from inside, begging for an audience.

Carefully opening the envelope, the letter, written on expensive white paper, slips out easily.

Holding it in my trembling hands I see cursive script written in black ink from his solid gold fountain pen that still sits on the desk downstairs, just as he left it.

Taking a deep breath, I feel the air rush from my lungs, that I am drowning under the weight and significance of this last piece of correspondence to me.

"Come back to me," I wish, though nothing will grant me the one thing I want more than any other.

Quickly pulling myself together, I begin to read;

Serena,

How do I begin to write this letter, especially when I hope you will never have to read it?

I don't know where to start although I sit here and hope with every fibre of my being that when the time comes, we slip away peacefully, together, wrapped in one another's arms.

The truth is, even the thought of writing these words rip me apart because when I said I do, never since that day have I envisioned a moment without you.

And now, if you are reading this, the time has come for you to carry on without me, and while I know your heart will break, I want you to hold your head up, smile, and remember the good times—it won't be too hard because we never had anything else when we were together—the sun set and rose every single day without us having an argument, or a single crossed word.

Ours was a true love only death could tear apart.

Smile for me, baby, please, because I can't bear it if I'm not there to wipe away your tears.

Being apart isn't forever, and many years from now, I shall be waiting to carry you in my arms up to the heavens. And then nothing will ever tear us apart again.

You are every beat of my heart.

You are the one that makes me the man that I am.

You are the breath I need to survive each day.

You are my protector.

You are my love.

You are my life.

You are my joy.

You are my happy ever after.

And everything I am, is because of the woman you are.

For now, I leave my soul in your capable hands.

Return it to me in time but promise you will live a long and happy life before then.
It isn't au revoir, but à bientôt.
Until we meet again...
Jamie x

Wracked with sobs, every emotion I've bottled up for months pours out like toxic sludge.

I pick up my telephone and dial his mobile number. His voicemail message kicks in, and peace covers me like a warm blanket. I should have cancelled the contract but couldn't bring myself to do it.

Dabbing at my eyes, then returning to his letter, I read it over and over again then do something I've avoided.

"Alexa, play *In Dreams* by Roy Orbison."

Playing *In Dreams* by Roy Orbison, Alexa responds.

"Alexa, volume ten," I demand.

I'm conflicted as the music begins, but I'm playing this for Jamie and nobody else.

My imagination takes over. I hear his voice in my mind. *Dance with me, Serena.*

"Why, thank you, kind Sir," I reply, standing and swaying in time to the music. Pressing the letter to my chest I feel a closeness to him that brings a fresh wave of grief crashing down upon me. Still, I shut my eyes and sway, imagining his body pressed next to mine, his hand resting at the small of my back.

The song ends, and suddenly I'm motionless in the middle of the room. I drop into a quick curtsey and imagine his response.

I hear his voice again. *Ah, you didn't forget, my love.*

"Alexa, play it again." And she does, on repeat until I'm dizzy and can't dance anymore.

Flopping down on the bed, I'm exhausted but I decide to throw caution to the wind and open the bedside drawer aware I'll be confronted with more things I've successfully managed to put off, until now.

Letters from the transplant coordinator catch my eye. And while I'd convinced myself I'd forgotten, fear stopped me from reading the contents until now.

Feeling a surge of strength, I read the first of three from a recipient who breathes through Jamie's lungs. Aside from gender, it gives no clue as to his identity, but I don't need to know. The fact he lives as a result of Jamie's gift means the world to me, and while I'd sell my soul to have him back, I am thankful the family of the recipient will never know what it feels like to lose a loved one.

The second letter is from a child given the gift of sight thanks to a cornea transplant. With it, there is a request to meet me. It's not something I am strong enough for yet, plus it's not as easy as it seems, and every request must go through official channels.

"One day, I promise," whispering into the ether.

It's the third and final letter from a young mother that touches me deeply with its simplicity. Although it doesn't reveal anything aside from basic information and it's no more than five lines, I read it over and over again.

I need to tell you what it means to me, but I cannot seem to find words that would adequately convey how I feel.

So, I say thank you, and promise to treasure the wonderful gift of life and guard what I have been given.

With eternal Love and gratitude.

I'm reduced to tears because Jamie's life not only mattered to me but made a difference to others who never knew him, and there is no greater testament to a life well lived.

Proud of his achievements, even in death, I push back the ever-present feeling of longing to hold him as I swing my legs onto the bed and hug my knees.

There is a sense of peace I haven't felt since his passing and though I know I'll wake up tomorrow feeling hopeless all over again, I'll take these moments when and where I can.

Chapter Seven

I'm Not Alone

It's gone nine when I wake up.

Unsurprisingly, I'm hit with the same sense of loneliness, but also with the knowledge I'm wasting my life and all I should be thankful for.

Swinging my legs out of bed, I decide to make today a constructive one. I take the stairs and feel lighter than days gone by.

Strolling into the kitchen I find myself humming a song I haven't heard in a while.

"Alexa, play *Wake Me Up Before You Go-Go* by Wham."

Alexa springs to life and talks to me. "Playing, *Wake Me Up Before You Go-Go* by Wham."

The familiar beat kicks in and in seconds my bum is wiggling in time to the music. It feels good to be alive though a betrayal to Jamie, but nobody other than me would see it that way.

I strut like John Travolta in *Saturday Night Fever* over to the fridge and pull it open. Feeling peckish I decide on a cheese and onion omelette with well buttered granary toast but am side-tracked by my phone beeping on top of the microwave.

Picking it up, I'm surprised to see two notifications flashing at me.

MISSED CALL FROM BETTY.
VOICEMAIL MESSAGE FROM BETTY.

We usually email, and at my request, she's the only one that has kept in touch from the hospital.

I click the message icon and await her sweet tone. I've missed her, and am genuinely touched she called, even though I have no idea what she is going to say, or why she had to say it so early in the morning.

"Press 1 to listen to the message," the computerised voice tells me.

I do as I'm told and press 1.

"Message received today, at 5:12am."

"Christ, Betty, did you really think I'd be awake then?" It's not really a daft assumption on her part because I would be if I was on a morning shift.

Hearing her voice makes me smile.

"Morning, sleepy head. Listen up! Grief Support at Violet Lodge. 6pm tonight. Go! It'll do you good to get out. No arguing. Call or text and let me know how it went. Miss you and hope to see you soon. Big kiss."

I don't think so, is my immediate thought instantly followed by *what are you scared of?*

I'm not sure I'm going to go, but rather than a flat refusal, I decide to think it over while eating my breakfast.

I have all day to talk myself out of it, but at 5:30pm I walk into the grounds of Violet Lodge and stare at the old brick building that looks like it's been left abandoned in another era.

"What the hell are you doing here, Serena?" I've found myself having these chats a lot lately, so maybe this is where I truly need to be.

Taking a deep breath and big strides, I'm on edge as soon as I walk through the doors of the quaint village hall. But I know if I don't take this first step into whatever my new world is, I'll be left behind to wallow in memories and a life that once was but will never be again.

GRIEF SUPPORT MEETING at VIOLET LODGE.
Every Monday, Wednesday & Friday from 6pm – 9pm.
ALL WELCOME!
Tea, Coffee & Refreshments provided.

I read the words written in big white letters on the chalkboard and almost turn on my heels at the ridiculousness of the situation.

"Are you here for the group?" An older lady of about sixty with a shock of bright purple hair, kind face and warm smile calls out as she walks toward me. She's every inch an Earth Mother, that much is evident from appearance alone. The wind blows and gently lifts her kaftan, but she's seemingly unfazed and carries on regardless.

"Erm…" I detect the smell of lavender. The scent is comforting as is the warmth that seems to radiate from every pore of her skin.

"My name is Louise." She holds out her hand. "And you are?"

"I'm Serena." I reach out and take hold, her skin remarkably smooth to the touch. "It's nice to meet you."

"Is this your first time here, my love?" I suddenly note the Bristolian twang to her accent. She's a fair way from home, but I don't know her circumstances, or anything about her.

"Can you tell?" I must have that deer caught in the headlights look.

"Yes, but you are most welcome regardless."

"I'm not sure I can do this."

"There is a little time before the start of the meeting, would you like to take a walk in the gardens with me and clear your head beforehand? Then you can decide if you would like to stay."

It's a lovely gesture from a stranger, but a much needed one I won't refuse. "I don't want to put you out."

"Don't be daft, it would be my pleasure, and besides, you look like you need somebody to talk to."

"That would be wonderful, thank you."

She links her arm through mine and although we'd never met before this moment, I feel secure with her. "You're shaking, you poor girl."

"I'm sorry."

"Never apologise for how you feel, Serena."

"Even the notion of considering a group like this is strange, for me at least."

She looks at me with understanding eyes. "When I started, I was feeling exactly the same way you do now, in fact, everyone who comes to the group did."

"You're part of this grief support group too?" How did I not realise? She wouldn't be loitering in the village hall, or its grounds, for the sake of something to do. Though she does have that look of a green goddess about her; a lady who is at one with nature and all that surrounds her. The brightly coloured kaftan is a nifty garment that lends her an air of freedom though it clashes horribly with the purple hair.

"Yes, and I have been for a couple of years now."

"Years?" I'm stunned, but bereavement knows no bounds and has no definitive time limit where it can wreak havoc on those left to face it. I'm at the beginning with no end in sight.

"I lost my daughter five years ago…" She takes a deep breath as a lump sits in my throat. "And that very same day, I lost a part of myself too."

"I'm so sorry." I hold onto her hand that little bit tighter and admire her bright pink shiny nail polish. "Although I didn't lose a child, I can certainly relate to losing part of myself."

"Everyone that comes here knows how it feels to lose somebody, whether it is a child, a parent, or a—"

"Husband," I interrupt, needing to tell her something about me and why I've ventured here. Admitting it's the reason I am there isn't as hard as I imagined it to be. "He was killed in a road traffic accident." I don't tell her how bad it actually was because it hurts too much to relive it.

"How awful." She pats the top of my hand. "I shall keep you in my prayers."

A lot of people have said that same thing to me and while it should offer me comfort, it doesn't, instead it makes me angry that God took him away from me. It's not her fault and I graciously accept her offer. "You said you lost yourself, and this might be a silly question, but did you ever find yourself again?"

"Now, that is a very good question, Serena but I like to look at it another way."

"How so?"

"The day I lost my daughter was then, and this is now. My life will never be the same, but I learned to find joy in other things again, though I can't help thinking I'm betraying her memory when I find myself laughing or enjoying whatever I'm doing."

"I've forgotten what it is to smile, but I know how you feel. Last night was the first time in months I felt a sense of normality though wrong on every level."

"One day, Serena..."

"It still hurts so much, Louise." I can't believe I'm pouring my woes out to a complete stranger but the old adage that it is easier to do so rings true. "And every day is that much harder than the last."

"I won't lie and say it gets better. It doesn't, and you will hurt for the rest of your life, but it becomes easier to bear, and while some days are better than others, there is no magical cure for what you're going through." She pats my hand reassuringly. "And as wonderful as this little haven is for us here, it's not designed to take away your suffering but to help you navigate through it."

I understand what she's saying even if I can't envision a time my life will resemble what it was before. "I'm too weak to fight."

"I don't know you, but it takes strength to take this first step into the unknown, and you did it."

"I haven't actually made it into the meeting yet."

"You will, when you are ready to, and that might be today, it might be another day, but you will, eventually, if you want it enough."

I squeeze her hand again. "Thank you for being so kind to me."

"Whether we like it or not, death is a bloody big part of life and a right pain in the arse to boot."

Her way of interpreting tragedy impresses me. "Did you always look at it so philosophically?"

"Bugger me, not at all," she replies. "For the longest time, I was mad with the world and everyone in it. I'd buried my daughter and no parent should ever have to suffer that."

I think of my in-laws and how I've neglected them since Jamie's passing. "I can't imagine how hard that would be."

"Looking back, Laura dying wasn't actually the worst part but her constant suffering, day in and day out, broke me, and there was nothing I could do to take the pain away. She was my little girl, and I was helpless and that left a dark stain on my soul."

"I don't know what to say to make it any better for you."

"She was only twenty-four-years-old and diagnosed with cervical cancer." She takes another deep breath as her eyes shine with unshed tears. "Then lockdown happened and appointment after appointment was cancelled and by the time she was seen by the consultant, it was too late to save her. My little girl died screaming in agony and fear, and that's what my nightmares play on repeat, night after night."

I'm ashamed of my selfishness and daring to assume I'm the only person to experience such pain. "God, that's awful."

"She barely had a chance to make her mark on, but I was there when that little miracle came into the world, and I was there when she left it. There is no greater privilege for a mother, no matter the cost to me." A single tear rolls down her cheek, but she is dignity personified, and I like her immensely, already. "Laura knew she was loved right until her last breath, I made sure of it."

Her tribute to Laura touches me deeply. I can't hold onto my emotions and bury my face in my hands. "I feel like such a horrible person."

She rubs my back to offer comfort. "Why, darling?"

"Because I thought it was just me."

"Don't you dare apologise for grieving, my flower, because it means you experienced your own form of true love."

"But you've suffered more than anyone should have to bear."

"As have you, but being here, it opens one's eyes, and we see, it happens the world over, and it doesn't matter if you're black, white, gay, straight, whatever, we deal with the same horrors life can throw our way. When we lose a loved one, their number is up, and it's left to us to soldier on without them."

"You're so brave, Louise."

She shakes her head, unwilling to accept my praise. "If you'd seen me back then, you wouldn't think so."

"Why?"

"It took me a whole year to find the strength to speak and introduce myself to the other members of the group, let alone do anything else."

"I'm definitely not a fan of public speaking and will probably find a spot at the back to hide in." The thought of opening up so publicly fills me with dread and despite liking Louise, I worry I've made a mistake coming here.

"You don't have to say anything until you're ready, Serena, but from my experience, it helps to listen to others at first, to know you're not alone, and that our little community are here and waiting when you need us."

"How many attend the meeting?"

"It depends. Sometimes it can be a good gathering, other times much smaller numbers." She tucks a strand of hair behind her ear, lined with piercings. "Whether we want it to or not, life goes on for many of us and for some, they find the strength they need from us and take it back out into the real world."

"Will I be the only newbie?"

"Most likely, but we're a friendly bunch and you're going to be just fine."

"It's silly, but I'm scared to introduce myself to the group leader in case he or she thinks I don't belong here."

"You really don't have to be scared of her."

"I don't." Her words reassure my worried mind. "Are you sure?"

"Crikey, Serena, not at all." She pats my knee. "I know for a fact because *I* run this little gathering, and you are most welcome here."

Relief soars through me but I should have seen her place here before now. She has that commanding air about her, that she is a true leader. "Thank God for that."

"Please don't be scared of me, or anyone else for that matter. We are all here to help and guide you to a place where life isn't so hard, and not to force you to do something you aren't ready to do."

I'm won over and any misgivings melt away in the Spring sunshine. "I'm glad I came."

"Trust me when I say that once you're inside, you'll feel a common bond with many of those going through exactly what you are. I did, and still do though we don't revel in our misery but share and take strength from it."

"I don't want to upset anyone, Louise."

"Oh, heck, ducky, people are going to cry, so will you, so will I, but it means we can still feel emotion and that's the most important thing. Tears are a form of expression, and nobody will think any the less of you for seeing you at your most vulnerable."

"I was terrified to take this step, but I feel better than I did ten minutes ago."

"And in an hour, you may feel hopeless all over again, but think of your emotions like waves. Some crash to shore and cause untold devastation while others will roll in gently and caress the sand. It's part and parcel of grief. There is no right or wrong way to deal with loss, it's personal to you, but take strength from us and embrace the fact you are no longer alone."

"I'm ready, I think."

"Are you sure?"

"It's now or never, Louise."

"Then take my hand and let's do it. But remember, you're not there against your will, so if it becomes too much, you are free to leave the room though I'd like it if you will wait for me in the back room if that happens, just so I know you're okay."

"Deal."

"Come on then, let's get you settled inside with a nice cup of tea, or coffee."

"Tea for me please."

"Whatever you fancy." She links her fingers through mine as we stroll back toward the village hall. I no longer feel nervous, but I'm still not sure how much I'll contribute toward the proceedings.

"You're too kind, Louise."

"I'm good to all my friends, and please call me Lou."

"You got it!"

Chapter Eight

Grief Support

A few hours have passed, and I still haven't uttered a single word. My silence aside, a weight seems to have lifted from my shoulders because there are others in the world who know how I feel. I take comfort in the fact I'm no longer alone.

I've listened intently to people from all walks of life speak their truths; those women who have lost children like Louise, to a twenty-something man who lost his mother to breast cancer or the blonde guy whose wife died in horrific circumstances.

All were experiences relayed with such harrowing realism that I was reduced to a sobbing mess. As sadness coursed through me, all I really wanted to do was hold each of them in turn, to tell them I understood, that I felt a camaraderie and that perhaps we were stronger together than apart.

But just as I wrestled the strength to introduce myself, Louise call the meeting to a close. "Okay, that's it for tonight, folks. See you at the next meeting."

The room emptied fast but there were those who hung around to chat to one another while others helped stack the plastic chairs neatly at the back of the room.

"It's lovely to meet you, Serena," a pretty young girl says as she passes by.

"You too." I'm hopeless with names, especially when hearing so many in a short space of time. "Take care."

An older gentleman with white hair relying heavily on his walking stick shuffles forward next. I can't help but be charmed by his lovely warm smile. I stand to greet him. "See you next meeting I hope," he says in what I detect is a Glaswegian accent.

"Oh, yes, I'll definitely be here."

"We're all in the same boat, hen, just remember that," he added. "But we'll look after you."

I felt warm inside, charmed by his Scottish brogue. I kissed his cheek. "Thank you..." I couldn't put my finger on his name.

"Hamish," he reminded me.

"Sorry, yes. You are very kind, Hamish, and it means a lot."

"Keep smiling, Serena." And with that he hobbled away.

"Well, how was it and how do you feel?" Louise asks, as she approaches.

"It was okay, and I feel calmer than before," I reply. "Better than I have in a long time."

"You do?"

"Selfishly, I don't feel like it's just me anymore, and I know that's because others have suffered too, but when I hear their stories, it's the kick up the arse I needed, to tell me I'm not the only one and to stop wailing."

"It's not hard to lose ourselves in our own problems, Serena. I still do it now."

"I know, but it's given me something to think about."

"Quite!"

"I do need to apologise to you though."

"Whatever for?" She plonks herself down next to me and kicks off her sandals.

"I made a bit of a fool of myself crying so much when people were telling their stories."

"Serena, you can relate to them, there is nothing wrong with that at all."

"I know, but still..."

"Look at the positives. You survived the first meeting and got the hardest part out of the way."

"I can't stop thinking of that poor man who lost his wife."

"Do you mean Elijah?"

"Is he the blonde guy who was sat near to the front?"

"Yes, that's Elijah, quite a delightful man, but as you witnessed, there is a melancholy within him he can't seem to shake off."

"I did notice, but he tries to cover it with that dazzling smile I can see right through."

"You are perceptive, Serena, which is why I believe you would make a fantastic group leader yourself."

"Me?" I'm taken aback anybody would think I am of sound enough mind to help anyone when I can barely help myself. "I didn't say a word."

"No, you didn't until the meeting was over, then I watched with fascination as some gravitated toward you. They instinctively feel safe with you, I see it already."

"You're crazy if you think I could do what you do so brilliantly because I can barely be trusted to look after myself."

"I see you too, Serena, and the empathy you feel for others. It's embedded in your DNA."

"My work as a Nurse meant the world to me."

"Ah," she said as her face lights up with realisation. "Now I get it. You are one of Earth's angels."

"Hardly."

"It's wonderful individuals like you that saw my Laura through her final days and gave her as much dignity as they could, and for that I am profoundly grateful. The sick and dying need you, go back to what God called you to do."

"I can't, not yet."

"Why not?"

"It's that place, I can't stand the thought of it."

"What place?"

"The Royal."

"You used to work there I take it?"

"For years, and I loved every moment, but–"

"You didn't say as much but it's where your husband…"

"Jamie," I added.

"…where Jamie was taken after the accident, right?"

"Every one of my nightmares ends with that final journey, of him being wheeled toward the operating theatre doors so they could take his organs for donation."

"My Lord, what a wonderful man he must have been."

"Yes, he was in every way, but as thankful as I am that he thought of others, I've never made peace with that decision and there were moments I initially wanted to say no, to leave him intact, but how could I even contemplate such a thing when giving life to others meant so much to him?"

"I get it."

"So, you see, while I miss my job and helping others, the thought of returning there terrifies me."

"Can you not put in for a transfer to another hospital?"

"Yes, I suppose I can, but there's a small part of me that thinks I'll wake up one morning and be ready to face that place again."

"And if that day doesn't come, what then?"

"I wish I had the answer, Lou."

"You have time on your side."

"Do I, really?"

"Yes, of course you do. Use it, get your head straight then decide on the future. Perhaps helping me out here can keep you busy for a while?"

"You need my help?"

"I've not spoken to anybody about this, but Laura always had plans to travel to Thailand, Cambodia and Vietnam, you know, a bit like when students take a gap year, though she never got the chance."

"And you're planning to walk the path she planned to take?"

"Is that silly, at my age?"

"God, no, I think it's a marvellous idea, and if you don't do it, you'll regret it."

"Which is where you might come in helpful?"

"How?"

"Divine intervention," she whispers, though I am clueless in which direction her mind is travelling in. "Maybe you would agree to look after things here for a few months if I were to start my journey in December?"

We've only just met so it's a tall order taking on any responsibility. "Is making sure your group is taken care of all that is holding you back?"

"Sometimes I think I can hear Laura spurring me on, to just get on with it, and lately, I've felt a few creaks in my old bones, so I think it's got to be sooner rather than later."

She doesn't answer my question directly, but I get the gist of what she is saying. Why I'm doing this, I don't know, but it's something different that I can sink my teeth into. "In that case, if you teach me what I need to know and get me up to speed, yes, I'll take care of things here while you're away, as long as you know it's only temporary."

"You will?" She clasps her hands together and looks up at the sky.

"We've only just met, but I owe you so much already, Lou, and if this is something I can do for you, and it will bring you genuine peace and joy, then absolutely, and without reservation, I'll make sure things run smoothly here."

She throws her arms around me and pulls me into a tight hug. "You're the most darling of girls and I truly believe God sent you here to me today."

I return her embrace because she doesn't realise how much she has given me in such a short space of time. For somebody that just came into my life, I had that feeling we'd been friends for the rest of our lives. Don't ask me to explain it because I can't. "I adore you, Lou, and that might seem strange, but you came into my life when I needed you most."

She kisses my cheek. "I think better days are just beyond the horizon."

"I really hope so."

"Trust me. I'll put in a word with the big guy in the sky."

Just then, Elijah walks past carrying a leatherbound file. His big blue eyes meet mine, and for a moment I see a flicker of recognition until a breeze comes from nowhere and blows through the room, distracting me.

"See you at the next meeting, Lou," he calls out with a wave.

"Bye, Elijah and thanks for coming," she replies, waving back.

He strolls by then turns on his heel. "Nice to meet you, Serena."

"You too, Elijah, take care." With a nod he rushes away. "Aw, he seems like a nice, genuine guy."

"Thoroughly decent as I like to say."

"Can I just say, meeting these people, I realise that life is bloody shite at times." I'm not one for profanity but sometimes it's the only way to say what is needed.

"You're telling me, but I'd have put it far less ladylike than that."

"Yeah?"

"Sometimes I stand in the gardens out there and scream, FUCK, FUCK, FUCKITY, FUCK, FUCK, FUCK..." I almost fall off the seat at her foul-mouthed tirade, but I'm fit to burst as are the other volunteers around us. "...in the hope Laura is listening because it will make her laugh." She crosses herself, and I guess she's a good catholic girl at heart.

With a titter, I share my thoughts. "You two were closer than close?"

"She was my best friend from the moment I held her in my arms."

"Jamie was mine, and sometimes I think that makes losing him worse because I shared every little thing with him and now he's gone, I don't know who to talk to."

"You can talk to me any time you like, Serena."

"Would you like to go out for coffee sometime?"

"How about we do it now?"

"Really?"

"There's no time like the present and my mouth is as dry as Gandhi's sand shoe so yeah, let's go." I can feel laughter brewing at her choice of words. "I know a lovely little Vegan place in town. They sell the most delicious brownies."

I wonder what's in these brownies that makes them so delicious, but I won't judge, even though my new friend is the embodiment of the hippy-dippy lifestyle. "I rode my bicycle over, you know, I like to do my bit for the environment."

My green goddess assessment was correct and more power to her for having conviction in a worthwhile cause. "If I take the basket off the front, it folds in half."

"I'm sure it will fit in the boot of my car."

"What are we waiting for then?"

Chapter Nine

A Kindred Spirit

A couple of weeks have passed, and my tenth meeting is over and done with. It's taken quite a while to settle myself into unfamiliar surroundings but today I had a breakthrough of sorts.

I'm busy stacking chairs at the back of the room while Louise is with a lady who attended for the first time tonight. I know how it feels so I will exit graciously without interrupting and text her later.

Ready to leave, Elijah, the handsome guy who usually sits at the front of the room approaches me. He appears nervous and does that thing I've noticed on other occasions when his eyes dance about the room. It's as if he doesn't want to make eye contact for fear of somebody looking into them and seeing the real him.

He lifts a chair and stacks it onto another, then onto another. With barely a grunt he lifts five of them. "Can I get you a coffee, Serena?"

Looking up, it dawns on me how tall he actually is. I'd guess six foot three and compared to my height of five foot two, he's practically a giant. "A tea would be lovely, Elijah, thank you."

"You know, you did really well today."

"I hadn't planned on saying any of that stuff, but it just came from nowhere."

"But you did, and from my point of view, I understand you more now than I did at the last meeting where you only spoke briefly."

"I felt such a fool sobbing like that in front of you all."

"Why? Each and every one of us has sat in this room and lost our shit at one time or another."

"It feels good to talk to others that understand. Thank you, Elijah."

"Like it or not, we're all in the same boat here, Serena."

"Opening myself up to others doesn't come naturally as you might have guessed."

"I was the same way, and still feel guilty but Kara would want me to move on."

He's mentioned Kara every session and it's obvious her death is still raw for him. "How long have you been coming to the group?"

"I first found this place a few years ago though I took a little break for health reasons a while back."

"I'm sorry to hear that. Are you better now?"

"Much better, thanks, though Kara still occupies my mind, even when I want some respite from it."

"I get that, totally. But as Lou says, why try and fight it?"

"I thought I'd got my life together then losing her sent me back down a path I'd tried so hard to step off. Her death pushed me into self-destruct mode, and though I blamed her at first, I always had the power to control myself but used her death as an excuse to behave like an animal."

"You're too hard on yourself." He hands me a cup of stewed tea way past its best, but I'm grateful anyway.

"It took me nearly dying to bring me to my senses but that's a story for another time."

He doesn't want to talk too in depth about whatever his health issues were, and I respect his choice. As a nurse I knew boundaries mattered and would never dare cross them uninvited. "I'm pleased you made it through."

"Yeah, by the skin of my teeth." He takes a gulp of his coffee. "So, tell me more about you."

For groups such as these, it's a cardinal sin to pry but I don't mind. I know he means no harm. "I'm a mess, that's the top and bottom of it." I laugh which surprises me because I've only expressed sorrow in front of him before now. "Sorry…"

"I spent too long apologising simply for being human so give yourself a break."

"You know I lost my husband but what I didn't tell you all is that it was in a road traffic accident. He was hit by two cars while trying to stop a thief who had robbed a local off-licence."

"Bloody hell." He blows his cheeks out. "That's awful."

"So, when I tell people I'm a mess, that's why."

"Obviously, and nobody would blame you for feeling that way."

"I haven't learned to live without him yet or come to terms with how he died."

"Do you realise you just said the magic word?"

"I did?" I scour my mind, wondering what it was. "What did I say?"

"*Yet*, which means you're open to the possibilities of carrying on and living a good life."

"I can almost hear Jamie in my head telling me to stop wallowing and get on with things."

"And would he be right?"

"Probably. But talking myself into action isn't the easiest option."

"We've all been there, Serena, but the past is the past for a reason, and we don't have to forget, but find a way to carve a path to the future, or what's the point in living at all?"

"I thought we'd be together forever."

"Nothing is forever and as crap as that sounds, it's the truth."

"I know that now, but I dreamed of us old and grey, shuffling about like the lovely Hamish, comparing hip replacement scars."

He's amused by my words and chuckles. "You will find your way back to one another when the time is right?"

"Do you really believe that?"

"Absolutely, and without that belief, darkness comes and threatens to consume me." I feel a kindred spirit in him because his thoughts reflect what is on my mind. It's what I need, rather than well-meaning but useless platitudes. "Death really is only a heartbeat away."

"That's a nice way to look at it."

"It's true, and when yours beats its last, there he will be, waiting for you."

I feel a rush of warmth because his spiel might be considered cheesy, but I'd rather look at things from his point of view than mine. It gives me food for thought that Jamie and I weren't meant to have our together forever here on Earth, but when my time comes, perhaps an eternity in Heaven lies in wait. "You're a wise man, Elijah."

"Wisdom comes from making too many stupid mistakes," he says, trying and failing to hide the misery of his past.

"Have you really made so many?"

"More than I care to dwell on."

"I'm surprised, because you seem so tuned in."

"To myself?"

"Well, yes…" He doesn't seem the type of guy that isn't aware of his own actions.

"Ha, you're talking to the biggest idiot that ever walked the Earth."

"Now you're being too hard on yourself."

"I've made some terrible decisions, and most led me to ruin."

"No, not to ruin, Elijah. If that were the case, you wouldn't be here talking to me."

"Okay, well let's say I pushed things as far as I could before fate stepped in and forced me to look at the direction my life was heading in."

"Intriguing."

"Maybe I'll tell you one day."

"If that day comes, I'll gladly listen."

"Sometimes it's all I need, for somebody to hear me."

"Do you ever feel like you're screaming your lungs out and nobody can hear?"

He closes his eyes and shakes his head. "Wow, you actually get it."

"I do?"

"You hit the nail on the head because that is exactly how I feel."

"I won't be the only one, Elijah."

"Perhaps not, but I don't often have one on one conversations so it's like hearing a symphony for the first time."

"Well, I'm glad whatever I said struck a chord."

"You're a wise lady, Serena."

"Wisdom comes from making too many stupid mistakes," I reply, mimicking his words, though our mistakes won't be the same. I've made many since Jamie died, but soon I will have to take stock and put them right. "You're not the only one... I've learned that much already."

We're interrupted by a familiar voice. "What are you two yapping about?"

"Oh, just life, Lou."

She links her arm through Elijah's, and while she's taller than I am, he still towers above her. "And how are you, my blue eyed boy?"

"Oh, you know me, Lou, plodding along."

"You're doing better though, yes?"

"Every day is better than the last."

"That tells me you're living your life, good for you."

"Without you, I'd be up shit creek without a paddle."

"She's amazing, isn't she," I add.

"Yes, and you're not so bad yourself, Serena."

"This lady is a diamond," Louise adds.

I feel my cheeks burning. "Oh, shush, you two."

"Right, I need to get going, I have a date with The Walking Dead on Disney Plus."

"Argh, Elijah, I can't watch that, it terrifies me."

"After what we've experienced, nothing scares me anymore."

He has a point, and though he probably doesn't realise it, his words have a profound effect upon me. "You're right."

"Well, gotta go."

"Night, Elijah." Louise unlinks her arm from his. He bends down to kiss her cheek.

"Goodnight, ladies."

"Thanks for the tea," I add.

"Any time." I watch as he walks away and still feel my cheeks burning. "What a lovely boy," I say.

"Boy?" Louise queries.

"Yeah, what is he about twenty-eight?"

With a cocked eyebrow and the hint of a grin she corrects me. "Behave yourself, he's thirty-five."

"Well, he doesn't look anywhere near it."

"He should look as old as I do after what he's been through."

"I don't know the ins and out of it, but I do feel for him."

"Is that Nurse Serena poking her tongue out again?"

"What do you mean?"

"Empathy, there it is again. Are you sure that hospital isn't where you need to be?"

"Maybe, but not right now."

"You know, I won't hold you to taking care of the group if your old job is your calling."

"I don't know what it is, but I'm happy doing what I'm doing now, and helping you out here gives me something to focus on. So, no, there won't be any backtracking. I am doing this for you, and for me, then when you return, who knows?"

"Slowly but surely, you seem to be coming back together again."

"Although my longing for Jamie is just as it was, I don't feel as broken, but I am spurred on by the members here. They've suffered so much."

"As have you."

"Yes, but if you and all these wonderful people can find a way, I'm damned sure I can too."

She cups my face in her hands. "Well said, my beautiful flower."

"I'm only where I am because you helped me find the right path."

"Nonsense. I just provide the tools and you're doing the rest."

"You don't know how grateful I am to have you in my life."

"We're a meeting of mind and spirit, Serena, I truly believe that."

"I love your way of thinking."

"It's gotten me through some pretty tough times, but now, we're heading for brighter times."

"Absolutely. And by the way, I stopped by the travel agents on the way and picked up some brochures for Thailand, Vietnam and Cambodia."

"You did?"

"Yep, so how's about we go back to mine and I fire up the pizza oven and we raid the wine cellar?"

"Are we cooking?"

"We are. No frozen pizza for me. Fresh all the way."

"Then you have a deal."

"Come on then, let's get this place tidied up, a bottle of red has my name on it."

"Something tells me you're about to become a bad influence upon me, Serena."

"Ha! I don't think so."

"I'm a good girl, I am." She mimics Eliza Doolittle from My Fair Lady.

"Louise Geller, I'm no fool. Something tells me I only know a fraction of what has gone on in your life."

"You might be right but add a bottle of Gin or two to the evening and I'll tell you everything you wanna know."

"Deal!"

Chapter Ten

Facing the Past

Today is the day my past and present collide.

It's been a long time coming but I'm prepared to accept whatever consequences come with it.

Driving along the country lanes toward my mother and father-in-law's cottage fills me with dread but I've put it off for far too long. They deserve better from me.

Pulling into the driveway, the gravel rattles under my tyres. I park in my usual place, right in front of the sitting room window.

As expected, Miriam, my beloved mother-in-law, peeks from behind the curtain.

I deliberately avoid looking at her because I couldn't bear it if she appears angry or unwelcoming.

To my surprise she opens the door with a beaming grin on her face. Her hair is a little longer and greyer than the last time I saw her, and the extra pounds she proudly carried are now gone.

I know the feeling well; having struggled with weight all of my life, now I seem to have little appetite, and the calories I do consume are burned away through nervous energy. I'm now what is considered the perfect size ten though I'd gladly balloon to a size thirty to have Jamie back.

Reaching into the back seat, I grab my green canvas bag, then step out of the car and lock the door with the fob though she has no neighbours for miles, and it's unlikely to be stolen.

I speak before she does because there are pressing matters that I have to get off my chest, and if I don't do it right away, I might never do it. "I hate myself, Miriam, and owe both you and Jimmy a massive apology."

She ducks down as the archway around her front door is still surrounded by multi-coloured roses that are a little overgrown. Holding open her arms she walks toward me.

I fall into them, comforted by her touch.

"Oh, my darling girl, you have nothing to be sorry for."

Contrite, I look directly into her eyes. This time there can be no hiding behind events of the past. The present is more important. "It's been too long."

"Yes, it has, but we both understood your need for time alone, but now you're here my heart could burst with joy."

"You've always been so good to me. I don't deserve it, not now anyway."

"Serena, you will always be a part of this family, no matter how far you go, or how long you're gone for."

I cry happy tears, but ones mixed with relief. "I don't want to lose either of you."

"That was never on the cards. We're here for you as long as you want us to be."

"It's been so hard without him, you know–" I stumble on my words and remember who I'm talking to. "You know that better than anybody."

"Jimmy and I have one another and if truth be told, even that's not enough at times. But we try our best to get through the days and nights."

"I miss him so much it hurts." I fall back into her arms and cry.

She pulls me close for a moment then holds me at arms-length, looking me over. "I hate to see your tears, Serena." With her index finger she wipes under my eye. Leading me into the cottage, familiar surroundings envelop me. I place my bag on the work surface behind the door.

"Crying is all I'm good for right now."

"Now that I can relate to, but you made the right decisions and we've never thought any differently."

"We'd talked about what would happen as you do, but never did I think I'd ever be forced into that position."

"It's one that nobody would ever wish to be in but that's the way the cards were dealt, and you did what you could in the worst of circumstances."

"Wherever Jamie is, I hope he can forgive me for letting him go so easily."

"There was nothing easy about what you did, Serena. It was the bravest thing and not something I'm sure I'd have had the strength to do if left for me to decide."

"I was so scared the family would hate me for it, for allowing parts of him to be taken away."

"Jamie would have hated an existence with machines breathing for him, you know that as well as I do." The smell of her famous cheese scones baking in the Aga tells me I'm hungry. She pulls a chair out and sits me down before taking one for herself and positions it opposite me. "Every single one of us admires your decision because it was made out of respect for him, and there is no greater love than putting your own grief aside and honouring another's wishes."

"What if...?"

"There's no point torturing yourself with what ifs because by the time the machines were turned off, he'd already gone and no matter how many wishes we sent to the heavens, or prayers offered, nothing would have brought him back, but this way, a part of him lives on in others and I take some comfort in that."

"I can't, not yet anyway because I hate that he's not here and they are."

She looks at me with an understanding, knowing there is no malice, just selfishness that I want him back. "Did you ever speak to the transplant coordinator?"

"Not yet, but I did read the letters. I just don't want to meet any of them yet—"

"I read them right away, but you don't have to explain yourself to me. I get it and when you are ready, just pick up the phone and I'll be right there if you do want to take that step."

"Thank you."

She pats my hand and I feel the never-ending love and affection that has warmed me since the day we met. After losing my own parents the year before I married Jamie, she became my surrogate mother. "You've never been far from my thoughts, and so many times I wanted to knock on your door, but I had to let you come back to me."

"I would never have stayed away forever, but I admit that joining the grief support group pushed me into accepting a future I wasn't sure I wanted."

"You're going to counselling?" She's misunderstood what I was saying.

"Not counselling, no. It wasn't really for me, but I am going to a local support group three times a week."

"Oh, really?"

"Yeah, and it's way out of my comfort zone but I find it helps to talk about my problems to others who've experienced the same thing, even if they are strangers."

"That's good, Serena. You're finally getting out of the house and talking to people and hopefully making friends."

"I didn't need friends when Jamie was here, but I should have confided in you and Jimmy,"

"Then why didn't you?"

"I couldn't bear the thought of my torment adding to yours."

"Losing a child, no matter how old, is not something any parent gets over, but I have faith, and it teaches me to have belief that one day we will meet again."

"Do you really believe that?"

"I have to, because if I don't, all I'm left with is anger and questions as to why it was my baby and not somebody else's that was taken."

For the first time since I'd known her, Miriam looks her age. With the greying hair, lines I hadn't noticed on her face before today told of the strain losing her eldest child has brought on her physically. I'd yet to see Jimmy but would never forget the sorrow etched across his face when the purple velvet curtains closed around the coffin.

It was a day I'll never forget for obvious reasons but to witness a man who had only ever shown strength reduced to a blubbering wreck is something I'll struggle to shake off. Memories that still bother me on days when guilt stabs at me over my enforced separation from them. Something tells me he cries every day, away from the watchful eyes of his loving wife.

"How is Jimmy?"

"If I'm honest, a broken shell of the man I married," she replies. "And no matter what he says I know him better than I know myself. He can't lie and never could." She dabs at the corners of her eyes with her clean crisp apron. "Day by day, he's hanging on by a thread, and it's only Ben and Helena that keep him from slipping away into the quagmire of grief each of us skirt around day to day."

"Oh, God." I don't want to cry again, not now. I bury my face in my hands. "I'm so sorry…"

She pulls my hands away from my face and smiles. "Now don't be silly, you cry all you like, I do."

"I should have been here to help you both through it."

"You haven't been in a fit state to help anybody, let alone a pair of old duffers like us."

"I love you, Miriam, Jimmy, Helena and Ben too. To me, you're the only family I have, and nothing will ever change that."

She holds out her arms. There is comfort and security in being held once more. Tenderly, she kisses the side of my head then speaks. "We feel exactly the same way you do, Serena, and together we'll find our way back to the world, even though right now it hurts to take a breath." She rests her chin on the top of my head and though she is upset, I'm safe in her arms. "Ten seconds at a time is how I manage."

I know what she means. If she can get through ten seconds, and then the next ten, then the next, it's easier than thinking about hours, days, weeks, months, or years. "You know Jamie would be so annoyed looking down at the pair of us. He'd say you're wallowing, Serena, knock it off. I can almost hear him now, but he meant so much, and still does that I can't let go of him so easily."

"None of us ever will, but we will get through it and live again, if only for him."

"How can you be so practical?"

"My whole family would fall like dominos, and you know what they say about us Northern women being the backbones of the family."

"You're the strongest woman I know, Miriam."

"I don't know so much—you have the makings of a lioness."

"Do you think?"

"I know it."

"Thank you."

"For what?"

"Not hating me and sending me away."

"What's all this nonsense?"

"I wouldn't blame you or Jimmy if you did—after all he was on his way home to me when he was hurt."

"Exactly the same way he was every other day of the week," she sighs. "It was his time, and that's that."

I find it hard to think of the human race existing with pre-assigned numbers. "Do you think we're here for a pre-ordained amount of time?"

"What God gives, he taketh away, and I stand by that—Jamie was needed up there..." She points a finger to the ceiling, but I know where she means. "...and who are we to argue with his plans?"

For the first time in years, I feel the call of the Church and make a mental note to stop by on the way home. "You look at it in such a beautiful way. I envy you."

We're standing face to face again when she taps the side of her head. "Memories are mine to keep, Serena, and nobody can take them away." It reminds me of something Louise once said to me. Then she places her hand over her heart. "Jamie has lived in here from the moment I knew I was carrying him, and he's still here, with every beat, my son was and is still a part of me."

"I talk to him, you know."

"So do I," she replies with a little cackle. "When I'm cleaning, or washing the dishes, I give him a running commentary of my day. I bet he's up there rolling his eyes and telling me to shut up yapping."

I find comfort in the fact she does the same as I do. But we're both clinging on, refusing to let go. "No, I think he would love that you still talk to him."

"No matter what the future holds for us all, Jamie is never going to be forgotten."

"I don't really see any future without him, Miriam, how can I?"

"But there is one, a bright one, for you, because you are still a young, vibrant, intelligent woman, and right now, living your life without him might seem alien, but it's what we've all been doing for the past twelve months."

"It feels like only yesterday that I said goodbye to him."

"For me too, but as cliche as it is, life goes on, it has to, and one day, when you say goodbye to Jimmy and me, that won't negate what we meant to you and vice versa."

"I can't stand the thought of any more loss, especially the two of you."

"We all die, sweetie, in the end, but it's about what you do with your life—don't waste it, you have that lovely big house, the business, and while you might never have to work again, find something that brings you joy and cling onto it."

"I'm glad you mentioned the business." I'd been worried and unsure how to broach the subject.

"Oh?"

I decide to just spit it out. "I've had an offer to sell it."

"Right." Her eyes tell me it's not what she wants but she won't tell me that.

"But I haven't made any decisions because it feels wrong right now to even think about it."

"You have to do what is right for you."

"If I sell it, I might not be able to live with the decision afterward, so I had another idea, and wanted to run it by you first?"

"Let me get those cheese scones out of the oven. You can tell me what's on your mind, and I'll give you an honest answer."

"May I have one?"

"A scone?"

"If you don't mind."

"You can have as many as you like, and you know what's strange is that today is the first time I've baked since Jamie died. Perhaps the universe was telling me you were planning to visit."

"I've not had much of an appetite, but I can't resist your cooking. You know me and anything savoury." She pulls two trays out of the oven and the delicious aroma intensifies making my tummy rumble. "Gosh, how many did you make?"

"More than enough for you to take a batch back home and enjoy."

"You're too good to me."

"What are mum's for?" Those four words fill me with warmth and for the first time in a long while I'm where I need to be. "Now, would you like Lurpak, or perhaps you want to eat it plain?"

"Lurpak is good for me." It's the best butter on the market and one I avoid buying because I'd smear it over everything.

"Full fat or the light spread?"

"I need the calories so let's go for the bad stuff."

"That's my girl." She sets a plate of scones down in front of me then retrieves the Lurpak butter from the fridge, a side plate, and a knife from the drawer next to the Aga. "Go on, tuck in, then you can tell me what's on your mind."

I do as instructed and take a bite of the warm scone. It's all I can do to stop my eyes rolling to the back of my head. It tastes so good, but also like home if that makes any sense. "Oh, yummy."

"You always did love them."

With a mouthful I answer. "Heaven..."

She loves to tease me and makes a piggy noise. "Well, there are plenty more and I can always whip up another batch of the mix, but before I do that, I'm itching to know what you want to talk to me about."

Reluctantly I put the second half of my cheese scone down then take a deep breath and blurt it out. "I wondered if Jimmy would be interested in taking over."

Wide eyes tell me it's the last thing she'd expected me to say. "You want my Jimmy to take over Jamie's business?"

"Yes, and I know it seems like a crazy idea, but I can think of nobody better."

"He knows nothing about computer software, Serena."

"But he knows about people management, and if he agreed to come on board to oversee that side of things, I could hire a permanent consultant to take over from Jamie. That way both sides of the coin are taken care of."

"You're serious, aren't you?"

I eye up the scone, yearning to take another bite. "Deep down, I don't really want to get rid of what Jamie worked so hard to build, but I'm not equipped to deal with everything needed to keep it going. And if Jimmy doesn't want to, I'd rather sell than see it go to ruin."

"Then ask him outright, no skirting about the issue, lay it on the line and tell him your reasons why."

"You don't think he'll be mad at me for suggesting it?"

"Mad with you, never? But sock it to him straight, tell him you need him, and it might give him a sense of purpose that's missing in him right now."

"I don't want to put any pressure on him."

"Jimmy is at his wits' end right now, and nothing I say or do can rescue him."

"It hurts me to hear that."

"You have to see it through his eyes–Jamie was his eldest child, but still his baby and losing him goes against the natural order of things." She pauses because the same can be said of her loss. "Ask him for help. He won't refuse you I guarantee it."

"But I want him to do it because he wants to and not out of some foolish loyalty to either of us."

"He will think of you at first, but keeping Jamie's legacy alive will soon take precedence, and who knows, it might help him navigate a route back to living, rather than existing, again."

"I really don't want to hand the company over to strangers."

"Then talk to him." She nods toward the door. "Now's your chance."

Chapter Eleven

What the Future Holds

"Talk to who?" Jimmy pushes the door open and steps into the room.

Miriam nods my way. "We have a visitor."

He looks like he's aged ten years in months. A lump pushes its way into my throat, and I try hard not to cry. He opens his arms to me. "My beautiful girl, how I've missed you."

I'm shocked by his gaunt appearance and sunken cheeks. But he's still the same man who walked me down the aisle because nobody else could do it. I stand then rush to embrace him. "I've missed you too, so much, and I am sorry it's taken me until now to come."

"I understand."

"I wanted to see you both so badly, but there is another reason I am here, albeit a more selfish one."

"Hit me with it and I'll tell you what I think."

"I want you to take over the company."

"Oh aye, what company would this be?"

Miriam tuts then rolls her eyes. "She wants you to take over the running of NASA." She always was the mistress of sarcasm. I've missed it.

"Eh?"

"What company do you think she means, soft arse?"

He holds onto both of my hands. "You want me to take over Tate Technology, is that what you're asking me?"

"If I don't have somebody I trust in there, it's going to fail." I debate internally whether to tell him the next part but want to be honest. "I've had an offer from some big American firm to buy it lock, stock and barrel."

"And?"

"I don't want to sell what Jamie fought hard for. I want to make it into a continuing success in Jamie's name, but I can't do it without you."

"Then that's what we'll do."

It seemed too easy, and I fear he's only doing it to help me and not because he wants anything to do with the company. "Really?"

"Have I ever let you down before?"

"Never."

"Well, today isn't a good day to start. But I have one condition."

"Go on."

"I want you there with me, at least for a little while because you know the staff, and by my side, it might make the transition smoother."

"If I say no, will you still help me?"

"You know I will. But I'd like your help, plus I get to spend time with my daughter."

I'm not actually his daughter but he has never treated me any less than one of his own. If he needs me, I'm there for him. "How can I say no to you?"

"You can't."

"Okay, then, and of course, you'll be paid as any Managing Director would." I feel like a weight has been lifted from my shoulders. "I'll stay for three months to help ease them all into this new era with you, will that be okay?"

"Let's take it day to day, shall we?" Jimmy always played hardball, but I appreciate him agreeing to help so quickly. "All that director stuff can wait. Pay me what's fair then down the line, we can make it more official if we're both suited to the new arrangement."

"Whatever you say, boss."

"Now that's sorted, I better drive myself into town and buy myself a new suit."

"And a couple of new shirts too," Miriam adds helpfully. "Plus, those dress shoes of yours have seen better days, so find something that matches whatever you buy. Oh, and double up on everything, in fact, you want five suits, five matching shirts, socks, ties, two pairs of dress shoes, anything you forget I'll go out for tomorrow."

"Christ, woman, I'm going to work in an office not a fashion show in Paris."

"Just do as you're told, Jimmy, and don't ever call me woman again." She shoots him that 'behave yourself' look then follows it with a smile. Theirs is a true love I envy.

"Are you sure you don't want that old assistant of Jamie's to run the company for you? She'd have it ship shape in no time."

"She never wanted any responsibility, and nor did I ask her because I think you're the perfect person for the job."

"And I agree," Miriam says. "Plus, it will get you out from under my feet for a few hours a day."

"Yeah, the less nagging I hear from you, the better."

Their banter fills me with joy. It reminds me of times now past. "Now we've got that out of the way, there's something else I'd like to ask."

"Spit it out then."

"I'd like it if you would agree to take Jamie's old office?"

He hesitates for a moment. "Why would you not want that for yourself?"

"I don't intend to stay working at the company because I have other plans, but right now, I think it might be too overwhelming, and I will totally understand if you feel the same way. There are plenty of other places we can settle in."

"Let's see how we both feel tomorrow morning, shall we?"

"Tomorrow morning?" I ask.

"There is no better time—let's not put anything off. 8am, on the dot."

"It's been a long time since I got up that early." I'm almost dreading the ring of the alarm, but routine might push me back into accepting I am still a part of the world, and not some crazy shut-in only venturing out to talk over my woes with a crowd of mostly strangers.

"It will do us the power of good, so I'll swing by and pick you up, and that way you don't have to drive." He pulls me into his arms and kisses the top of my head. "Thank you."

"What for?"

"For giving my life purpose again."

"Oh, Jimmy," Miriam adds, overcome with emotion. "You will always have a purpose."

"But this is important, and if I can help carry my son's legacy into the future, I can die a happy man."

"You'll be here for years yet," I say.

"Oh, I know that but it's nice to think I'm shuffling out of retirement rather than toward my grave."

"Don't talk like that, Jimmy," Miriam protests, shaking her head. I know what is going through her mind right now. The thought of existing without him is unbearable.

He stares at the plate of scones and raises his eyebrows. "You've been baking?"

"Or perhaps the Easter Bunny dropped by while you were tinkering about the garden."

Their banter is legendary within the family. Sarcastic to their cores, each one compliments the other perfectly. "Wouldn't that be something." He swipes a scone off the plate and bites into it. "Mm, still warm. Right, I'm heading into town." Another bite is followed by a smile, that something from before losing Jamie has crept back into the present. "Will you be here when I get back, Serena?"

"If you want me to be, yes, of course."

"I'd love you to stay for dinner, that's if you have enough room after polishing off Miriam's goodies."

"I'll be here, and I'll be sure to save some space for whatever we're having."

"Homemade Steak and Ale Pie, how does that sound?" Miriam points to the side where it sits ready to go into the oven. "Cabbage and carrots too."

"You have been busy."

"I had a feeling we'd have guests today, and we do, a very special and welcome one."

I'm overwhelmed with a feeling of love and being wanted. Standing again I open my arms. "Group hug."

The three of us are united in our grief but also with the sense of a brighter if different future than any one of us anticipated ahead. Crying happy tears mixed with a tinge of longing, I kiss each of them on the cheek. "I feel like I'm home, thank you."

"This will always be your home," Jimmy reassures.

Do it now, I tell myself. It's the secret I've wanted to share since the day we released Jamie's ashes at Lulworth Cove. Edging backward, it's now or never. "There's something I want to tell you both, but I don't want you to be angry with me because I did it with the best of intentions."

"What is it?" Miriam asks.

I grab my canvas bag from the work surface, sit back down and open it. Reaching in, I retrieve four small black velvet boxes and place them side by side on the kitchen table. Inscribed on the top of each one is an initial—J, M, B, and H. "I've had these for a while."

"You don't have to bring us gifts."

"It's not exactly a gift, Jimmy." Rather than going around the houses, I hand Jimmy his box first, then pass Miriam hers. "Please, open them."

They do so in unison. "Ooh, how lovely," Miriam coos at the small gold band. "What's it for?" Jimmy stares at the silver band in his box but remains silent.

"I know we talked about Jamie's ashes as a family and decided to sprinkle them all, but a part of me worried it was all too soon, and I didn't want any of you to be left with nothing, so I had these made…" Both glare at me wide-eyed and I can't read how they truly feel though I pray they see my good intentions. "Each ring only used a tiny amount of Jamie's ashes, but I wanted something you could all hold onto, and while I know…" I was rambling now as nerves took hold. "…it was done with the—"

Jimmy holds a finger up to silence me. "You did this for us?"

"For all of you, yes."

"Even though you were falling apart, you set that aside to think of what we were going through?"

I shrug my shoulders, not wanting or deserving of any praise. "You're my family, what else was I going to do?"

Miriam allows her tears to fall as she slips the ring on her third finger left hand. It would forever sit next to her wedding ring.

Jimmy followed her lead, then to my surprise he walked out of the room closing the door behind him. Hearing him sob on the other side of the kitchen door cut me in half.

I look to Miriam, clueless as to what to do next. "I'm so, so sorry, I didn't want to upset either of you."

She reaches for my hand, and I gladly accept. "You didn't upset him, my darling girl, but what you did do is give him a little piece of his son back. He won't have the words to tell you how grateful he is, but I can speak for all of us when I tell you we will never forget this kindness." She stares at the ring on her finger, and I see a flicker of light return to her eyes. "...not ever..."

"So, you don't think Ben and Helena will be upset that I took some of the ashes?"

"No, not at all, but if you don't mind, I should ring them both. I'm sure they would love to see you, and I think you should be the one to give them their gifts."

"Oh, gosh. Do you really think so?"

"I know so."

"I've missed them."

She picks up the landline and presses in a series of numbers. I hear the speakerphone click in. "Ben, it's your mum."

"I know, most of us have mobile phones that tell us who's calling." He inherited the sarcastic nature from his parents.

"I'll slap your legs if you give me cheek again."

"Just kidding, Mum, what's up."

"There is somebody here that wants to say hello."

"Oh?"

She nods my way. "Hi, Ben."

There is silence on the line for a moment. Then he speaks. "Serena, is that you?"

"Yes," I reply. "I've missed you."

"It's so good to hear your voice." Then more silence, and I'm sure I hear a sniffling sound. "Let me call Helena, and we'll be right over, okay."

"Okay, darling, see you soon," Miriam replies. "Drive safely."

He ends the call.

"No matter how he sounded, I'm worried me being here will upset them."

"Trust me. Both of them have missed you and will be delighted you're here." She stares at her ring and smiles. "And they are going to love their gifts."
"I really hope so."

Chapter Twelve

The Deep End

The afternoon sun beats down on my face. But I'd take it over the cold any day of the week. I'm just locking the front door as my mobile phone rings.

Looking at the screen I see Louise's name flash up and answer.

"Hey, Lou."

"Where are you?" She sounds flustered.

"At home and just leaving for group. Why?"

"I wondered if you would do me a favour."

"If I can, sure."

"I'm not going to be able to make it tonight and wondered if you would lead for me?"

"Are you okay?"

"Yeah, but I ate some leftover Vindaloo from the takeaway. It must have been off because I've had the flying shites for the last hour."

"Oh, no." Toilet talk always makes me laugh and this time is no exception. "I'm—"

"Are you laughing?" She suddenly has a coughing fit.

"Sorry, but I can't help it."

"My arse is on fire... oooh..." More coughing and then she groans.

I lock my legs at the knees. "Stop it or I'll wet myself."

"It's bloody awful." She burps down the line. "It's coming out both ends now."

I'm fighting back the urge to laugh. "Gosh," is all I can think of to say.

"I can feel my tummy bubbling," she added. "Will you do it for me?"

"Yes, of course, but how am I going to get in and open up?"

"Bob, the caretaker will be there, but I'll call him now and let him know the situation."

"Okay, but I'm nervous that–"

"Look," she says, cutting in, "I gotta go before I poop all over my brand new laminate floor...you'll be fine, call me when you're done."

She hangs up before I have time to answer. I chuckle to myself though I'm suddenly presented with what I see as an impossible task. How to conduct a meeting and whether those in attendance will even open up with a new face leading them.

Jumping into my car, I head over to Violet Lodge.

Louise was right and the cantankerous old caretaker is waiting inside for me. "Hi, Bob," I say."

"Good day to you, miss."

"Did Louise call you?"

"She sure did, and don't worry, I'll have it all set up in a flash."

"Let me help."

"No fear, I've got everything under control. You just get yourself prepared 'cos that whingeing lot will be here soon."

I ignore his unkind barb when I really want to put him in his place. "Thanks, Bob."

He waves away my gratitude and cracks on while I think about what I want to say.

Half an hour later, I'm stood before a group of people requiring an explanation. "Hey, everyone, I know you're all a tad surprised, but Louise is a bit under the weather and asked me to help out. I don't mind admitting I'm terrified and out of my depth, and will totally understand if you don't want to talk but–"

Elijah is the first to speak up and I'm beyond grateful for it. "You're one of us, Serena, and we're all friends here."

Nods of agreement and smiling faces stare back at me.

"Here, here," Hamish adds. "Go on, hen."

"Thanks everyone."

"Is Louise okay?" Dawn asks.

"Yes, she's fine, a dodgy curry caught her unaware." And though I shouldn't be surprised, I'm suddenly laughing at the mental image of Louise racing to the toilet with flames billowing out of her back passage. As it happens my laughter is infectious and soon, we're all having the time of our lives. Though this isn't how Louise would manage the meeting, it's the best I can do and wonderful practice for when I temporarily take over. "So, I've been thrown in at the deep end, but if anybody wants to take the floor, the rest of us are here to listen."

Time flies by and suddenly Bob is hovering about at the back of the room waiting to lock up. He taps his watch and I look at mine. It's twenty past nine in the evening, and I'm grateful he allowed me more than the allotted time.

"Well, you won't believe this, we've overshot, but I want to thank you all for being here tonight and giving me a chance."

A round of applause brings a wave of emotion I hadn't expected. Then, as usual, the crowd dissipates and this time only Elijah remains behind to assist with clearing up.

"You know, you were fantastic."

"I didn't do anything."

"You listened and that's all you needed to do. Lou made the right choice asking you to step in while she is on her travels."

"My legs were shaking."

"I noticed."

"You did?"

"We all did, but you found your stride and while it might be at Lou's expense, humour is a good ice breaker."

"Don't set me off again. She's probably glued to the toilet seat and we're all having a good laugh about it."

"Lou would be the first to find it funny, but something tells me she could have made it if she'd wanted to."

Suddenly, I'm suspicious. "Do you think so?"

"You said you were thrown in at the deep end, and while I don't doubt Lou is in dire straits, what better way for you to learn than to do it all by yourself."

"Well..." A sudden realisation hits that I've been played. "...the crafty cow."

"Lou marches to the beat of her own drum, you know that as well as I do."

"Yes, she does, and while I should be mad, I'm grateful for the opportunity and experience."

"People warm to you, Serena, have you not cottoned on to that yet?"

"I've never met such a wonderful bunch of people."

"They would say the same of you."

He stacks the chairs and lifts them with ease. "You have the strength of ten men."

"I used to work in the construction industry many moons ago, hanging off buildings, you know the thing."

"And now?"

"Drugs and heights don't mix."

I'm impressed by his ability to say it how it is. "I guess not."

"Most days I was off my head. How I wasn't killed I don't know, but now, I'm hovering between past and present."

"So, what do you do for work now?" I realise I'm overstepping. "Sorry, Elijah, that is none of my business, ignore me."

"It's fine," he replies. "If you want the truth, I'll tell you but only Lou knows."

"You can trust me."

"Would it be permissible for me to buy you a tea or coffee in town?"

"Yes, I don't see why not. Just let me get this place tidied and we can go."

"Sure thing," he adds.

"Are you in your car?"

"No, I only live on the other side of the park so walk here."

"That's fine, I can drive and drop you home when we're done. Do you know anywhere local that is still open?"

"There's a coffee shop called Milly's just at the bottom of my road. They do fresh jam and cream scones too."

"Oh, yes, I think I know it. Count me in."

"I'll get these chairs sorted and put the water urn away."

"Thanks, Elijah, and for your support at the start of the meeting. I'm sure it's the only reason they were so open to giving me a chance."

"Nonsense, it was you who got them to open up."

"Well, I appreciate you very much."

With a nod he stacks more chairs and places them where they belong at the back of the room.

Twenty minutes later, after a quick call to Louise, who has made the most remarkable recovery, Elijah and I sit in awkward silence as I drive us to Milly's.

Chapter Thirteen

Elijah Hart

Milly's Bistro & Coffee Shop is located on Waterford Lane in an affluent area of the town.

It's been a while since I've been there, but it's changed a lot. The interior is dimly lit, but warm and inviting. The staff all wear matching uniforms, a far cry from the grotty café I've been visiting of late. The sign on the wall tells me it's open twenty-four hours a day but right now there is only one other couple, cosy in a cubicle on the other side of the spacious premises.

Small lamps sit in the middle of the wooden tables covered with satin cloths. I wonder if the ambience is used to reflect the time of night and its patrons. Whatever, I'm comfortable as soon as I take my seat opposite Elijah.

The pretty young waitress takes our order.

The smell of freshly baked goods reminds me of Miriam's kitchen. I make a mental note to call her from the office in the morning. "This place is lovely."

"Yeah, I spend a lot of time in here when I'm working."

I'm confused. "You work here?"

"No," he replies. "I just do my work in here."

The waitress reappears and sets two large Latte's down and a tray of assorted cakes. "Thank you," we both reply.

"My pleasure," she says, though it's obviously directed toward Elijah and with a side helping of fluttering eyelashes. He seems oblivious to her desires.

"You should know I've struggled with weight all my life and eating these won't help."

"There's nothing of you."

It's true, there isn't much left, and while I'm down to a size eight, my boobs and bum have all but disappeared. I'm not daft and well aware the pounds can creep back on simply by looking at this tray of goodies. "Well, it took Jamie dying for me to shift the excess and that's not the ideal type of diet for anyone."

"Your face lights up every time you mention him."

"Does it?"

"Yeah, and it's nice to see, that love you still have for him."

"It'll never die,"

"Nor should it, Serena."

"This may be a stupid question, but do you still feel the same way about Kara?"

"God, yes." He's quick to answer. "I can't imagine anybody replacing her to be honest, but the realist in me knows that one day I'll meet somebody else, but it will just be me moving on."

"You seem so sure of it."

"Losing her pushed me onto a path I was always destined to travel down, and without sounding too religious, I think him upstairs did it to show me how precious life is."

"I can see why you'd think that."

"Before then, I was on a one-man mission to party and while it's fine in your twenties, it's a bit desperate when you're in your thirties."

"How old are you?" I already know because Louise told me. But I don't want him to know that.

"Actually, I'm thirty-six today."

"What?"

"Yep, I made it to the grand old age of thirty-six, and while many people bemoan ageing, I embrace it because I should have been dead a long time ago."

"Was it so bad?"

"Having a heart attack in your thirties isn't something to be proud of, but as the old saying goes, we live and learn."

"Gosh, I'm sorry to hear that. And yes, you're right, we do."

"It's all in the past, and I'm still here, who knew?"

I can see he doesn't want to go too deeply into it so don't push. "Happy Birthday, Elijah. I wish I'd known, and we could have gone somewhere a bit more special and celebrated."

"Sitting here with you and a tray of cakes is celebration enough, so thank you."

"It makes a nice change from me going home and sitting in an empty house."

"My apartment barely feels lived in. It's just somewhere I sleep."

"You said you work in here, and I'm intrigued. What is it you actually do?"

"Have you ever heard of Grace Hart?"

"The famous romance writer, of course, yes, I love her books, though I haven't read one in a while. But what about her?" He points at himself. "I'm confused." I lift the coffee mug to my lips praying I'm not left with a foam moustache.

"*I'm* Grace Hart."

"Who is?"

"I am."

"You're pulling my leg."

"Honestly, I'm her, him…"

"You're *the* Grace Hart?" I feel like I've missed part of the conversation. I take another sip of my drink.

"Yes," he replies. "I'm her, or she's me, whichever way you want to look at it."

Shocked by his admission, I almost cover him in a spray of Latte. "I'm so sorry. How embarrassing." Dabbing furiously at my mouth and then the mess on the table, I find my words. "You're really her, well him, oh, heck?"

"Don't worry, it's fine," he says with a smile while wiping himself down.

"Are you kidding me?"

"No, not at all," he confirms with a grin.

"But, how?" I'm beyond surprised by this revelation.

"My past isn't exactly squeaky clean as you'll probably gather from the little snippets I've revealed so when I submitted my first novel to the publishers, although they snapped it up right away, when I told them about my past, suddenly they were nervous about negative publicity affecting a title they truly believe in, you know, druggie, convicted dealer, wife killed after falling three storeys while high on cocaine. It's not exactly somebody your average romance reader can relate to."

"Wow."

"I've shocked you."

"Absolutely, but I'm just in awe of your talent and the way you've worked through adversity to deliver such wonderful books. Your words are powerful, and I don't think you realise how affected we are by them."

"That is very kind of you to say, but like I said earlier only you and Lou know the truth so please keep it to yourself."

"I'm having coffee and cake with *the* Grace Hart." I can't believe I'm saying it but I'm genuinely star-struck now.

"Well, technically, you're with Elijah Hart, but yes, I see what you mean."

"I'm fan-girling but at the same time, I really don't think your readers would abandon you if they knew the truth. Had I been oblivious, and the news leaked to the press, it wouldn't have made one iota of difference and my support would have been unwavering, especially due to the fact you travelled through adversity to who you are now."

"I'm not so sure. My publishers didn't and still don't want to take that risk."

"Your writing is so touching, so real, so moving, and now I know why–because you've experienced true love and loss."

"It feels good to tell somebody else the truth of who I am and what I do."

"Do you know, if you ever revealed yourself to the wider world, you'd never know a moment's peace."

"What do you mean?"

"You're kind, caring, talented, handsome, you're the stuff of romance readers' dreams."

"Handsome, ha, I don't think so."

"Look at the waitress if you don't believe me."

He turns his head discreetly. "What am I supposed to be looking at?"

"She hasn't taken her eyes off you since we walked in."

His cheeks flush a deep red and highlights his cute dimples. "Since Kara, I've not even gone on a date."

"You will, I'm certain of it."

"I will, but what about you?"

"Well, that's one thing I'm not so certain about. But for you, it's been a touch longer, and without sounding disrespectful it might be a little lighter at the end of the tunnel for you, and while it's coming up to a year since Jamie's death, I'm not there, yet."

"There's that word again, *yet*."

"So it is." I can't argue with it. He's master of the word and knows what he's talking about.

"Don't close yourself off to the world, Serena."

"I'm slowly opening up again, just like a flower does in the first throes of spring though only to the possibility of life without Jamie."

"That's a nice way to put it. I might use the flower part in my current work in progress."

"Feel free." Suddenly, he rubs at the centre of his chest. His whole demeanour changes and concern pushes away his smile. "Are you okay?"

"Yeah, I'm fine, but sometimes my scar itches."

"You've got a scar there?"

"I had surgery and sometimes it irritates me still."

I don't ask what the surgery was for, it's not my business unless he chooses to make it mine. "Do you need me to take you home?"

"No way, not when there's a tray of cakes for me to polish off."

"Are you sure, I really don't mind."

"Like the rest of me, it's healing and gives me a bit of trouble every now and again."

"You are quite a remarkable man, Elijah, and it's a pleasure to have you as my friend."

He picks up his coffee mug. "A toast?"

"To?"

"The future."

Our mugs touch and in unison we toast to times ahead.

I've had such a good night with Elijah that when I glance at my watch and it's almost midnight, I almost topple off my chair. I haven't been out this late since the night Jamie died.

"Crikey, have you seen the time?" I push the empty tray away and the half-drunk cup of hot chocolate I switched to earlier.

He looks at his phone screen. "I hadn't realised."

"I should drive you home."

"It's fine, I only live two minutes away."

"No arguments, it's too late to be cutting through that park."

"I've had a lovely night, thank you."

"It's your Birthday, and you didn't spend it alone, that's important."

"Means a lot. Thank you for being my friend."

"I have an ulterior motive."

"Go on." He's suspicious of what is coming next.

"Would you sign my books for me?"

He seems genuinely pleased by my request. "You know I've never signed one of my own books, so if I do, it might be worth a lot of money in the future."

"Oooh, how much?"

"About twenty quid."

I slap the top of his arm. "Silly..."

"Joking aside, I'd be honoured to do it for you, but keep yours and I'll order brand new copies from the publisher."

"You'd really do that?"

"With pleasure. I'll order them tomorrow and sign them as soon as they arrive."

"I'll gladly pay for the copies."

"Don't be daft. Consider them a gift from a grateful author to a special fan."

"I'm chuffed, thank you."

"I'll bring them to the group as soon as I have them."

"Call me and I'll swing by and pick you up, I don't want you walking through the park loaded down with a bagful of your classics."

"Classics...if you say so." Elijah hands me his iPhone. "Pop your details in there and I'll text you, so you have my number."

I do as he asks. "Thank you, Elijah."

"Anytime." He rubs at his chest again.

"Scar giving you jip?"

"Yeah, but I have some cream from my specialist. I'll apply it when I get home."

My protective nature creeps in, and every instinct from my nursing days kick their way back to the forefront to remind me of the person I was, and still am. "Come on then, let's get you home so you can get that scar sorted."

Chapter Fourteen

Changes

I'd spent the morning in the office working alongside Jimmy, and while I enjoyed the challenge, it wasn't my world. Still, it was wonderful to see my father-in-law wake from unhappiness. Being there made me realise I'd go back to nursing once my commitments to Louise had been honoured.

Jimmy had decided to take over Jamie's old office and while I was pleased, going in there still presented a problem for me. "How's it going?"

"Great," he replies, not lifting his eyes from whatever he is reading to look at me.

"Are you busy?"

Now he looks up. "Never too busy for you."

"Oh, good." Tentatively, I walk in, memories assaulting me from every angle and take a seat opposite.

"What's wrong?"

"Nothing."

"Come on, this is me you're talking to. I know you."

"I'm worried."

"About what?"

"Something I did last night."

He purses his lips together and narrows his eyes into small slits. "Nothing daft I hope?"

"God, no, but I want to be honest with you and Miriam because I'd hate you to find out and think I'd kept it a secret from you."

"You can tell me, or Miriam, for that matter, anything."

"Okay, but please don't hate me." His approval means everything to me, not that I did anything that needs to be approved.

"Never." He twists the memorial ring on his finger.

"Well, that group I go to three nights a week, I ran it last night for my friend because she was ill, and when packing up, one of the guys talked to me..." I notice him shifting in his chair. "But he has been there for two years, a nice guy, and long story short, we went for a coffee, as friends."

"Is that it?"

"I feel like I've betrayed Jamie's memory."

"You went for a coffee with a friend, is that what you're telling me?"

"A male friend, and we ended up having cake because it was his birthday."

"So, what are you fretting about? Coffee and cake. It's hardly anything to get riled up about."

"Everything about it was wrong."

"Serena, Jamie is gone and yes, I know it's not been quite a year, but I know you well enough to know you're not there yet. But if that day does come when you find happiness again, I will not stand in your way, okay."

"You're going to make me cry."

"Well, don't do that 'cos you might set me off and it's not good for the bosses to be seen blubbering."

"I just don't want you to think I've forgotten."

"You are one of the most honourable women I have ever met, and I trust your word, so if you say he is just a friend, that's all I need to know. But if that changes, I want you to tell me that too."

"Will you tell Miriam?"

"Yes, because I don't keep secrets from her, but expect a phone call to tell you to stop fretting. You are a grown woman and can choose your own friends."

"You don't know how relieved I am. I've barely slept for worrying over it."

He rolls his eyes. "Did you have a good time?"

"It was nice being out of the house."

"And this guy, he's a gentleman?"

"Yes. He lost his wife in quite awful circumstances then had some form of surgery."

"Heck, that's quite a run of bad luck."

"I know he won't mind me telling you, but he knows how it feels, and sometimes it's therapeutic to sit and listen to somebody else's problems rather than dwelling on one's own."

"This group of yours, it really helps, doesn't it?"

"Yes, and it's also given me the strength I need to decide I am going back to nursing, but not until next spring."

He claps his hands together and beams with delight. "I'm thrilled. It's exactly where you should be."

"I've missed it but going back to The Royal might be too hard, so I've decided to give it a try and then if it's not for me, I'll put in a transfer request."

"That's a good idea, but I think you'll fall right back into step– you're too good at your job to let your personal life interfere."

"What would I do without you?"

"You'd survive, but luckily for our little family, we still have one another to fall back on."

"I wouldn't want it any other way."

"Me neither, but while you're here, I do have something to say but I suspect Miriam might hang me by my toes because she wants to tell you herself. But in the spirit of sharing, it seems only right."

"Should I be worried?" Adrenaline flies round my body at breakneck speed because I can't handle bad news.

"Not at all."

"Go on then, put me out of my misery."

"Helena is pregnant."

"Aaaaaarrrggghhh." At first, I don't realise I've leapt out of my chair and shrieked so loud, but hope fills me completely, so I don't care who sees and hears me. "Oh, my God, that's the best news I've heard in ages."

"You're going to be an aunty and I'm going to be a grandad." His joy is evident, and nothing can hide it. For the first time in a while, I see the old Jimmy back again.

I race around the desk and throw my arms around him. He squeezes me tight. "I'm so happy for you all. How far gone is she?"

"Six months, but she only told us last night."

"Wow, so not long to go. How long has she known for?"

"Apparently she suspected it right away but didn't want to say anything because of Jamie."

"Oh, no, he would hate that."

"I said exactly the same thing, but that girl is as stubborn as her mother."

"Jamie worshipped Helena, and was fond of Keegan too, He only ever wanted them to be happy so wherever he is, he'll be whooping with pride." Before I can stop myself, tears fall again. "Oh, damn, I'm sorry, Jimmy. I seem to cry at everything these days."

"Come on now, there's no need for that."

"These are happy ones, trust me."

"That's a good thing then. Miriam sobbed for about two hours until I plied her with enough Brandy that she finally went to sleep."

"I have to go and see her, but I swear not to drop you in it."

"Oh, tell her, she'll guess anyway but if you would, give Helena a call and put her mind at ease. She's worried."

I grab a tissue from the box on Jimmy's desk and dry my eyes. "I'll soon put a stop to that. In fact, I'll drive out tomorrow and see her but before I do, a shopping trip is in order." I feel like I've been covered in a warm fluffy blanket. "Aw, my first niece or nephew."

"This baby will be spoiled rotten. I can see it coming."

"It's a gift from God."

"Or someone else," Jimmy adds in hushed tones, though I know who he is talking about.

I like to think Jamie is up there pulling strings but right now a baby is the very best news. Miriam is going to dote on her new grandchild, and I couldn't be happier.

Eager to hear feedback of my maiden voyage as group leader, I'd agreed to meet Louise at Luigi's for lunch before I headed out for a shopping expedition for baby goodies.

Having been here many times before, I knew her favourite dishes and ordered a feast for both of us to indulge in.

She drifted in, her candy floss pink hair windswept and wild, looking flustered, but it was the dayglo Tracksuit that drew my attention and that of the other diners. I've never seen as many colours in one outfit. I've given up trying to get her to colour co-ordinate.

"Are you okay? You look a little off your game." She covers her mouth with her hand. The cough that has been driving her mad for a while seems ever present.

"I'm fine, flower, just trying to do a million things at once and these allergies are playing havoc and making me sneeze all the time."

"Aside from your allergies, how are you feeling today?" I ask out of politeness though I'm sure I was hoodwinked into leading the meeting last night.

She avoids any mention of the out of date Vindaloo. "You were a roaring success." Louise's faith is misplaced because I actually did very little and at times it seemed the group led me, rather than the other way round.

"Well, that's kind of you, but the group ran itself."

"As it does for me, but you had to experience that for yourself."

"You didn't have the flying shites at all, did you?" I accuse, though I am not remotely bothered. After all, she really did do me a favour.

"Anyway, tell me how it went." She's desperate to avoid incriminating herself.

"How what went?"

She leans in closer as though she is about to divulge military secrets. Her voice drops to barely a whisper. "Bob told me you drove off with Elijah."

"That nosey old goat," I snap. "It wasn't like he's probably made it sound."

"Oh, come on, any fool can see you and Elijah have the makings of a genuine friendship."

"And that's all it is, Lou." I shouldn't have to say it, but I feel the glare of suspicion thrust upon me.

"Come on, Serena, don't you think I know that already?"

"I don't want people assuming otherwise."

"You're worrying too much, and if you've found a friend in Elijah, then good for you, because this crap that men and women can't be anything other than fuck buddies is exactly that, crap."

"It was his birthday yesterday."

"Was it?"

"Yeah, thirty-six, so we went out for coffee and cake, but I didn't know it was his birthday when I agreed to go."

"What did you talk about?"

"Life," I reply. "Sounds boring I know but it was nice to sit in pleasant surroundings with good company and just relax. Of course, getting out of the house was a bonus too."

"Sounds ideal to me. When Laura died, I missed the human contact. I wish I'd have had a friend like you back then."

"You have a friend who thinks the world of you now."

"I know, but for somebody like Elijah, who doesn't open up that often to many, he must see that thing I keep banging on about."

"Not empathy, again."

"It matters, Serena, and to those of us who have lost trust in the world, it's vital we feel we have somebody in our corner."

"He's a nice guy and I enjoyed our chat, but I can't help compare it to times spent with Jamie. It didn't feel right being with another man."

"You're only friends, where's the harm?"

"I don't have male friends, Lou, never have."

"Correction, you didn't have male friends, but now you do, one, Elijah Hart."

"I guess."

"There is nothing wrong with male company as long as all parties know their boundaries, and trust me, Elijah hasn't let go of Kara so won't contemplate the idea of another woman."

She's wrong but I won't betray a confidence. Elijah made it clear he is open to moving on, but I'm not that person.

"He's a very interesting guy, but that's where it stops. I just hope Bob doesn't repeat what he told you to the whole group."

"I asked him to keep it to himself."

"Thank God, but if he gives me any trouble, I'll wipe the floor with him." The waitress arrives with our starters, and I realise my appetite is slinking back slowly but surely. "This looks delicious."

"Tuck in," she replies, tearing then biting into a chunk of garlic bread. "Ooooh, this is yummy"

"Perhaps I should have ordered you something a little less spicy, especially after that dodgy curry."

"Shut your face and eat."

I take that as her admission of guilt, but she's fast become my best friend, and there are worse crimes than trying to help somebody out.

Chapter Fifteen

Bump

Loaded with bags of clothes for mum-to-be and the little one cooking up a storm in her belly, I'm overcome with emotion.

Helena has always been the little sister I never had, so seeing her in full bloom and looking as radiant as she does, I'm thankful she, and the rest of the family have been blessed with the impending arrival of a child that will never know what he or she means to us.

I rest the palm of my hand on her bump. "I cannot believe you kept it secret all this time."

Miriam is lifting something that smells loaded with calories out of the Aga.

The aroma fills the kitchen and kickstarts my hunger pangs. I'm dying to tuck into whatever it is.

"Me neither, Serena, but you know what Helena and Ben are like." There is a hint of annoyance to her tone.

I see both sides of the argument but keep my opinions to myself.

"If I hadn't exploded like a space hopper, I'd have kept it to myself a bit longer." As most expectant mothers are, she is thriving. Pregnancy suits her.

"You didn't have to do that, not because of Jamie."

"It's hard being this happy, and then feeling so sad at the same time."

"Your big brother will be watching and grinning from ear to ear to know you're having a baby."

"I wish he was here, Serena. It's not right he won't get to meet this little one." She cradles her stomach.

I can't catch what she is saying and give up trying. "So do I, but your little darling will have the best guardian angel, think of it like that."

"Keegan said the same thing."

"He's right."

"Yeah, but don't tell him that though."

"Is he thrilled about the prospect of being a daddy?"

"He's shitting himself to be honest."

"Language, Helena!" Miriam snaps. "The baby can hear everything in there, which is why I keep telling you to play something soothing, it helps."

Helena pokes her tongue out, but Miriam is busy preparing food. "I'm not playing Brahms to my unborn child."

"It's better than that head banging rubbish you call music."

"Excuse me, there is nothing wrong with BTS."

Even I'm shocked she's mad about this particular boyband. She's not exactly a teenager but has never been any different with her musical tastes.

Miriam isn't convinced at all. "Take the t out and you'd have a better description of that racket."

It takes me a moment to figure out what she means—BS, I get it.

"Oh, ha ha, mother, very funny."

I try and sway the conversation away from playing music to the bump. "I don't know how it feels but I know you are going to make amazing parents."

She lifts her T-shirt up. "I'm such a fat cow."

I paw at her protruding stomach. "Aww, I just wanna squeeze you."

"Go on then but remember I'm baking a baby in here." She taps her stomach and I go in for a hug. "It is lovely to see you again."

"And you, but now baby is on the way, we can't leave it so long. I want this little one to know his or her Godmother."

It takes a few seconds to register what she just said. "Say what?"

"You heard–I want you to be the baby's Godmother."

I fan my face with my hand, desperately trying not to cry. "Oh, oh–"

"Say you will."

"I-I would be honoured...but are you sure?"

"Aside from Ben, there is nobody else I want more than you."

Throwing my arms around her, I allow a few tears to fall but I don't want to make anyone else cry so pull myself together. "I'm going to love him or her so much."

"Him," she whispers in my ear.

"What?"

It's a boy, she mouths. *Don't tell Mum, I want it to be a surprise.*

Okay, I mouth, while trying not to cry again. It'll be a dead giveaway, so I swallow back my swelling emotions and try to pretend I don't know.

"What are you two whispering about?"

"Nothing," I lie.

"Hmm," Miriam replies.

"Mum, what are you cooking?"

"Chicken and Leek Pie, Roast Potatoes, Sweetcorn, Sprouts and glazed Carrots."

"The baby just did a spin in my belly, even he likes the sound of that,"

I cringe at the mention of *he*, but Miriam doesn't seem to pick up on it. It won't be a secret for very long, I know that much. Though I suspect both grandparents will be choked to discover a grandson is on the way.

"Me too."

"You look well, Serena."

"I've put a bit of weight back on."

"It suits you. The last time I saw you, when you gave Ben and I the rings, you looked a shadow of your former self." I look down at her finger and see the ring firmly in place. I definitely made the right decision in keeping some of the ashes.

"I've found my appetite again but won't go mad."

"Listen, I was going to call you anyway to discuss something a bit sensitive so I'm glad you came today."

"What is it?"

"Next week, it's a year since Jamie died and I wondered if there was something special you wanted to do in remembrance?"

Miriam stops what she is doing and turns to focus on us.

I blow out a breath because I've thought of nothing else for the last few weeks. As it looms closer, I worry it will put me right back to where I was again. "I don't know. Do you have any ideas?"

"To be honest, I think it would be nice to just spend the time together and talk about him as a family. I'm not ready for anything public and I know Ben won't get involved in that, so a quiet family dinner, how does that sound?"

"How about I make Jamie's favourite meal and you all come to mine for the night?"

"Ugh, you're going to make us eat stew?" She pulls a face, then laughs. "If there is one day of the year I'll agree to eat that slop it's then, so yes, if Mum is okay with it, let's do it."

"Sounds good to me." She's quieter than usual and I know the day will hit her especially hard. "And there is nothing wrong with stew, Helena."

She pokes her tongue out playfully and rolls her eyes.

"Will Ben be okay with that plan?"

"As long as it's just us then yes."

"I'll look forward to it." Then I realise how bad it sounds and correct myself. "I only mean it will be nice not to spend the day alone."

Miriam places a serving dish down on the table full of steaming roast potatoes. "It's okay, Serena, we know what you mean."

"I'll go and get Dad and Ben."

"Let me come with you."

"No dilly dallying, either of you."

I follow Helena into the hallway. "You nearly gave your own secret away."

"I know, which is why I want to tell everyone next week at yours, if you don't mind?"

"Great idea, and it might cheer everyone up."

"There is one more thing, but I'll understand if you say no."

I already know what she is going to ask. "You want to call him Jamie, don't you?"

"How did you know?"

"It's exactly what I would do."

"Do you mind?"

"Right now, I want to cry again because you've made me so happy, but I can't think of anything that would honour your brother more."

"Oh, don't start with the waterworks, you'll set me off. I was a mess when the milk man was late yesterday."

"That's hormones for you."

"DINNER," Miriam suddenly calls from the kitchen.

"We better go and get the boys or she will be out here wondering what we're doing."

"You go," I say, "and I'll keep her distracted."

Chapter Sixteen

One Year On

Groundhog Day is one of those movies I hate, yet as I stand chopping vegetables for the stew, I realise the significance because I was preparing this very meal, well re-heating it, when the police arrived to deliver the news about Jamie.

Maybe it's a bad omen, I say to myself before quickly stopping myself from dwelling. *How can anything be worse than that?*

"Can I do anything to help, Serena?" Ben slinks in behind and startles me.

"No, thank you, I'm good. Nearly there then they can go into the pan."

"I can't believe it's a year already."

I stop what I'm doing and focus my attentions on him. He looks the spitting image of his brother and at times it's distracting, but he's still struggling to deal with life without him. "Time goes so fast, and as much as I hate the saying, life goes on."

"Doesn't seem fair though, does it?"

"No, but we have to take the good and the bad, and Helena's little one is the best news we've had lately."

"I'm so happy for her, but—"

I stop him because I feel it's important for him to allow himself to celebrate the news. "You shouldn't feel guilty for looking forward to being an uncle."

"I just think about what the baby will miss out on."

"We have decades of memories between us, and Jamie won't ever be forgotten, I know you'll make sure of that."

"It's just not the same."

"What isn't?"

"It was always the three of us. Even though he was older by a lot of years, we still grew up together and shared everything."

"He talked about it a lot and had the best time with you both."

"I still want to pick up the phone and call him whenever something goes well. Now everything is different."

"I do it too, want to call him, I mean."

"He should be here, especially for moments like this.

"Helena had two brothers to look out for her, now you have to be the responsible one and pick up the slack."

"You know what Helena is like. She's as batty as she always was and still thinks she's sixteen."

"I think motherhood will change her entirely, and yes, she might still have that flighty, girlish persona but this baby will rock her world in the best possible way and give her something to channel all that love into."

"He'd be ecstatic, wouldn't he?"

"Jamie would be singing it from the rooftops, whether it was you or Helena who made him an uncle."

"Do you regret not having kids?"

It's the million pound question I'm often asked. "Yes, and no," is my reply. "But with my condition the decision was kind of taken away from us. We could have opted for surrogacy or adoption, but I dread to think of myself as the widow trying to put myself and a child back together again."

"We would have stood by you whatever, and you'd never have done it alone."

"As families go, you're the best."

"Are you getting past it?"

"Gosh, no, and I never will get over losing him in such a horrible way, but lately, I have thought more and more about how he would react if I had been the one that died."

"And?"

"Jamie would have struggled for a while, but he had a zest for life and would see wallowing as a waste, so right now I'm living my life the only way that I can, and while I feel immense sadness he's not here, I'll carry on and hope there is a place for me somewhere."

"You'll always have a place with us."

"And I couldn't be more grateful, now come and help me put all this into the pan."

"You're just like my mother." He stands next to me in front of the sink, rinses the vegetables and drops them into the casserole pan.

"That's the nicest thing you've ever said to me, Benjamin." I've forgotten to chop the leeks.

He bumps me with his hip. "I only ever get my full name when I'm in trouble."

I hand him a knife. "Chop those leeks or you might be."

"Are you two having fun?"

I turn as Miriam enters. She looks tired and drawn, but today will be hard for her. Remembering her son with a smile when she probably wants to batten down the hatches and retreat from the world takes courage. "We're fine. How are you?"

"I didn't sleep well last night."

"When have you ever slept properly since Jamie died?" Ben added, slicing the leeks, and dropping them into the pan.

"Few and far between if I'm honest, but it'll get better." She's always been one to look at the positives, and though she is probably lying through her back teeth, time will ease the pain somewhat. Her grandson will bring joy and light back into her life.

Soon enough, we're joined by Helena and Jimmy too.

"Is Keegan not coming today?"

"No, he said he'd sit this one out, being the first anniversary and all."

"Call him and tell him he's more than welcome."

"It's okay, he's fine to leave us be for the day." I wonder if his absence means Helena won't share the news about the baby's gender. "Besides, he'll probably be with his mates watching football, golf or some crappy sci-fi show."

"As long as he doesn't feel left out."

"Keegan sails with the wind–trust me if he wanted to be here, he would've said so."

"He's a good boy," Miriam adds. "And he's going to worship that baby."

"Talking of babies, I have something to tell you all."

"Oh?" Miriam looks frightened for the moment. "Is everything okay?"

"Baba is just fine, Mum, stop worrying."

"What is it then?" Jimmy asks.

"I have some good news."

Ben puts down the knife and turns. "Well, spit it out, or are you waiting for the birth of your second child?"

"Shut it, pig face."

"Don't start bickering you two," Miriam warns. "Good God, you're like school kids at times."

They always were, I want to say. But with their banter comes much love and if somebody crosses one, the other will always step up with swinging fists. "Come on then, let's hear it."

Helena takes a deep breath. "We're having a boy."

Miriam's hands fly up to cover her face as Jimmy rushes to congratulate his daughter. "That is wonderful news, isn't it, Ben?"

He's visibly moved but I see more of a reaction from him than I've seen in a long time. "Yeah…"

"And if it's okay with you all, I'd like to call him Jamie."

Everyone looks to me. "I think that's wonderful." I don't want to go too overboard and drop Helena in it for revealing the news to me before anyone else.

"But you knew already, didn't you?" Miriam suddenly announces.

"No, not at all." I shake my head, but as terrible a liar I am, she sees right through me.

"That's what you were whispering about last week." She looks at Helena, her bottom lip quivering. "But I'll let you both off because I'm so happy."

"Are you, really?" Helena asks. "Even about the name?"

"I think it's a lovely idea, and so would your brother."

"I agree."

"Come here and give me a cuddle." Miriam opens her arms to Helena. "Oooh, you are the most scrumptious girl in the world and this baby is going to be so lucky having you as his mummy."

"You're crushing me, Mum."

"Whoops," she says, releasing her vice like grip. "Sorry."

Later on, we sit around the dining room table chatting.

"I'd like to raise a toast to Jamie," I say, raising my crystal glass. "He was simply the best, and wherever he is, I want him to know we all love him."

"To Jamie," assembled company repeat as we clink glasses.

Being together, it's a bittersweet moment, and while we all celebrate Helena's news, the truth is, without Jamie, what should be a light-filled moment is dimmed somewhat. Looking around I see eyes shining, but it's not what I want, nor would Jamie have.

"Today is not about grieving but remembering how lucky we were to have him in our lives, okay."

Jimmy nods. "You're right! I miss him but I know one day we'll be together again."

Miriam forces a smile but through it I can see her suffering all over again. It tears me apart, so I reach over for her hand. "And very soon, you're going to be a Granny." I choose my words carefully.

Helena chuckles.

"Less of the Granny, thank you very much. I'm going to be Gaga and Jimmy is going to be Opa."

Ben pulls a funny face.

"You're going bloody gaga if you think any grandchild of mine is going to call me that."

"Suit yourself," Miriam snaps without missing a beat. "You miserable old fart."

"Gaga and Opa," I say. "It has a nice ring to it."

"I agree," Helena adds as a mischievous grin settles across her painted red lips.

"You're all barking mad," Jimmy says, though I have my suspicions that Miriam will win this battle. "I'm going to be plain old Grandad, okay. I don't want no faffing about."

"Whatever you say, Opa." Ben chimes in, knowing what Miriam wants, she usually gets.

We all burst out laughing, and it's exactly what is needed right now to diffuse the tension and lift the mood. As a family we have to learn to be happy without the inevitable guilt. Nobody wants to bring a child into the world under a cloud.

"I give up with you lot." He takes a sip of his wine.

"Have you not learned yet, Jimmy?" I raise my glass to his.

"I expected more of you, Serena."

"You know I adore you…"

He winks at me, and I know there is a genuine love and respect between us. Since working together, we're closer than we've ever been, and I know when the time comes for me to step away, it will be in safe hands. Tate Technology is thriving and while Jamie laid the foundations, it will be his father that carries it into the future. It's the best legacy I could hope for.

Chapter Seventeen

Just Good Friends?

Anniversaries will come and go for a multitude of occasions but learning not to fear them is going to be tricky.

As a family, we navigated through Jamie's birthday and the day of his death but once there, I felt a weight lifted from me. If I could cope with that, almost anything was possible.

I had things to do and buried myself in learning as much as I could about leading the group. It had become a source of comfort to me, but I looked at it selflessly. If I could help at least one person learn that life didn't stop for them, I would be happy.

Louise dashed about, muttering to herself while stuffing papers into the rainbow coloured canvas bag I found in a local market. "Thanks so much for closing down for me." She kisses both of my cheeks then rushes toward the door. "If I don't leave now, I'll never make it." There's some sort of emergency at home but I won't stop her and ask, she'll tell me later.

"No problem. Call me tomorrow."

"Okay, toodle-oo."

She flies out of the door as Elijah approaches me. I hear her coughing from the hallway. He looks troubled and there isn't the usual shine to his blue eyes, but I won't overstep and ask him anything outright. I hope he will volunteer whatever seems to be bothering him. "Hey, Serena."

"Hello, stranger. I haven't seen you for a few weeks." I take a seat and tap the one next to me, inviting him to chat.

He takes a seat as his eyes dance about once more. "I've been crazy busy with deadlines for the new book."

"How exciting." I don't believe him entirely, but don't question it.

"I thought of texting you to let you know I wasn't going to be here for a bit but decided not to."

"Why ever not?"

"Oh, you know, people do like to gossip about stuff."

"What stuff is this?"

"The two of us being friends."

Instantly my mind travels to Bob and him telling Louise about us leaving together some time back. "If people have nothing more exciting to talk about than two people enjoying one another's company, sod 'em."

"Yeah, you're right, but Bob needs to learn to keep his mouth shut."

"I might've known that twit would be involved, but don't you worry, I'll sort him out."

"Pardon the bad language but he's a nosey old bastard and forgets that this is supposed to be a sanctuary for us, and what we say or do here should remain within these four walls."

"I hope you haven't stayed away from the group because of it?"

"I really have been busy," he reiterates. "I'm not lying..."

"But not too busy you couldn't have made it here perhaps once a week, am I right?"

"Well, I thought a few weeks away would make a refreshing change and that I didn't need to rely so heavily on everyone here."

"And how did that work out for you?"

"Not too well, I had more time to think than I'm used to."

"So, you'll be here for every meeting going forward, yeah?"

"You're bossy, do you know that?"

"I've heard that a few times lately, but you are my friend and I care about you, and what happens to you."

"I care about you too."

"Then we're on the same page, and if our friendship warrants gossip, let it be."

"You're stronger than you make out."

"In all honesty, Elijah, these last few weeks, I've walked through a few milestones–the anniversary of Jamie's passing, his birthday, I even cleared his wardrobe out and donated stuff to charity shops."

"Wow, that's major. It took me a long time to part with Kara's stuff."

"But the thing is, we did it, and life goes on."

"You've had some sort of epiphany it seems."

"I wouldn't go that far, but there are still good things happening in the world, and when I really sit and think about things, if I shy away for life, what am I left with?"

"Profound..." is all he says.

"As much as I loved, and still love Jamie, I didn't exist solely because he did. Yes, we were blissfully happy, and I wish I could go back and change things. I can't, so I have to forge ahead to whatever my future will be."

"You're amazing, do you know that?"

I see the twinkle in his eye and while the compliment is nice to hear, he should realise his own progress is inspiring. "Do you have time for coffee?"

"Sure, and if you wouldn't mind, can I run some of my new manuscript by you?"

Excitement courses through me. Recently, I've re-discovered my joy of reading and have devoured all the Grace Hart titles, even the ones I've enjoyed before. "Are you pulling my leg?"

"Nope, and while I'm here, I have a few things for you." He taps his satchel and dips his voice. "Your signed books."

"I told you to call me and I'd collect you, rather than have you hoof about with them."

"It's not a problem, but I don't want to give them to you in here."

"Tell you what, let's go back to my place, and we can talk properly over coffee, and I think I have some nibbles in the fridge that need to be eaten."

"Are you sure? I don't want to put you out."

"I've missed talking to you, Elijah, so yes, I'm sure."

"What about–?"

I turn to see Bob loitering. "Something wrong, Bob?"

"Erm, n-n-," he stammers. "Nothing, miss."

"I'm having a *private* conversation, so if you wouldn't mind waiting outside until our time is up, I'd appreciate it–you know how it is, too many people repeating things that are no business to anyone else." I eyeball him so he knows he is the intended recipient of my statement.

"Well, yes, yes, if you insist."

"I do, goodnight, Bob, and close the door after you leave."

I wait a few seconds and hear the door slam shut.

"Remind me never to piss you off."

"He deserved it, and I know he's a little old man, but careless talk is unnecessary."

"What if he complains to Louise?"

"Then I shall tell her exactly why I said what I said and there won't be a problem." He looks nervous. "Don't worry, Bob had it coming. I won't have him gossiping about me, or you."

"You're right." He stands and holds out his hand. "Shall we go?"

I reach up and take hold. "Thank you."

"You have a gorgeous home, Serena."

"Thank you."

He looks about the entrance hall wide-eyed. "It's huge."

"Too big for one, but the truth is, it was too big for Jamie and me, though we both liked the space." I guide him toward the sitting room. "Make yourself comfortable."

He sits on the sofa and puts his satchel down next to him. "My apartment is pretty spacious, but I just seem to occupy my office and bedroom."

"You don't sit and relax in front of the TV?"

"Not often these days."

"Why?"

"Writing takes a lot of time. I usually get up then sit at my desk, intending not to stay there all day, then darkness comes, and I realise I've done the opposite of what I should have."

"Your books are works of art."

"Aw, that's kind of you to say but–"

"No buts. I've just re-read them and they're so good."

Elijah reaches into his satchel and pulls out a stack of books bound together with silver ribbon. "These are..." He holds them out. "...for you, and with my compliments."

"I know I asked you to sign them, but I'm genuinely touched to have these in my possession."

"It's my pleasure."

"Do you mind if I read the inscriptions?"

"Not at all."

I sit next to him and open the first of four. He has neat handwriting. "How lovely," I say, then I move onto books two and three. "Such kind words." It's the inscription in the last book that brings a lump to my throat.

When a person is lost at sea, finding a beacon of light that slowly pulls them back to the safety of the shore is the difference between fighting for life and surrendering to death.
You are that light for me.
A true friend, and one I feel I've known forever.
Thank you for listening.
Thank you for understanding.
It is a privilege to know you.
Elijah (Grace) Hart

Feeling a swell of emotion, I use both hands to fan my face. "I think I'm going to cry."

"Oh, please don't," he says looking scared. "I didn't want to upset you."

I reach for his hand and hold it in mine. "Thank you, Elijah, you don't know how much your kind words mean to me. I shall treasure these forever."

"I do feel like I've known you forever."

"Yes, I know what you mean, but before I make a complete fool of myself, let me go and make a pot of fresh coffee, unless you would prefer something else?"

"Coffee is fine." He seems reluctant to let go of my hand. "Sorry."

"Don't worry." I stand, placing my signed books on the bookshelf. "I won't be a minute."

Standing at the kitchen window I take a few breaths to control my nerves. I hadn't anticipated a reaction like that. But it was a genuine moment between two people who have experienced something similar.

Returning to the living room with freshly brewed coffee and a plate of Danish pastries, with serviettes on a tray, Elijah's eyes follow me until I take the seat opposite.

"Are you okay?"

"I'm good."

"Coffee and Danish, is that okay?"

"Perfect."

"Please help yourself."

He picks up a pastry and holds it on a serviette. "I'm quite messy with these things."

"Me too, but I'll hoover up any spillages."

"You're so easy going."

"If life taught me anything, it's to embrace the moment and not worry about the silly things."

He bites into the pastry as bits flake all over his T-shirt. "See…"

"Just enjoy it. We'll deal with the fallout later."

Chapter Eighteen

Open Your Heart

We sat in silence for a while listening to a wide variety of music.

Eerily, we both listed Eric Clapton as one of our favourites. *Tears from Heaven*, written in tribute to his son who died following a tragic accident, played.

It resonates with me because I remembered the news reports, and how the little mite died.

Once the song finishes, I speak. "Tell me what really happened to you." I don't know why now but suddenly I need to know more.

He seems shocked at the impertinence of the question. "It's not something I like to talk about."

"I promise I won't judge, but you're hiding something, and whatever it is, you'll feel better if you unburden yourself."

"You might not think so if I tell you."

"I promise, I won't judge, no matter what it is."

"Are you sure you wanna know?"

"Truly, I do."

He picks up his mug of coffee and takes a sip, then sets the cup down again. "A few years ago, I was a bit of a bad lad."

"What does that mean?"

"It means I lived my life on the wrong side of the law. Arrogantly, I thought I was invincible and almost paid the price."

"You went into cardiac arrest, I know that, but I want to know who you really were back then."

"I wasn't a nice person."

"Were you an addict?" I lift my knees to my chest and wrap my arms around them.

"The worst kind, and with my addiction came a nasty side, a lack of empathy for anyone. I did whatever I wanted to do. I lied, cheated on those I loved, and stole to fund my habits."

"I'm not going to pretend this is easy to hear because the man I see now is so far removed, but you seem to have come through the other side."

"I have, but it doesn't negate who I was."

"What started you down that road?"

"A crappy upbringing, violent father, mum who didn't care, I could list so many things, but ultimately my own decisions led me to it. Plenty of others suffer far worse than I did growing up, but they live normal, healthy, respectable lives."

"Isn't that what you do now?"

"Yeah, but it took me a minute to get there."

"You did it, and that's not to be sniffed at." Suddenly he breaks out in a fit of laughter. "What did I say?"

"A Freudian slip if ever there was one."

"I don't follow, sorry."

"Sniffed at..." He's still laughing when I eventually get the joke.

"Oh, dammit, I'm so sorry."

"Don't be, it cheered me up, but I do know what you mean. It wasn't easy and I did it, though you haven't heard everything yet."

"You turned your life around, that's the main thing. I don't need to know everything."

"Not right away, I didn't, but I'd like to tell you if you'll listen."

"Okay, but please don't think I'll judge because everyone has a past."

"Mine is a doozy, and worthy of a novel."

"I'm intrigued."

"Well, I thought I was invincible, and despite being warned never to indulge again, I did, right after I got the all-clear from the doctors."

"Were you so hell bent on destroying yourself?"

"Absolutely and I couldn't have put it any better myself."

"I've seen it many times working in a hospital."

"Even as sick as I felt at first, I had that urge to get wasted and as soon as the cardiologist had discharged me, some sort of God complex took over. I believed that nothing like that would ever happen to me again, so I carried on, worse than before—"

"You had more cardiovascular issues?"

"I suffered a second heart attack that damaged it so badly which left me with one option, a transplant."

"It must have been a lot to deal with."

"I'm still battling with myself over it."

"Over what?"

"The transplant."

"Why?"

"There must have been far more worthier candidates than me."

"Worthy or not, you turned your life around."

"How could I not? What right would I have to slip back into my old ways and throw that in the faces of those grieving his loss."

"His?"

"Yes, but that's all I know. I did write a letter to the donor family, but I never heard anything back. I don't know anything else because the rules are so stringent."

From a personal perspective, I know what he's talking about. I should share my own story about Jamie and how I struggled with allowing his organs to be harvested. But this isn't about me. It's Elijah's desire to cleanse his soul that takes precedent here. "What about Kara?"

He shifts about and I detect the notable change in his demeanor. "We were three floors up. Both of us had taken so many pills, that when she climbed up onto the railings, I cheered her on..." He blew out a breath. "So many occasions before we'd played dangerous games but this time, she lost her footing, and I was too late to grab her and stop her from falling."

"Oh, God."

"She hit the ground...I can still hear the thud as she struck the pavement."

"I'm so sorry, Elijah."

"I looked over the edge and she was splayed out like a ragdoll with its strings cut, lying on her front with blood oozing from the side of her head. I knew she was dead..." His breathing became more erratic, and I feared he was about to have a panic attack.

"Take a deep breath, you're okay, I'm here with you."

"So, you see, I was responsible for her death—misadventure the coroner called it, but I knew the truth, I even went to the police, wanting them to arrest me, but according to them, there was no crime to answer for."

"Exactly."

"But I knew, I killed her."

I hold his face in my hands and my eyes meet his. "Listen to me, it was an accident, plain and simple."

"I should've stopped her, Serena."

"Would you have listened if she tried to stop you from climbing up there?"

"No."

"Then what makes you think Kara ever would have?"

"She was my wife. It was my duty to protect her."

"And you were her husband, but you were both addicts and too far gone at the time, you have to see that."

"I held her and spoke softly, telling her I loved her over and over until the ambulance arrived."

How could anyone hear this and not be moved by the horror of somebody seeing their spouse die? "It's awful, and I don't know what to say."

"You could say what her mother did and tell me it was my fault, 'cos it was."

"No, Elijah, it was a tragic accident, and nothing you say will convince me otherwise."

"You'd never condemn anyone, you're not the type."

"The man that robbed the off-licence has never been caught, yet I'd gladly watch him hang, and though he never actually killed my husband, he just played a part in it."

"That must be awful knowing he is out there somewhere, and you could pass him in the street."

"It is, but what do I do? Scouring the streets for him won't help, it's just something I have to live with, which is exactly what you have to do regarding Kara."

"She died on my watch, Serena." His hands trembled furiously.

"Kara was an adult and made her own choices, and nobody can hold you responsible for that."

"If only..."

"Don't do that, Elijah, because there is no going back. Learn to remember the good times and cherish them. Don't hold yourself accountable for somebody else's mistakes."

"I can't help thinking it should be me in that grave."

"Why you and not her?"

"Because..."

"Go on, give me a reasonable answer as to why your death would be anything less than hers."

"I can't, I just know how I feel inside."

"You were given the chance of life."

"And I took it."

"No, what you accepted was a half-life of sorts. Yes, you live and breathe, but are you really living?" Though I'm talking to him, I hear my own words and am spurred on. I make total sense, I see it now, he just needs to.

"I don't deserve to be alive."

"Then why did you agree to the transplant?"

"Dunno." He shrugs his shoulders and reminds me of a moody teenager.

"You want to live but guilt weighs you down."

"I've tried."

"Try harder," I snap, refusing to let him wallow. "Do you know how much happiness your books bring to people like me that need a few hours away from the torture their own brains inflict on them?" He shrugs again. "Well, do you?"

"You've said before."

"Take a look online and see for yourself—you bring hope to those who feel they have none, and it's not just empty words, but how you feel deep down though you won't allow it to come to the surface."

"Nobody has ever really listened to me before, not even Louise."

"Have you ever spoken loud enough for people to actually hear you? Have you ever truly opened up?"

"Not to anybody but you."

"And did I judge you?"

"No."

"Why is that?"

"Because we're friends."

"Yes, but also because I care about you and know what happened was an accident, and not something you planned or wanted."

"I loved her so much, Serena. She was my everything, and even through the drugs and drink, as long as we had one another, the rest of the world could fade away."

He has the soul of a poet, and his words touch me deeply. "Kara's death should force you to do one thing."

"What's that?"

"Live your best life in her honour."

"I'm trying."

"Try harder," I repeat. "I'll help you."

"You will?"

"Yes, and if you wouldn't mind me speaking of something that's been bothering me."

He looks a little wary but nods his head. "You're hiding behind Grace Hart when Elijah should be front and centre."

"I can't reveal myself to the public."

"You should stand proud of who you are and what you have achieved. Don't you realise that telling the world will open up so many possibilities for you and help others to see the good that can come from tragedy?"

"I didn't think of it like that."

"Because your publishers care more for money than they do for you."

"Isn't that always the way?"

"Yes, it is, but is it right, no?"

"You really think I should tell the public who Grace Hart really is?"

"Too bloody right I do dnd if your publishers don't like it, tell them to take a hike and self-publish, at least everything you earn will go to you."

"It's a lot to think about, Serena."

"Then think on it, and if you decide it's what you want, I'll be with you every single step of the way."

"You're amazing, do you know that?"

"I know," I kid, "and fully expect to be written into your next book as the buxom heroine."

"I don't think the written word could ever do you justice."

My face flushes and the moment I never wanted or craved seems to be right before me. I'm leaning in closer than is decent, but he seems to sense my reticence and draws back. "Think about it," I say, pushing myself to my feet. "Fresh coffee?"

"That would be nice."

I open the back door and allow the cool breeze to wash over me. I don't know what happened then but thank God Elijah moved away. Guilt is bogged down with confusion, and I don't know if inviting him here this evening was the best idea.

Suddenly, I hear the front door closing. "Elijah."

Stepping into the hallway, I glance into the living room, but he's gone.

"Damn," I say out loud, realising he's run away, although I don't know what state he's in.

My phone beeps. After rummaging in my handbag, I pull it out and read the message. It's from Elijah. He needs time to think. I understand but send a reply and tell him I'm here if he ever wants to talk. There is no reply.

Sliding under the cover that night, my mind replays the conversation between us. I can't change it. I just hope I don't lose my friend because of it.

Chapter Nineteen

The Real Me

It's six-thirty am.

I'm sat at the breakfast table indulging in half a pink grapefruit. I grimace at the sour taste. It's disgusting and I wouldn't feed it to a dog, but it's supposed to be healthy, so I soldier on even though every mouthful makes me gag.

My phone beeps. *Jimmy is awake early*. But looking at the screen I'm surprised to see it's a message from Elijah apologising for last night. Rather than text back I press dial.

He answers on the second ring.

"I didn't wake you with the text, did I?"

"No, not at all," I reply. "I'm sitting at the table trying to eat this grapefruit."

"Ugh, rather you than me."

"Quite, so what has you out of bed this early?"

"I want to apologise for bailing on you last night, it was inexcusable."

"There's no need, I get it totally."

"Do you, really?"

"I think so." I have conflicting feelings, but that's my issue to resolve.

"Aside from that, I want to talk to you about something else."

"Go on."

"I'm going to do a live chat later this morning on Instagram, and I hoped you'd watch."

His words mean nothing because I'm not tech savvy at all. "You'll have to forgive me, but social media is a mystery to me."

"Basically, I'm going to reveal to my fans who I am."

"Oh, my, I wasn't expecting that."

"I think you were right and it's time."

I push the grapefruit away, resolving never to try one again. "Did you tell your publishers?"

"I called my Manager when I got home last night, and she called her contact there. They aren't impressed and there was some mention of cancelling my contract."

"This time tomorrow, they'll be crawling to you on their bellies praying you don't drop them."

"You have more faith than I do."

"What time are you going live, if that is even the right thing to say?"

"About ten am I think."

"Why don't you come and do it from here, you know, for a bit of moral support."

"I'd feel cheeky, especially after abandoning you last night."

"Don't be daft, I'd like to be there for such a momentous occasion. The world will finally know who writes such majestic books."

"Are you sure you're reading the right ones?"

"I'm not that daft, yet."

"Shall I pick up some croissants from Milly's?"

"Yes, please, I just tried to force that grapefruit down, but it tastes awful."

"I'll stick to coffee and croissants if you don't mind. Give me about an hour and I'll be there. If you want, I'll set you up with an Insta account and you can join in the conversation."

"Deal!" I still have no clue what it is I'm agreeing to. "I'll put fresh coffee on, and Elijah..."

"Yeah?"

"No matter how scared you are right now, I'm proud of you, and believe you are making the right decision."

"That means a lot. See you soon."

He ends the call as I jump up from the table. My hair needs a brush running through it, and my face needs more than a hint of makeup. "Jimmy," I say as I climb the stairs. Once in my bedroom I call him.

He's on the ball and answers pretty much right away. "Morning, Serena. What can I do for you?"

"Hi, Jimmy, do you mind if I take the day off?"

"I'm not your boss."

"Oh, I know that, but I don't like to let you down."

"Is anything wrong?"

"No, nothing, but a friend needs my support, so I said I'd help him out."

"Is this the same friend you were worried about some time ago?"

I detect no accusatory tone although I'd wonder if I were in his shoes. "Yeah, that's him."

"There's no trouble I hope?"

"God, no, but you might see something about it on the news later. Just keep your eyes peeled for reports about Grace Hart."

"Isn't she that soppy author Miriam reads before she goes to sleep?"

"Yeah, we're both huge fans."

"So, you know her, the author I mean?"

"Kind of but once it's out there, you'll see why I'm being a touch evasive right now."

"Whatever you say but take care."

"I'll be in tomorrow, I promise."

"Serena, you do what makes you happy."

"Are you happy at Tate Technology?"

"It's a joy being here and using my brain, plus it gives me purpose and you can't buy that from any store."

"I'm glad."

"You rescued me when I needed it most."

"Ha, you're the last person that needs rescuing and I think you'll find it was you who is the knight in shining armour on this occasion."

"Well, we both have our opinions but thank you for saying that, it means the world."

"There's no need."

"There's every need, Now, get off this phone and go help your friend. I hope he realises how lucky he is."

"Speak to you soon."

"You will."

I end the call and sit in front of the mirror. My blonde hair is a shaggy mess from my attempt at cutting it myself. "Christ, you look like you've been electrocuted." I resolve to book an appointment at the salon as soon as possible.

Elijah steps into the house loaded with his laptop bag, two plastic bags stuffed with files, and a box of croissants that smell delicious, and a lot more inviting than the grapefruit that sits at the bottom of my bin.

"Here, let me give you a hand."

"Oh, thanks." There is the hint of a smile and a touch of regret for last night but I'm not one to hold grudges.

I take the carrier bags and box of croissants from him and lead the way to the kitchen. "Are you nervous?"

"Absolutely bricking it," he replies. "I know I'm doing the right thing but what if my readers turn on me?"

"They won't, now take a seat and settle your nerves." He does so while I pour the coffee and plate up the croissants. "It's all very exciting."

"My publishers have been ringing me non-stop since I got off the phone to you."

"Did you answer?"

"Nope. If I do, they might talk me out of it."

"Then turn your phone off and let them wait it out. I have a feeling you'll have them eating out of the palm of your hands by the time this day is over."

"Or I'll be sued for breach of contract."

"They wouldn't dare."

"Would you mind if I set my laptop up in here, it's brighter?"

"Not at all, but forgive me for saying this, are you going to go on camera looking like that?"

He appraises himself but can't see what I do. "What's wrong with me?"

"You're sweating, your hair is a mess–people will think you've just rolled out of bed, and this is too important for them to focus on anything other than what you have to say."

"What do I do?"

"Upstairs, first floor, last door on the right is the guest bathroom. There is a bath and shower, take your pick, clean towels, and toiletries are there too, take advantage of them."

"Jeez, do you want a job as my manager?"

"Being your friend is enough, now scoot, you have plenty of time–I want the viewers to see what I do."

"And what's that?"

"Your sparkling blue eyes for a start, now off you pop."

"I'm going."

He slinks off and I hear him climb the stairs then I remember his T-shirt could do with an iron running over it. I rush into the hallway. "Elijah, before you go…"

"What's up?" He looks over the banister.

"Throw your T-shirt down and I'll iron it."

"You don't have to do that."

"Do as you're told," I scold.

"Yes, Boss." He does something I don't expect. He pulls it off there and then revealing a rippling six pack, pecs and the scar that seems to bother him so much. "Catch."

"Ready." Elijah throws it my way and being totally useless where hand-eye coordination is concerned, I miss. It ends up hanging off my face, his scent filling my senses.

"Oops, I'm sorry."

Pulling it off my face, I feel the flush creep up to my cheeks but laugh it off. "Don't worry, you just get yourself ready for your adoring fans."

He turns and my eyes linger on the small of his back. There is a tattoo, but I can't make out the design.

Chapter Twenty

True Confessions

Elijah reappears looking clean and fresh. His hair is pushed back from his face, but what I'm interested in, his eyes, they twinkle in anticipation of the moment he probably never thought would come.

"You look ready to face your fans."

"Thanks to you."

"Did you find everything you needed?"

"I did, and I hope you don't mind but I used the deodorant and some hair wax I found in the cabinet."

"I don't mind." I remember Jamie buying both. He was finickity about his appearance and would never leave the house looking less than perfect. I'd ask why he fussed so much, and his answer was always the same. *You never know, Serena, I could get hit by a bus*, was one of his favourite sayings. Not quite a bus, but prophetic, nevertheless. Now isn't the time to dwell. More pressing matters need addressing. "Do you know what you're going to say?"

"I wrote a few words. Do you want to see?" He holds out a piece of paper.

I take the paper from him and cast my eyes over his words. "Nice, but if my opinion means anything, use these notes as a guide then speak from a place of truth and you won't go wrong."

"You're probably right."

"Do what is good for you at the end of the day, but to get who you truly are across, a script will only make you appear...well, scripted."

"What would I do without you to point me in the right direction?"

"Something tells me you'd manage."

"So, if I set the laptop up here with my back to the window, I think it will look better."

"Camera angles aren't my thing, but do what you think will work, but if you want to go out into the conservatory, the gardens are beautiful."

"I think that might tie in more to the books I write."

"Let's do it, there are sockets out there for you to plug the computer into."

"This place really is amazing."

"Jamie designed every part of it."

"He was a talented man."

"The best," I reply, thinking of what he would make of this moment.

"It's nine thirty now, so if I send an announcement via all my socials, Facebook, Twitter, MeWe, TikTok, and tell them I will be going live on Instagram to make a special announcement, it should give people enough time to tune in."

"Whatever you say."

The next twenty-five minutes is spent in silence while Elijah sets an Instagram account up for me, checks WiFi connections, cameras and God knows what else. But I'm not worried as he seems to know what he is doing. "I'm so scared."

"You're going to be fine, and if you struggle, I'm right here, remember."

"Don't go anywhere."

"I'm not moving."

"Four minutes." He mutters to himself though I can't catch his words.

"Take deep breaths and in ten minutes, you'll have told everyone who you are, then there is no going back."

"That's what worries me."

"Just be yourself and they'll love you."

"Three minutes."

"Close your eyes and take some time for your thoughts, breathe, and focus on what you want to say and how you're going to achieve it." He turns to speak but I put a finger to my lips.

Two and a half minutes is over in the blink of an eye and suddenly I see the countdown on the screen. "Here we go," he says.

I cross my fingers on both hands and hold them up in the air. *Good luck*, I mouth, taking a deep cleansing breath for him. Staring at my phone, I see 23,000 viewers waiting for him. No pressure.

"Hello, my name is Elijah, but you will know me by my pseudonym, Grace Hart."

I look at the varied reactions.

Heart emojis.

Shocked face emojis.

Smiling faces emojis.

Angry face emojis.

It's a whole range of emotions flashing and scrolling before my eyes.

"My publishers did not want me to tell you this, but I can't live a lie any longer, and while I know some may feel deceived, I want to use this time to explain why."

I try to read the messages as they appear.

I knew it.

Shit, she's a dude.

Wow, he's HAWT!

#WTAF???

Liar! You've lost a fan.

#Waiting for an explanation.

From what I see the overwhelming majority seem willing to allow him to explain. He does it with passion, conviction, contrition but most importantly, sincerity. Nothing is left out to be misconstrued and he lays bare the person he was, losing Kara, and tells of the person he is now.

Crying emojis follow.

We still love you, Elijah.

Thank you for being honest.

Hugging emojis.

#marryme.

A lie is a lie. Not buying it!

I want my money back.

#SobStorynotbuyingit

More heart emojis.

What a man!

#HotterthanHADES.

I watch, awestruck, and swallow down the lump in my throat. He's the bravest man I know, and only deserves applause.

My phone beeps. It's a message from Jimmy telling me Grace, well, Elijah, has hit the national news.

I turn my phone to Elijah. He reads it and doesn't miss a beat.

"So, while this is not me trying to excuse lying to you all, I felt it important you know everything. And now you do, this is me, Elijah Hart."

He answers a few questions from supporters but looks weary. It's taken its toll. The truth always does.

Wrap it up, I write it on a sheet of paper and turn it toward him. I open Google on my mobile phone and type in the name Grace Hart.

"For now, I'd like to thank you all for tuning in to this livestream. I pray you accept my apology. Your support means the world to me, and just so you know that I'm not trying to hide away any longer, I will arrange a longer Q&A session in the near future. Bye for now." He blows a kiss to the camera then ends the livestream.

"Wow!" I'm genuinely overcome, and I contributed nothing.

"I can't believe I just did that."

"You were amazing, Elijah."

"The world knows."

"More than you realise."

"What do you mean?"

"Look at BBC News on the internet, it's already breaking."

He types on his laptop. "I better turn my phone on, my agent and publisher will be freaking out."

"Wait until you catch your breath." I stand to put a fresh pot of coffee on. "Looking at the livestream while you spoke, the reactions were mainly positive."

"I wasn't going to win everyone over, right?"

"Never, but those who were negative are probably just blowing steam, and those same ones will buy your next book just to see if they spot any difference."

An hour later, he turns his phone on. "I'll give it five minutes before it rings."

Less than a minute later it rings. "It's my agent."

"Answer it."

"What if I'm being dropped?"

"Then find another agent who prefers dealing with real clients."

Tentatively he presses the answer button and lifts it to his ear. "Hello, Elijah speaking...Penny, hi!"

I'm a ball of nervous energy, and never have I wanted to hear the other end of the conversation so much. Then, he clicks on the speakerphone.

"I just got off the phone with the publishing house and since you went rogue, sales on KDP alone have gone through the roof."

"Really?"

"Up 3000% on this time yesterday and the numbers are growing across all of your titles."

I smile for him because it must be a relief.

"I don't know what to say."

"You were right–throw in a good-looking guy who's gone through hell and the audience is yours."

Immediately, I'm appalled she would use the worst moments of his life as reason to sell books.

"It's not about what I look like or what I've gone through, Penny, but living an honest life." He's pissed off and rightly so.

"I didn't mean to offend you."

"It took me a long time to walk a straight and narrow path, and never again will I be convinced to do otherwise."

Pride swells inside.

"It's your career, darling."

"Yes, it is, so, it's about time you justified your twenty percent commission–I have something I want you to do."

"What is it?"

"Speak to the publisher and tell them I want all my titles rebranded using the name Elijah Hart, plus I want the picture updated to one of me in the dust jackets."

"They might not go for it."

"Then I won't write another word for them, it's their choice."

"You're under contract."

"Then sue me."

"Elijah, listen, I really–"

"Call me back with the good news once you've spoken to them."

He ends the call and I silently clap, thrilled he stood his ground. "You were spectacular."

"Perhaps I was a bit rude then. Should I call her back and apologise?"

"Don't you dare." I stand in front of him. My cheeks hurt from smiling. "You took control of the last aspect of your life and if she doesn't like it, tough, well done."

"I couldn't have done it without you." He pulls me into a hug and holds me for a moment. His touch feels wrong, but right at the same time. "You're the best friend I think I ever had."

Pulling away, embarrassed by the closeness between us, I look into his eyes, hoping he can see my sincerity. "And I'll always be here for you."

Chapter Twenty-One

Taking Charge

Six weeks pass by in a blur.

I've settled into my role within the group and begin to lead more classes, allowing Louise the time to plan her trip, plus get her affairs into order.

She's decided to sell her house and downsize to something smaller.

I think about doing the same thing but I'm not yet ready to leave my marital home.

Jimmy is thriving in his role of Managing Director of Tate Technology and no matter what we agreed, I'm there less and less, though I'm sent daily reports I rarely read. From the meetings with accountants, the company is going from strength to strength which is why I decided to sign over a twenty percent stake to Jimmy and Miriam, plus another fifteen percent each to Helena and Ben. They all protested, but it's very much a family company and Jamie would be happy to know they were all taken care of. Plus, my remaining fifty percent brings more money than I know what to do with.

For me, having those shares in the company brings peace of mind and although money is not an issue for Jimmy and Miriam, they will never have to worry again. For Helena and Ben, it means they can buy their properties outright without a mortgage hanging around their necks.

Miriam is busy planning for the arrival of her Grandson while Helena is enjoying the last few weeks of being fussed over.

Ben called me a few days ago, asking if he could visit. "I'd love to see you." He arrives, looking bright-eyed and better than I've seen him looking in a long time. "Come in."

"These are for you." He presents me with a gorgeous bouquet of pink and yellow roses, my favourite. "I hope you like them."

Bringing them closer to my nose, I inhale the scent and smile. "They are so beautiful, thank you." I kiss his cheek. "Now come into the kitchen while I find a vase for them." He follows dutifully and takes a seat at the table. "Coffee or tea?"

"Vodka," he replies.

I instantly turn and look. "Uh-oh, what's wrong?"

"Nothing really but get me that drink and I'll tell you."

"Okay." I reach into the freezer and pull out the bottle of Grey Goose and a bag of ice. "Neat, or mixer?"

"Tonic Water please."

"You got it." I grab the Tonic Water and put ice in two tumblers. Armed with the Vodka, I take a seat opposite. "I'll let you pour."

He pours two single measures and tops it up with Tonic Water. Taking a swig, he seems a little more relaxed. "I needed that." Mind over matter is in play because the drink hasn't had time to do anything.

"Are you going to tell me what has you so jittery?"

"I've got something to tell you, but you have to promise to keep it to yourself for now."

Bile rises to the back of my throat. "Oh, God, you're not ill, are you?" It seems to be the first thing that enters my mind when anything is wrong. It's the thought of losing somebody else that terrifies me.

"No, not at all."

Relief washes over me. I take a gulp of the drink. "So, what is it?"

"I've met someone."

"Is that it?"

"Yes, but—"

"You frightened the life out of me, Ben."

"Sorry, but I've met somebody."

"I'm pleased for you but all this cloak and dagger nonsense because you've finally met a boy you like?"

He's stunned I've hit the nail on the head. "Hang on, how did you know?"

"I've been part of this family a long time, and you seriously think I don't see the real you?"

"You never said anything."

"Because you're still the Ben I love, no matter who you love."

"Did Jamie know too?"

"He did, in fact, he told me, then it all clicked into place."

He has a nervous look on his face, like he's waiting to be handed the death sentence. "And he wasn't bothered about it?"

"The only thing that bothered him was the fact you didn't feel comfortable enough to tell him yourself."

He holds his head in his hands. "I regret it so much that he died not knowing."

"But he did know, and loved you anyway—do you think he really cared about you being gay?"

"I mean hearing it from my lips."

"Why didn't you tell him if you don't mind me asking?"

"I worried he wouldn't accept me."

"Whatever made you think he wouldn't?"

"You know what Jamie was like, so straight-laced, so formal, and everything had to be just right."

"Where he was concerned, yes, but he never insisted others live the same life as him."

"I really screwed up, didn't I?"

"Your private life is yours and Jamie didn't need confirmation, neither did I, and no matter how many girlfriends you paraded in front of us, we were always waiting for the day you felt you could truly be yourself."

"I can't live a lie any longer, not after everything we've all been through."

"Then don't lie, simple."

My mind is immediately taken to Elijah. It's been weeks since I saw him last. Currently, he's on a promotional tour buoyed by the incredible success of his own 'coming out'. Telling the truth freed him and offered him opportunities he never imagined. Ben will experience the same sense of freedom but on a different scale.

"What about Mum and Dad?"

"Do you really think they will turn their backs on you?"

"I'm terrified they'll be disappointed."

"What did Helena say when you told her?'"

"You assume she knows."

I roll my eyes and shake my head. He forgets how well I know them both. "The two of you are thick as thieves, and my bet is, she's known for years and has helped you keep your little secret."

"She has and thinks I'm finally doing the right thing."

"This boy you've met, do you love him?" He shifts uncomfortably in his chair, unused to discussing such personal matters. "Yes, or no, it's quite simple, Ben."

"Very much so."

"Then tell your parents. They know, like the rest of us, that life is too short sometimes. Trust me, they will love your man just like they love you."

"Thanks, Serena. I really needed to hear some words of encouragement from somebody other than Helena."

"Prepare yourself for an ear bashing from your mum though."

"Why?" he asks.

"For keeping secrets."

"She never did like secrets, did she?"

"And for good reason, now as much as I love seeing you, get out of here, call your parents and tell them you're on your way, then be honest with them, okay."

"Can I have a hug before I go?"

"Anytime." I hold onto the man I consider my baby brother, squeezing him a little tighter than needed. "I'll always be on your side."

"I hope you know we all feel the same way about you."

"You have my back. I've always known that."

"And if the time comes when you do meet somebody new, I hope you know we'll all be happy for you too."

"That isn't on the horizon, Ben."

"What about your friend Elijah?"

So, they have been talking about him amongst themselves. I hold him at arm's length. "Just a friend."

"Any chance of things developing beyond that?"

Now, I'm the uncomfortable one. "Too soon for that I think."

"Do you like him?"

"He's a great guy, but as you can probably see from the news, he's somewhat an international celebrity now, and I'm not sure when he will be back in the UK."

"Have you asked him when he's coming home?"

"No."

"Then perhaps you need to give him a reason to hurry back."

"We're just friends, Ben."

"Look, I've never met the guy, and you were the one that spoke about the importance of honesty."

He wants the truth, so I'll tell him. "Jamie's only been gone a year or so."

"I'm not saying jump into marriage, just don't close yourself off to meeting somebody new."

"It's too hard to contemplate giving myself to somebody else, body and soul."

"So, join a convent."

"What?"

"If you've given up on the idea of love, join a convent, take the veil, charity work will give you something to focus on." His mouth is turned up at the sides. He's dying to laugh.

"I should slap your legs–the very idea of me, a nun, ha!"

"All I'm saying is, you're the most amazing person, and we all want to see you happy again, and while we're not trying to shove you into the path of somebody, we can all see this group you go to has brought something to your life, and if what Dad says is right, this Elijah is a good guy."

"Your dad has never met him."

"Dad might not say much, not that he can get a word in edgeways with Mum, but he listens. Not much goes past him. Plus, he trusts your judgement more than most."

"You've grown into quite the wise man, Benjamin."

He scrunches his handsome face up. "Oh, no, not you as well. Less of the Benjamin, please."

"Jamie would be so proud of you, hold onto that, and be who you want to be."

"I will." He kisses my cheek. "I better go and get this out of the way."

"Go in with an open mind and you'll be fine."

"Still scared, Serena."

"You've no need to be, not where Jimmy and Miriam are concerned. As parents, you've got the best."

"I'll call you later and let you know how it went."

"You'll have to beat your mother to it."

"Yeah, that's true."

With one last hug, he races out of the door.

I pick up my mobile phone, find Elijah's number and stare at it. I don't know where he is in the world, but Ben is right.

My finger hovers but I've nothing to lose and hit dial.

I hear the international dialling code and consider hanging up, then he answers.

"I was just thinking about you."

"You were?" Hearing his voice, I feel warm inside.

"Yes."

"Did I wake you?"

"No."

"Where are you?"

"Right now, I'm in Antwerp, Belgium."

"How's it going over there?"

"I'm shattered and all talked out. I can't wait to come home and sleep in my own bed."

"When are you back?"

"On Saturday morning." It's Tuesday now. Only four days. "I'd love to see you."

"You would?"

"I've missed you, Serena."

"I've missed you too," I admit. "I could cook dinner for us, then at least you can relax and tell me all about your trip."

"Sounds like a plan to me."

I hear a voice in the background calling his name. "Do you have to go?"

"Yes, sorry, but I'll call you when I get to my hotel later on, if you'd like?"

"I'd like that very much."

"Okay, I'll speak to you later, and Serena…"

"Yes?"

"I'm so glad you called."

"So am I."

"Big hugs," he says, then hangs up.

I stare at my phone, conflicted but knowing I made the right decision for me.

Chapter Twenty-Two

Breath of Life

I'm wiping down the tables with disinfectant spray at Violet Lodge when I hear a phone ringing in the background.

"Serena, I think that's yours," Louise adds.

"Is it?"

Louise rushes over for my handbag and passes it to me. "Yep."

Digging deep I find it and answer. "Hello."

"Serena, it's Miriam."

"Oh, hi." I'm expecting her to call me and regale me with tales of Ben's long overdue coming out but it's something entirely different. "Helena's gone into labour."

"But she's not due for another few weeks..." I try to calculate the dates in my head and fail spectacularly.

"I know that, but you know as well as I do that babies come when they want to," Miriam adds, sounding a touch flustered. "And this one wants out."

Time seems to be running away with me. It only seems like yesterday she announced her pregnancy. "Is she still having the baby at The Grange?"

"Yes."

"Okay, I'm just closing down the meeting and will get there as soon as possible."

"Hurry, we need you here with us."

"I promise, I'll be there."

She ends the call and I find myself shunted toward the exit. Louise had heard everything. "Go, I'll sort the rest out."

"But—"

"GO!" She points to the door before a coughing fit forces her to cross her legs. I know the feeling; the older I get the weaker my bladder seems to be. "Enjoy being an aunty."

"Thank you."

"Take Friday off and have some family time."

"I'll be here," I say. "Commitments..."

"Okay whatever, but for now, out!"

I rush to kiss her cheek then fly out of the door and jump into my car.

As bad luck would have it, the roads are jammed, and it takes me an hour to get to the hospital whereas it should have only taken me twenty minutes.

Rushing into the private hospital, I dart along the corridor and through the double doors toward the delivery suite where I see Miriam, Jimmy and Ben chatting quietly. Keegan is pacing the floors, chewing at his fingernails. I'm suddenly filled with dread. I rush over and hug him.

"I'm so sorry, the traffic was a nightmare."

"That's okay, love," Miriam answers. "You're here now." I swoop in to kiss her cheek and offer a comforting squeeze.

"How's Helena?"

"In theatre," Ben adds.

"What? Why?"

Jimmy speaks up. "The baby's heartbeat was a little unsteady, so the doctor decided a caesarean was the better option."

"Okay, well that's not unusual, so try not to be too worried."

"What if something goes wrong?" Keegan asks with a tremor in his voice. "I can't stand this."

"Nothing is going to go wrong." I try to reassure him. "These things happen day in, day out where childbirth is concerned but it's only to protect both mum and baby." I look to Jimmy and Ben. "Trust me."

"I do, but I'm shitting myself," Ben admits while Jimmy nods.

I know what's going through Jimmy's mind. *What if I lose another one?*

"Helena will be just fine," I say.

I hear a noise behind me and see a scrubbed-up nurse approaching from the other end of the corridor. She approaches Keegan. "Mr Washington."

"Yes, that's me. Is Helena okay?"

"How is she?" Miriam asks, "and the baby?"

"Mum and babies are just fine and still with the team. Congratulations to you all."

"Thank God," Keegan replies, blowing out a long breath of frustration.

"Hang on," I say, suddenly realising what the nurse just said. "You said babies, plural?"

"Yes," the nurse replies. "Helena has two healthy little boys, a little smaller than we'd like but both are doing just fine."

Miriam, Jimmy, and Ben stand open-mouthed as I turn to Keegan. "Did you know she was having twins?"

"Yeah, we decided to keep it secret."

"Can I see her?" he asks the nurse.

"Yes, would you like to come with me now?" Keegan follows close behind. I see him wringing his hands as he walks away.

"Send our love," Jimmy calls out.

"My children seem to keep a lot of secrets," Miriam snaps, though I know it's only the residual fear of having her child in the operating theatre. She doesn't seem to notice Keegan is gone. "Oh, dammit, I wanted to send my love."

"I just did, Miriam." Jimmy wraps his arm around her shoulder. She leans her head against him.

"Don't start, Mum," Ben warns, not wanting a scene.

Jimmy diffuses the tension. "She doesn't mean anything by it, son."

"I'm sorry, take no notice of me. Your dad and I are happy for you and your young man, but it's the most terrifying thing having one of your children in surgery."

We're all pulled back to the day we said goodbye to Jamie. Though there is a much happier outcome. "See, I told you, didn't I?" I feel like I've just put my foot in it by revealing Ben had come to me. "Sorry…"

"Don't be. I know how close you are to them, Serena, and I like they can come to you when they feel the need."

"As long as you don't think badly of me."

"I'd think so if you ever turned them away."

"That will never happen."

"Twins," Ben said.

"Did you not know either?" I ask.

"She never said a word to me, for the first time ever."

"It's wonderful though, two little ones in the family."

"Will Helena be okay?" Miriam asks, "You know after being cut, and what about the babies?"

"Helena will heal just fine. There is nothing to worry about because there are plenty of us that can rally round and support her and Keegan. The babies might be a little underweight and struggle to eat because of mucus in the lungs, but once that's cleared, they will feed just fine and soon get to a more desirable weight."

"I can't believe I'm a Grandma." Emotion gets the better of her.

"Erm, what about GaGa and Opa?" Ben teases.

"Grandma is just fine, thank you, Benjamin."

He can't keep a straight face. "And what about you?" He looks to his father and smirks.

"I'm sticking with Opa."

Ben chuckles while Miriam shoots him a filthy look. It doesn't last long before she bursts out laughing. "I might have known, you vain old man."

"Our grandchildren will keep us both young, okay GaGa."

"Whatever you say." She leans in for a kiss and I'm touched to see the love they still have for one another. "Those babies are going to be smothered in love."

"Baby Jamie..." Miriam coos. "...and baby, oh, I wonder what other name she decided on?"

"I have no clue. She never mentioned an alternative to me."

"We'll soon find out. Here comes Keegan."

When he approaches, I see tears of joy. "How is Helena and the little ones?"

"Helena is a little tired but excited they're finally here."

"Can we see her?" Miriam asks.

"Soon, they're just doing some checks. She's been stitched and is eager to see the babies, and all of you."

"My baby has babies of her own."

I see her jaw wobble, but the moment hit me for one thing; it's true testament that life goes on. People live, people die, babies are born, it's one thing that is guaranteed. *You should be here,* I think. "Have you and Helena decided on a name for the other little one?"

"We decided on Alexander James, what do you all think?"

"Oh," is all Miriam can say. I know how overwhelmed she is right now because Jimmy was born Alexander James but always used a derivative of his second name. "That's adorable."

"It's perfect," Jimmy adds. "All bases are covered."

"And we also decided on a middle name for little Jamie."

"Not Benjamin I hope?"

"Your name is lovely," I add.

"Ben is a dog's name."

"Oh, hush," Miriam scolds cosying up to her beloved son. "It's perfect, just like you."

"Aww, thanks, Mum."

"What did you decide for the little tyke?" Jimmy asks.

"Jamie Sereno Tate-Washington and Alexander James Tate-Washington."

"Sereno?" I feel warm and tingly and desperately try not to cry. I've cried enough for a lifetime.

"After you," Keegan adds, which reduces me to full blown sobs. "It's of Spanish origin and means exactly the same as your name—serene."

"I-I don't know what to say." Miriam hands me her handkerchief. "Oh, gosh, I really did try..." I blow loudly into it, sounding like a trumpet, making everyone laugh.

Chapter Twenty-Three

Reunited

Excited to see him again, I rush to open the front door.

"Hey, stranger," Elijah says, looking a tad embarrassed. I can't help noticing the tan, whiter than white teeth and blonder highlights in his hair. He looks like he's had the full-on Hollywood treatment. But he looks well, and more importantly, happy.

"It's so good to see you."

Tentatively, he approaches for a hug. I reciprocate and wrap my arms around him. "It's lovely to see you, Serena."

"You too, now come in and let's have a proper catch up."

He follows me into the conservatory. I've already set out glassware and crockery. "I hope you're hungry?"

"For good old-fashioned British grub, famished."

"It's nothing special, just a homemade Chicken and Leek Pie with Mashed Potato and Green Beans. I got the recipe from my mother-in-law."

"Can't wait!"

"I thought we'd keep it casual and eat out here if you're okay with that?"

"Whatever you want." He sits and reaches into his bag and hands me a gift wrapped box. "This is for you. Don't go mad but I thought of you as soon as I saw this."

"Oh, Elijah, you didn't need to bring me a gift."

"I wanted to."

"Well, thank you."

"Open it, I hope you like it."

Carefully I unwrap the box, roughly the same size as a bag of flour and lift the lid. "Oh, my…" I'm rendered speechless by its intricate beauty and the generosity behind it.

"Do you like it?"

It's an intricately carved crystal wishing well. "I've never seen anything quite like it."

"I saw it in a little shop while wandering down a back alley in Italy. It seemed to call to me, so I had to buy it."

"It must have cost a fortune."

"I'm a worldwide bestselling author, don't you know?" He says it tongue in cheek. "But forget the price, I truly believe it was created just for you."

Lifting it out of its protective wrapping, I hold it up, mesmerised by the light shining through it. "Oh, Elijah, it's absolutely perfect, thank you."

"You're so welcome."

I can't take my eyes off it. "It's going to have pride of place on top of my fireplace."

"You know, I guarded it with my life, through Italy, France, Holland, Croatia, Greece, Germany and finally Belgium."

"And I will treasure it forever." I lean in to kiss his cheek, but as unaccustomed as I am to kissing other men, I balls it up. He turns his head as I do, and our lips meet. It's quite the transcendental moment and by his expression, it hits us both in equal measure. It wasn't a kiss exactly but there was unexpected intimacy. "Oh, erm, erm, I didn't mean to—"

"Don't, it's fine."

"I'm so embarrassed."

"Please, don't be. I've wanted to do that since the first time I saw you."

"You have?"

"If I'm being honest, yes, but my respect for you and Jamie was, and is such, I would never want to overstep and ruin our friendship."

"You're just the loveliest man, Elijah, but—"

"It's not what you want, right?"

"Wrong," I say, surprising myself. "It is what I want but I'm still very much Serena Tate, wife of Jamie, and I think it will take me a while to stop seeing myself that way, so if you're okay with whatever this is, can we take it slow?"

"We can do anything as long as it makes you happy."

I reach for his hand and interlock my fingers in his. "I'm not saying never, but I need a little more time."

"You got it."

"Are you sure?"

"I never looked at another woman after Kara, but meeting you, I felt like I'd woken from a long sleep. It took a while for me to figure out that it was you who brought me back to life."

"I can't lie and say knowing you hasn't made my life more bearable. It has, but with that comes confusion. It wasn't until you went on your promo trip, I realised I'd been missing you."

"Getting that phone call from you put everything into perspective."

"How so?"

"Right here is where I'm meant to be, and whatever comes of us, I know we'll be friends forever."

"That, I never want to lose."

"You won't, so no pressure, let's just carry on the way we have been and see where it leads us, okay."

I lean in, this time with meaning, wanting to find his lips. They're soft to the touch. We still don't have that full-on kiss, but the closeness is enough for me right now. Holding the side of his face with my hand, I'm exactly where I need to be.

After we've eaten, Elijah and I sit and talk about his promo trip and the overwhelming support he's received since his announcement.

"It's nothing I ever expected."

"So, your agent and publishers are rubbing their hands together dreaming of their commission, am I right?"

"I think so, but the trip made me realise something else."

"Oh?"

"I definitely don't have any desire to be famous."

"You don't think that ship has already sailed?" I've seen him in every newspaper I've picked up since he went away. His star is on the rise and about to go stratospheric.

"My face is too well-known, now I'd happily slip back into oblivion."

"What are you going to do..." I pour us both a glass of red wine and hand his to him. "...if you hate the celebrity part of it?"

"I'm going to tell my agent to deny any future interview requests."

"Really? That won't go down too well."

"I don't care, it's not for me. All I want to do is write, the rest, forget it."

"Won't you reach a bigger audience going on these trips?"

"You know, Serena, I can live with what I have."

"You're quite the unusual man, Elijah. Everything most would sell their soul for, and you turn your back on it."

"Hotel rooms in strange cities don't make me happy. And besides, I felt kind of lost without the support of the group."

"I wondered if you would ever come back."

"Would I still be welcome?"

"It's not up to me, but there is no way Louise would refuse you."

"I need that support, still, and while it might not be forever, there is something to be said about solidarity."

"Did you struggle while on the road?"

"More than I care to admit, but it's not so surprising 'cos the group has been my emotional crutch so ripping it away without warning was a bit silly."

"You do know the rest of the group are now aware of your dual identity."

"Let me guess, Bob?"

"That old fart couldn't wait to get in there with copies of the local newspaper."

"What did they all have to say?"

"They're happy for you, just like I am."

"Would it be okay with you if I came back?"

"It's not the same without you, Elijah."

"That settles it then." He moves and sits closer to me. "So, you're an aunty, tell me more."

It's my favourite subject of late. "Oh, they're the most darling little boys. Seeing them makes me wish I had children of my own."

"It's never too late."

"No, you're right, but with endometriosis, conceiving even if I wanted to at my age would prove difficult."

"I'm sorry. You would have made an amazing mother."

"But an even better aunty."

"They are lucky to have you."

"I find myself staring at them as they sleep while fighting the desire not to pick them up and hold them close to me."

"You're one of those that wakes the babies 'cos you want to play, aren't you?"

"I don't know what you're talking about." I manage to say it with a straight face.

"Yeah, I already know."

"I just love them so very much."

"That much is obvious," he says. "How are your in-laws doing?"

"They're all ecstatic. Jimmy is like a changed man and Miriam is the typical mother hen clucking around and making sure everything is perfect. I'm not sure Helena has managed to do much yet, not after the caesarean."

"She will when she's healed."

"And Ben, he's just gorgeous and so happy with his new man."

"He's gay? I don't think you ever mentioned that."

"Yeah, he is, and I've known for years. He came out not long ago and introduced us to Jonathan yesterday—what an absolute hunk."

"Oh, really?" He's wide-eyed but joking.

"Him and Ben make a gorgeous couple, and I'm thrilled for them."

"You don't have a judgemental bone in your body, do you?"

"Love is love, Elijah."

"You have my total agreement there, and in this world, if a person finds it, good for them."

"They're all going to be okay, and it's good because I feel I can breathe now. I'd been so worried and once I got over myself and went to see them again, I realised my bond to them as family would always remain."

"The babies have brought joy back into their lives, right?"

"Exactly, but even they didn't realise to what extent that would be."

"I'm happy for them all, but let me ask you a question…"

"Something tells me I'm not going to like this."

"How are you, really?"

"I'm going to be okay too." He slips his arm around my shoulder. I close my eyes, and for the first time in a while, I feel like myself again.

Chapter Twenty-Four

Three Letters

Today I face the part of my past I've been ignoring.

It's not that I want to do this, I feel compelled to.

Pulling the letters from the drawer, I read them again and feel the same rush of emotion as I did the first time.

"God bless you all," I say, picking up the phone, intending to speak to the transplant coordinator.

"Hello, Eleanor Parker speaking."

"Erm, hi, Eleanor, this is Serena Tate, I don't know if you remember me, but my husband Jamie was on the transplant register."

"Yes, of course, Serena, how are you?"

"Plodding on."

"That is good to hear."

"Look, I'm sorry to bother you, but I've just re-read the letters and would like to meet the recipients."

"Okay."

"You don't seem so sure, Eleanor."

"Forgive me, but it's you that needs to be absolutely sure it's what you want."

"I do."

"Right, first off I'll need to write to them and see if a meeting is still wanted."

"Okay, then what?"

"If they do, I shall contact you back with their decision and if it's a go, I will be in touch with the relevant people to make it happen."

"I'm nervous even talking about it, but it's something I have to do." I hold the letters close to me.

"Many in your situation feel the same way, but it's not always easy and can be quite upsetting."

"Seeing them with my own eyes might be hard but knowing they're living, and breathing will help to ease the residual pain of Jamie dying."

"Some see the patients as an extension of their loved ones. But I think it's important you see them as they are, individuals alive because of a transplant."

"I get that."

"Whatever you feel in the moment, the heart for example, no longer belongs to Jamie, but to the person it beats inside, can you live with that?"

"Jamie is dead, I know that, but a part of him still lives inside them. That's not to say I'll confuse any of them with him. He's gone and what he left behind is the gift of life."

"That's fine, Serena. Leave it with me and I'll come back to you as soon as possible."

"Thanks, Eleanor."

With that out of the way, I feel lighter. Now is the right time, but I want to keep it to myself for now. Telling Jimmy and Miriam might upset them. They're playing the dutiful grandparents, a role they relish and truly deserve. I don't want to interrupt that.

At a loss, I decide to call Louise and see what she is doing.

"I was just thinking about you," she says.

"All good, I hope?"

"Are you free for lunch?"

"You must have read my mind because I was calling for the exact same thing. Do you know Milly's? It's not far from Violet Lodge."

"Yeah, I've been there a few times. They have delicious vegan muffins."

"Ooh, nice."

"Sarcasm does not suit you, Serena Tate."

"I wasn't being anything of the sort."

"You're also a terrible liar, my friend."

"Okay, now you caught me out, shall we meet there in half an hour."

"Sounds good to me. See you there."

I race around, grabbing things I need; keys, handbag, photographs of Jamie and Alexander, and race out of the door.

Louise is already there and seated when I arrive. It has a completely different vibe from my last visit here with Jamie.

We have our customary hug and I sense something is bothering her.

I take my seat opposite her. She looks tired and drawn. "Are you sick?"

"Oh, thanks so much."

"Sorry, but you look a little peaky."

"Old age is creeping closer, Serena."

"There's more to it than that."

"Were you always so intuitive?"

"With people I love, yes."

"There is something I want to tell you."

"Am I going to need tissues for this?"

The waitress steps forward. "What can I get for you?"

"A Caramel Latte for me with only one pump of caramel please, and what about you, Lou?"

"Vegan Chai Latte for me."

"Two vegan muffins too, actually make it four," I add. "We might be here a while." At the back of my mind is the anticipation bad news is coming. I'm not prepared but in a public place, I won't wail like a banshee.

"Won't be too long."

"Thank you." I lean in. "Now, the truth please and don't try and spare my feelings."

"There is no easy way to say this, but I've got cancer."

The air rushes from my lungs. "Where?"

"Lung, but before you collapse into a puddle, its treatable."

"But not curable?"

"The oncologist said if I had come to him ten years ago the prognosis would have been bleak but as it is, he thinks I can live a relatively normal life for many more years to come."

I reach over for her hand. She takes it. "I'm so sorry, Lou." My lip quivers.

"Don't you dare cry, Serena, do you hear me?"

"I don't want to lose you."

"And you're not gonna, not for a long time anyway."

I know what she is telling me is factually correct, but as my best friend, I can't bear the thought of her suffering for even one minute. "Oh, Lou..." The floodgates open as I reach into my bag for tissues.

"I told you not to do that."

"I tried; I swear I really did."

She laughs and so do I. "Not bloody hard enough." She dabs at her eyes. "See, you've set me off now."

"That's it, you're moving in with me and I will take care of you."

The waitress arrives with our order. She can see something is wrong but maintains professionalism. "Anything else I can get you?"

"No thanks," Louise answers while I fight to compose myself.

"Absolutely not," she replies when we're alone again.

"I have loads of space."

"And a life, plus I still fully intend to take my trip."

"You're still going to go?"

"If it's the last thing I do, yes."

"I could come with you."

"Then who would look after my group, Bob?"

"Elijah." It's not the worst idea in the world.

"He's a lovely guy, but you're the ideal person for the job." She takes a sip of her Vegan Chai Latte.

"I'll be so worried about you." I follow suit and wince at the sweetness of my drink. There is more than one shot of caramel but I'm not making an issue of it.

"Don't because if one thing is giving me purpose, it's the thought of visiting all of those wonderful places Laura never got to see."

Something tells me her mission in life will end in Cambodia, but I don't want to dwell. This has become more than a journey for her dear daughter. Now, it's about finding her own path. "Can I at least suggest something?"

"You're going to whatever I say, so spit it out."

"And you are going to tire a lot easier and a train journey to faraway places won't do you any good."

"And?"

"it's important you see everything you need to, right?"

"Yes," she says, suspicious of where I am going with this.

"Then let me help."

"How?"

"Just leave it with me."

"Serena Tate, what are you up to?"

"I'm your best friend, and you are mine, trust me."

"You aren't coming with me and that is final."

"I know, but if you allow me to do this, I won't have to worry as much."

"Fine, but whatever you have planned, don't treat me like a charity case."

"I never would. Now, what I need from you is your itinerary."

"Jeez, I've not got that far yet."

"Even better."

"Why am I worried?"

"Don't worry, just leave me to it, and when I reveal my surprise, know it's been done with love."

"You're a good girl."

"You might not think so when I tell you my gossip." Before I continue, I take a bite of the Vegan Muffin. One chew and I spit it into a napkin. "Ugh, what did they make this with, sawdust?"

Louise bites into hers and chews furiously. "Tastes like shit." She waves her hand in the air and yells across the room. "Excuse me, flower, this muffin is out of date."

She has no shame. I hold my head in my hands. Even living with cancer, she's still the fiercest woman I know.

Chapter Twenty-Five

The Recipients

After another busy week. I relish the silence and slip into a hot bubble bath.

It's only two thirty in the afternoon but I've nothing else planned.

Two hours later, I finished my current eBook, *This Much is True* by revered acid-tongued actress, Miriam Margoyles, and thoroughly enjoyed reading about her past. It's her candour that was most endearing, and the fact she has been lucky in love—fifty plus years with the woman of her dreams while living on different continents is not easy. But she did it. I feel a sliver of envy but push it out of my mind.

Half an hour later I'm sitting at my dressing table, daydreaming, when my phone rings. It's a withheld number. Grimacing, I'm not in the mood for marketing calls but answer anyway intending to give these arseholes short thrift.

"What," I bark down the line.

"May I speak to Serena Tate please?"

Instantly my mood shifts, and my telephone voice makes an appearance. "How may I help you?"

"Oh, hello, this is Eleanor Parker speaking."

"Gosh, please accept my apologies. I thought you were one of those ambulance chaser compensation companies asking about an accident I've never had."

"That's quite alright. I'm sorry to call so late in the day but I have news and thought you'd want to know as soon as possible."

"You do?"

"Yes, some good and some which won't be what you want to hear."

"Okay."

"I've had correspondence back from the three recipients and two of them have declined your request for a meeting."

"Oh, really, that is disappointing?"

"For the moment, yes, though both asked if it would be okay to write to you and explain why, with the possibility of meeting in the future."

"Yes, certainly. Am I allowed to write back?"

"That will be fine."

"Excellent."

"The third recipient who received the heart is happy to meet with you as soon as next week if you are available."

"Wow, so soon?" Nervous energy flows through me but there is little point delaying. "When and where? I can do any date and time."

"That makes things so much easier. I'll sort it out and email me you the details. But it's more than likely to be at The Royal."

"Does it have to be there?"

"I can look for an alternative venue."

Do it, my inner voice urges. "You know what, let's do it there."

"Are you sure?"

"Yes, it's about time I laid that ghost to rest too."

"Okay, well keep an eye out for the email. I'll try and get back to you before the end of the day."

"Fantastic. Thanks for everything, Eleanor."

"It's my pleasure."

It takes a few minutes to take in the news. I can't quite believe it, though guilt stabs at me because I really should tell Jimmy and Miriam. Half an hour later, I can't live with deceiving them and decide to drive over to see them.

On the ride over, I rake over the possible ways I can introduce it into conversation, then decide to just get it out of the way. Walking on eggshells around either won't be appreciated.

"This is a nice surprise." She hugs me tightly. "And you're just in time for dinner."

"Oh, no, I didn't think about interrupting you."

"You didn't and I've cooked more than enough." She pulls me through the door. "Jimmy will be thrilled to have company."

"Is it just the two of you?" I follow her down the hallway and into the kitchen.

Jimmy is sitting reading a newspaper. "Hi, Jimmy."

"Hello, love, is everything okay?"

"Yes, all's fine, I just wanted to speak to you both about something."

"You're not sick, are you?" I'm certain it's Miriam's favourite question, mine too on occasion.

"No, not at all. Healthy as a horse."

"Sit down," Jimmy says.

I take the seat next to him as Miriam sets another place. "Whatever you're cooking smells delicious."

"Braised Steak, Mashed Potato, Carrot, Turnip, and Savoy Cabbage."

I'm almost salivating at the thought of it. "How can I resist that?"

"You can't." She dishes up quickly and minutes later I'm sitting in front of a steaming plate of food any good restaurant would be happy to serve. Jimmy tucks in, as do I. "So, what's on your mind?"

I'm in two minds because I don't want to ruin her dinner. "I don't mind waiting until we're finished."

"You might as well tell us," Jimmy advises. "Whatever it is, we can handle it."

"I've spoken to the transplant coordinator and arranged to meet one of the recipients."

"Right," Miriam says, while Jimmy remains silent.

"I feel terrible not telling you before I arranged it."

"Don't." Jimmy finds his voice. "It's your right to do that, Serena."

"I think the meeting will be as soon as next week and I wanted to know if it is something either of you would be interested in?"

"For me, it's a no," Jimmy advises, "and that's only because I've reached a certain point where I can focus on the good times and don't want to go backward."

"I get it."

"So, while I wish the recipient well, I'm sitting this out, but just so you know, and not that you need it, you have my full support."

"And mine," Miriam adds next. "But I'm with Jimmy for now. I want only the best for whoever Jamie helped, but I've got two new grandchildren who don't need to see me as a blubbering wreck and I fear meeting any of them will push me back to where I was."

"I thought the same for such a long time, but it feels like an invisible force pushing me to do it. Sounds crazy but I can't explain it."

"There's nothing crazy about it." She places her hand over mine. "You have to do what you feel is right, Serena."

"I thought you'd resent me for wanting to do it."

"Never," Jimmy says, shovelling mashed potato into his mouth. "Miriam is right."

"Don't talk with your mouth full, Jimmy."

He shakes his head.

"So, if you're both totally fine with me doing it, would you like me to tell you anything about what happens?"

Jimmy chews his braised steak.

Miriam answers. "Tell you what, love, if we want to know, we'll ask, how's that sound?" She's speaking for both of them.

"Perfect."

"Now, eat your dinner before it gets cold."

"There is something else." I hadn't intended to bring up Elijah but it's another thing that niggles my conscience.

"Okay." Miriam stabs at the cabbage on her plate, poised to taste it. "Go on." Then she finally chews on a mouthful of food.

I know Ben mentioned Elijah, but I'll carry on as though it's something new. "I've met a guy, but he's just a friend before you jump to conclusions."

"She already knows, I told her, Serena."

"I do," Miriam confirms. "And I'm happy that you've found somebody that has put a smile on your face, friend or not."

"Honestly, we're just friends. We met at the support group."

"He's lost somebody close too I assume?"

"His wife, she died in a fall."

"That's so sad," Miriam adds.

"He still misses her, like I do Jamie. But it's nice to have somebody to talk to, not that I don't have you all when I'm feeling down."

Jimmy busies himself with the food on his plate.

"You don't have to explain anything. As far as I'm concerned you were the best wife my son could ask for, and as long as we never lose you, we'll be happy when you find somebody special."

"What did I do to deserve you both?"

"We ask the same question about you. Now, you can tell us all about him once you've eaten your dinner but make some room for dessert."

"Dare I ask?"

"Rhubarb Crumble and Custard."

"You're going to make me fat again."

"You were never fat," Miriam says. "But don't worry, I have low fat custard if you'd prefer."

"Don't go to any trouble." My eyes are bigger than my belly but where Miriam's baked goods are concerned, I don't care.

It's late when I leave the cottage, but I take a chance and call Elijah anyway.

"Hey, pretty lady."

"Did I wake you?"

"No, I've been holed up in my writing cave all day."

"Ooh, the new book," I reply, excited for him. "How's it coming along?"

"Seventy-five-thousand words in, so another five or ten k, and I'm done."

"I can't wait to read it."

"I'll make sure you get an advanced copy but while you're on the line, I've got a signing tour next week."

"Where?" It helps me out immeasurably because I hadn't intended to tell him anything about my appointments for fear it would upset him "I didn't know you had anything in the pipeline."

"All over the UK, and yeah, but I forgot to say until I was reminded before."

He does have absent minded tendencies, so I forgive him. "That's better than a world tour."

"I've already told my agent no more foreign trips."

"I'll miss you."

"It's only a week."

"Just enjoy it but the positive is we're in the same time zone so I'll call you every day."

"I like the sound of that."

I hear the tapping of keys in the background. "Me too."

"So, how was your evening with the in-laws?"

"They're just the most amazing people—I told them all about you."

"Really, and how did they respond to that?"

"Jimmy already knew of you, but unbeknownst to me he'd already told Miriam."

"And they were fine with you having a new friend?"

"Totally, in fact, Miriam told me they're happy as long as I am."

"They sound like decent people."

"I think they're more worried about me meeting somebody else and phasing myself out of their lives."

"No way would that ever happen."

"Absolutely not, and I did my best to reassure them of that."

"I've never met them, but they mean a lot and whoever is lucky enough to win your heart, they'll have to get used to the fact you all come as a package."

"Exactly, and I'm so glad you understand."

"Kara was my only family, so I'm envious of what you have and would never dream of coming between that."

He's such a decent man and will hold a person up rather than tear them down. It's on the tip of my tongue, but I can't find the words to tell him about next week. I hate myself. But it's something I have to do alone. One thing is certain, I'll tell him everything when he returns.

"Listen, I know you're busy, so I'll let you get back to it, but I'll see you at the meeting, and perhaps we can have coffee before you leave."

"I'd like that."

"Okay, I'll see you soon."

"I'm counting the minutes."

Chapter Twenty-Six

Surprise!

It's Louise's last meeting before she leaves for her trip.

I'm emotional as are a few others, but we're all agreed, finally taking the trip in honour of her daughter, is no less than she deserves.

"Thanks everyone. I'll see you all when I get back, but in the meantime, I leave you in Serena's capable hands." Louise brings the meeting to a close, but I have a surprise for her before she leaves. "Goodnight."

At this point people usually rush for the doors but nobody moves.

I stand and interrupt the proceedings. "Before you head off there is something I want to say."

"Oh, God, I had a feeling you'd do this to me."

"Before you complain, it's not a big gushing speech, or anything like that."

"Hallelujah!" She replies in full on sarcastic mode.

"We all know you hate mushy stuff so rather than with words, we all want to say something with this."

I reach into my bag and pull out a large plain white envelope. "Here, and don't shout at us."

"What is it?"

"Sit down and read it," Elijah urges, already in on the surprise.

She peels open the envelope and pulls a handful of documents from inside. Seconds later, her hand works its way toward her mouth. "This is..." Her eyes take on a glazed look.

"An all-expenses paid trip to Vietnam, Thailand and Cambodia."

"I can't accept this, it's too much."

"You can, and you will." Hamish says as others murmur their agreement.

"But, why?"

Louise had been honest with the group regarding her diagnosis. Every one of us reacted the same way; sadness that one of our own is suffering, but all agreed it was our turn to take care of her. "Train journeys thousands of miles across the globe and queuing in packed airports will leave you too tired to enjoy yourself, so we clubbed together for first class flights, five star hotels and a trip on the Orient Express Thailand."

She lowers her head as her shoulders gently rise and fall. "I-I don't know what to say."

"We love you, Louise, and want to give something back. After all, every one of us is better off for knowing you."

"I do what I do because I care, not for free trips abroad."

"And we've done this because we care for you, more than you know, so go, with our blessings, good luck and have the time of your life."

Finally, she looks at us, and seeing how happy and relieved she is, even though she won't say it, she speaks. "I adore each and every one of you."

A chorus of cheers rings out. She means the world to us, and while I know this trip is everything she needs, I can't help feeling this is the last time I'll see her.

She hugs each of them before they leave but saves me until last. Elijah says his goodbyes then busies himself with clearing tables. "There is so much I want to say, and while I know I don't have to, what I need to say is, losing Laura shattered my existence, and then you came along, broken, needing me, and guess what happened?"

I'm sobbing now and won't apologise. "What?"

"Turns out all along I needed you too, and though I love my Laura with every fibre of my being, God gave me another daughter." She fights to control her emotions too. "I know I didn't give birth to you, but you were sent to help heal me and that's exactly what you did. Always remember when your days are dark, in here…" she taps her chest. "…you are mine."

"Oh, Lou, what am I gonna do without you?"

"I'm coming back."

"Promise me."

"I swear, I'm going to walk back in here feeling reinvigorated."

"I'll come and get you if I have to." I don't want to say it, but if she doesn't make it, I'll fly out and bring her home.

"Bring that man of yours along."

"He isn't my man."

"Yes, he is, you just have to open yourself up to the possibility."

"I like him a lot."

"He feels the same way too."

"I never imagined I'd be where I am now. It didn't seem possible."

"You're stronger than you give yourself credit for and I couldn't be prouder."

"Are you really going to be okay over there on your own?"

"It's an adventure with my name written all over it and thanks to your generosity, I'll be doing it first class."

"We'll worry about you a little less now."

"I know you're really behind this gift, and Elijah too."

"Honestly, it was all of us."

"This sort of thing costs an arm and a leg and while I'm certain the rest gave all they could, you and money bags over there, added the other zeros."

"I don't know what you're talking about."

"Sure." She chucks me under the chin. "I love you, Serena, and I'm going to miss you."

"You won't get chance to because you're going to call me and fill me in on your trip at least twice a week."

She holds my face in her hands and kisses the centre of my forehead.

"I don't want to say the word so I'm going to make a quick call and when I turn around, you'll be gone, okay."

"Whatever you want." Despite harrowing times, I've been so lucky in my life. With Miriam I always knew I was loved and wanted. With Louise I feel exactly the same way. One last squeeze and I whisper into her ear, "I love you too." I rush away before I make a fool of myself in front of the stragglers in the group.

Elijah waits by the door for me. "Shall I drive?"

"I think so. I'm too upset."

"Come on, you big softie." He wraps a protective arm around my shoulder and leads me toward the car.

"I don't want her to go but she needs to do it."

"You know that so let her have this time."

"What other choice do I have?"

"None." He's always the voice of reason. "Shall we stop off for a bottle of wine?"

"I have plenty at home but if there is something specific you want then I don't mind."

"It's fine, straight back to yours it is."

Too lost in my own thoughts, I say nothing on the journey back to my place. "Sorry I've been so quiet."

"Would you prefer I leave you to your thoughts?"

"No, I want you to come in. I just needed that bit of silence, sorry."

"I get it, Lou is a force to be reckoned with and it won't be the same while she's away."

I push the key in the door. "Give me a few minutes to get out of these clothes."

"Shall I grab a bottle and pour?"

"Yes."

"Any requests?"

"You choose."

I walk up the stairs, into my bedroom and sit on my bed. What I want to do is scream and shout, but it's not in me, nor do I want Elijah to think I've lost my marbles. Instead, I slip into comfy pyjamas–definitely not the sexiest item of clothing in my wardrobe. Elijah and I haven't taken that step, yet, so it doesn't matter.

Plus, I feel the need to discuss the changes in my life with Miriam and Jimmy. It's only fair plus I did promise to. Elijah and I are getting closer. It's only right they know.

Fixing a smile to my face, I find Elijah in the kitchen. He's poured two large glasses of white wine. "I hope this is acceptable."

"Right now, I'd drink anything."

"You will see Lou again, please don't worry."

"How do you know that's what I'm thinking?"

"I kinda know you, and how your mind works."

"What if you're wrong and tonight was it?"

"I don't think she's ready to give up yet."

"If anything happens, swear you'll come with me to get her."

"There's no way I'd let you go alone."

I down half the contents of the glass and top it up again. "I needed that."

"Just don't drink yourself into oblivion, or you'll regret it tomorrow."

"I probably will but it might be worth it."

"Shall we go into the living room?"

"If you want."

"It's comfier in there." He picks up the bottle of wine. I lead the way and sit on the three seater sofa. I bang the cushion next to me.

He flops down. "Did I mention I have the itinerary for my tour next week?"

"No, you didn't say. Are you going anywhere special?"

"The usual, London, Glasgow, Newcastle, Birmingham, Dublin, Belfast, Plymouth, Leeds, Coventry, and a few other places."

"I wish I could come with you, but looking after the group, I won't be able to, plus I need to drive over and see Miriam and Jimmy too."

"Are they okay?"

"Yes, totally, but it's a few weeks since I've been into the office so I'm well overdue for a catch up with both."

"Sounds good."

"It's always nice to see them." I drain more of my wine. "Now, tell me about these signings."

"Local bookstores, I think. Penny sorted everything, but I'll be gone Monday through to Friday."

"Why do I feel like everyone is leaving me?" I don't know where that thought came from or why I vocalised it.

"I'm not leaving you, just going to sit behind a desk and smile at strangers."

"You love the adoration."

"I'd rather spend my time with you."

"When Lou gets back, why don't we book some time away together?"

He appears surprised and perhaps it is a big step, but we enjoy one another's company and there has been a positive shift between us. We're comfortable around one another.

Add in the sunshine, beach, and copious amounts of cocktails, and what could go wrong?

Chapter Twenty-Seven

I Know Your Heart

Waking early, my first thought is to question my decision, and deciding I've made the right one, I make sure I look presentable, but for a change, I tie my hair back.

Miriam calls me. "How are you feeling?"

I'm filled with a mixture of dread and anticipation, But I instigated it and won't back out now. "Terrified."

"You need to do this, so I won't try and talk you out of it."

"Please try."

"No," she replies. "I think this will bring you peace, and a sense of closure."

"I'm not sure, but I'm going to be brave and do it anyway."

"You're going to be fine, and I'll be thinking of you."

"Shall I call you when the meeting is over?"

"Yes, I'd like to know you're okay, at least." It's her way of saying not to tell her anything more unless she asks.

"Well, I better get a move on. Thanks for calling."

"Stay strong, Serena."

"Will do." Though I am meeting the person who has Jamie's heart, it's doubly difficult as it's the first time I've returned to The Royal. It bothers me more than it should.

Thankfully, Eleanor Parker is meeting me.

Driving there is hard, but I focus on Talk Radio and lose myself in other people's problems rather than facing what is before me.

After slipping into the hospital, I'm relieved nobody spots me. I've shed a few stone since last being there, so colleagues would not necessarily realise it's me anyway. Walking through familiar corridors it's not as bad as I imagined it to be, but anxiety pushes me forward and ensures I don't make eye contact with anyone passing me by.

Stepping out of the lift on the fourth floor, I find the meeting room and see a pretty older lady styled to within an inch of her life waiting at the door. Her auburn hair is piled high on top of her head, but she looks amazing, and funnily enough, just as I imagined her to be.

"Hello," I say as nerves kick in.

"Serena?"

"Yes."

"I'm Eleanor Parker, lovely to meet you." She extends her hand to me.

I take hold, aware I'm trembling. "You too, thanks for meeting me here."

"Come in and take a seat while I run through how this will work."

I do as she suggests. The room is fairly large and has four two-seater sofas with a coffee table in the middle of the room which serves no purpose because the seats are too far away. "All the years I've worked in this place, and I never knew this room was here."

"We use it for these meetings, you know, somewhere impartial both parties can feel at ease."

"Do you do this regularly?"

She sits next to me, and I catch the unmistakable scent of Chanel No.5. "More often than you'd think. Sometimes these meetings can be awkward at first, but after a few minutes, the tension resides. Other times, there's joy from the moment the donor family and recipient meet."

"I'm terrified."

"You'll be fine, and the good thing is, you don't have long to sit and dwell on it."

"What should I expect?"

"The recipient will enter the room, but I will stay as long as you need me to, then if you wish, I can leave the two of you to talk."

I gather myself. This should be a wonderful moment.

Eleanor's phone rings. "Excuse me." She stands and walks to the other side of the room. I try not to listen in on the call, not that it lasts long anyway. "Okay, are you ready?"

"Now?" My pulse quickens and I feel beads of sweat forming under my hairline. I lean back and rest my head on the wall. I close my eyes to gather myself. *Calm down, Serena.*

"Do you need a little more time?"

"No, the more I have the worse my anxiety will be so let's do it."

"If you're sure, I'm just going to the lift. I'll be back in just a few minutes, okay?"

"Right."

"Just try to stay calm. The thought is worse than the deed."

She leaves the room and I suddenly feel I can't breathe. Dashing toward the windows, I look down and focus on the tiny people milling about unaware of what is about to happen.

Tick, tock–the noise from the wall clock intensifies my nerves but I don't have time to think on it for long as I hear voices. I'm too scared to turn and look as they approach.

"Just through here," I hear Eleanor say as I take a few deep breaths, ready to meet the girl.

Bracing myself, I fix a smile to my face and turn.

"Serena, I'd like you to meet–"

"What the hell is this?" Horror courses through me as Eleanor stands next to Elijah. He appears as confused as I am but says nothing.

"Is something wrong?"

"Elijah, what are you doing here?"

Eleanor's eyes dance from me to him. "Do you two know one another?"

"You could say that," I snap, feeling I'm losing my mind. "I-I don't understand, Eleanor."

"Elijah received Jamie's heart." She confirms what I don't want to hear.

He's stunned into silence.

"No, no, that's not true, a young mother got it."

"I don't know why you'd think that, Serena, but Elijah is the recipient."

I look to him, imploring him to say something but there's nothing in his eyes. "Elijah, did you know?"

"No." He looks to Eleanor. "This can't be happening."

"There has to be a mistake, somewhere, please, tell me it is." I slide into the nearest chair, holding my head in my hands.

The atmosphere in the room is one of panic. I don't know what to do, nobody else in the room seems to either.

"How is this possible?" Elijah asks, stepping further into the room.

"Don't come any closer," I warn. "I can't bear it."

"This is most irregular," Eleanor adds.

"Oh, God, oh, God," I repeat. "I felt drawn to him and now I know why." I look down and realise my feet are moving involuntarily. I want to throw up and press my hand over my mouth in case.

"Serena..."

Repulsed, I hold my finger up. There's nothing he can say I want to hear.

"Elijah, would you please come with me," Eleanor asks.

"I need to check she's okay."

"Please, I insist," she orders. "Until I find out what has happened, it's better if you come with me."

I jump to my feet, desperate to get out of there. But to do that I have to pass him. What if he touches me, tries to stop me?

Praying for strength, I tell my legs to move, and seconds later I've pushed past them both, standing in the corridor unsure which way to go. I feel dizzy and press my hand against the wall to steady myself. But it's too late as the floor rushes up to meet me. The last word I hear is my name called out before my eyes close and I'm lost to unconsciousness.

I'm aware of voices and can smell Chanel No.5.

"We had no idea there had been an error. It's unforgivable."

"When will she wake up?" Miriam asks.

"Soon," another voice adds.

My head is still fuzzy and hurts. "Miriam…" I open my eyes.

"Thank goodness. You frightened the life out of us." Turning I see Jimmy too.

"I didn't know, I swear."

He holds my hand but says nothing. His touch comforts me.

"What didn't you know, darling?"

"That it was him."

"We don't know anything, apart from there's been some sort of error with the correspondence between recipient and donor family."

"It's him," I cry, losing control of my emotions. I want to scream but a warm, fuzzy feeling quickly takes over me and I close my eyes again.

"She's coming round." I recognise Jimmy's voice.

"Serena, we're here," Miriam says as I open my eyes. "Try and stay calm, okay love, everything is just fine."

I feel hopeless, that any progress I'd made toward a future without Jamie has been ripped away. Then, thinking of the time Elijah and I spent together, and why I felt so comfortable. The words, I know his heart, echo through my mind, torturing me. "He was there all along."

"Darling, we don't know the full story, but you need to remain calm, or they'll put you back to sleep again." Jimmy rubs my hand, trying to stem the panic threatening to erupt from within me.

"I didn't know."

"Serena, listen to me…" Miriam stands next to the bed. "Whatever has happened, we'll get through it as a family, just like always."

Pushing myself up the bed, I don't know how I'm going to tell them. "Elijah…" It hurts to say his name.

"Your friend from the group?" Miriam adds. "Is that who you mean?"

"Yes."

"What about him?" Jimmy asks.

"Jamie's heart…" It hurts to breathe. "He's the recipient."

"That's not right, love." She looks at Jimmy. He shrugs his shoulders. Do they think I've finally cracked?

"It is."

"But how?" she asks.

"I don't know but he was here, I was supposed to meet the recipient and it was him." Why won't somebody tell me I've imagined it. Turning, I see Eleanor Parker lurking in the corridor. "Ask her, she'll tell you."

Jimmy waves her into the room and before she's in, he speaks. "Is what Serena is saying true?"

Eleanor steps into the room. She looks washed out. "I'm afraid it is. I've spent the last few hours on the telephone to various people and going through records. While we don't know how it happened, Mr Hart is the recipient."

"How the hell does this sort of thing happen?"

"I wish I had all the answers to give you. I am so sorry, but there will be a full investigation."

An awkward silence follows her confession. There is nothing left for me to say but I wonder where Elijah is and how he has taken the news.

Chapter Twenty-Eight

Time

Slowly, the days pass by but I'm still in a daze.

Elijah has tried calling me numerous times, leaving voicemails and text messages, but I can't deal with him, not yet.

It's taken a few hours, but Louise finally returns my call. Hearing her voice, I realise how much I've missed her. Trying and failing to stay calm, I tell her what's happened. She doesn't speak until I've got everything out.

"I can't believe it, Serena."

I know she will see something mystical in this latest development. "Please, tell me what to do. I'm so lost."

"Face up to the situation, that's all you can do."

"Do you believe in fate?"

"You're asking me, the world's oldest hippy, if she believes in stuff like that? I do!"

"It's like some sort of cosmic joke? Jamie is taken away from me, but a part finds its way back."

"You might not want to hear this but consider it could be the universe's way of telling you his heart is eternally yours."

"That sounds like a plot from one of his books," I bite back at her words. Then I'm angry at myself for taking it out on her.

"How else do you explain it, Serena? Of all the people in this world you could see a future with and it's the same guy who has your dead husband's heart beating in his chest you end up with."

"I can't even think of that, Lou."

"It's become your reality and the sooner you deal with it, the better for you both."

"I just want to turn back time and forget what I know."

"Elijah is still the same person he was before you knew."

"I don't know who he is anymore."

"You're being silly–he's exactly the same kind, gorgeous man he always was."

"It's Jamie's!" I cry again.

"Yes, it is but you're luckier than most because I'd give anything to be close to any part of Laura."

Selfishness slaps me across the face. Thinking of myself when she's lost as much as I have is wrong. "It's like something from a Hallmark movie. I don't know what to do, and yes, I might be acting silly, but how would you feel?"

"Don't get me wrong, Serena, I'd be as shocked as you are, but when that passed, look at it another way, that a part of him has found its way back to you."

"Do you really believe that?"

"Nobody knows what lies for us when we die, but who are you to say Jamie hasn't had a hand in this?"

"Elijah isn't Jamie."

"Whew, I'm glad you realise that, or things would get a lot messier."

"What do you mean?"

"Jamie is gone, but a part of him lives inside a man you've grown quite fond of–"

Rudely, I interrupt her. "I wouldn't go that far–"

She does the same, wanting to get her point across. "This is me you're talking to now, Serena, don't kid a kidder. You like him but only you know how much."

"He's just my friend." I'm lying but it seems easier to deal with this crisis if I tell myself that.

"Elijah's dazzled by you, so sometimes things are just meant to be, and you have to suck it up and get on with things."

"I haven't even spoken to him since."

"Why ever not?"

"What am I supposed to say?"

"Perhaps start with, Elijah, it's not your fault, but I need time to digest what's happened."

"Everything is so black and white with you."

"Okay, smart arse, give me the grey areas." She waits for my reply.

"I can't."

"Why?"

"Because you're right, as usual."

"It's not a question of right or wrong, Serena, but what is meant to be. You found my group and Elijah was already part of it. Over time you gravitated towards one another. Don't you find that odd, out of all the people that attend those meetings, it was him that caught your eye and vice versa?"

There's no way I can brush off her words with any other explanation than fate. "So, it was meant to be?"

"I think so, but the romantic in me sees it as the most beautiful thing rather than anything to be feared."

"I wish I could see it that way."

"You will, if you allow yourself to."

"Never in my wildest dreams did I ever imagine anything like this."

"Who would, but remember, it's not just about you, but Elijah, and Jamie's family too. You've been dating, and before you go mad, that's exactly what it is."

"I'm a selfish cow, aren't I?"

"Yeah, but I still love ya." She laughs. It's good to hear.

"I haven't even asked how your trip is going?"

"First class flights and five star hotels, there's nothing to scoff at."

"So, you're enjoying yourself?"

"The places I've visited are beyond words, but more importantly, I feel close to Laura, and that's what I wanted."

"And how are *you* doing?" I'm asking about her health but won't say the c word.

"I feel totally calm and at peace. The other thing is still there but I refuse to let it rule my life."

Her words scare me. "You're coming home, remember?"

"I made you a promise and intend to keep it."

"I miss you so much."

"Right back at ya, kiddo. But soon enough, I'll drag my weary old arse home and you'll soon be sick at the sight of me."

"You know, I'm terrified you're going to die while you're away." I hadn't intended on saying anything, but she deserves to hear my truth. "And I can't stand the thought of never seeing you again."

"If you think for one moment that I'm ready to pop my clogs, you're off your bloody rocker."

"Promise me."

"I've got no intention of rolling over and dying quite yet. There is so much more to do, places to see, friends to sort out."

She's talking about me and Elijah. "If you want to come home tomorrow, I'll pick you up from the airport."

"Nice try, but I've got open-ended airline tickets that means I won't be back until I've seen everything Laura wanted to see."

"Take no notice of me. I'm happy you're happy."

"Forget me for the moment and tell me what you're going to do about Elijah."

"No idea."

"You know I'm going to call him, don't you?"

"Kinda figured you would."

"I won't betray your confidence, but he means a lot to me, as do you."

"Time, that's all I need, to get my head around everything. Plus, I need to see Jimmy and Miriam to find out how they really feel about everything."

"Don't leave it too long."

"Can't promise that, but I'll talk to him, eventually."

"Make sure you do, now I've got to go, but I'll check in with you in a few days, okay."

"Thanks for calling."

"There's no way I wouldn't have–just screw your sensible head back on and think things through before you lose what could be the best thing you've had in a long time."

"Yes, Mum."

"Good girl. I love ya."

She ends the call and things don't seem quite as bad as they were minutes ago.

I stare at my phone, contemplating calling Elijah and no matter how hard I try, my finger won't touch the call button. "Time," I say to myself.

Climbing into my car, I'm looking forward to the drive to Jimmy and Miriam's cottage. It will afford me the chance to declutter my mind and think, and while I don't know what reception I'm going to get, I can't put it off any longer.

Miriam is standing at the front door as I pull the car to a stop in the usual place.

I open the car door but can't force a smile.

"I was hoping you'd show your face today." I don't know how to read Miriam right now. The welcome isn't as warm as it usually is. She turns on her heel and goes back inside, leaving the door ajar.

Jumping out of the car, I follow her into the kitchen. As usual, something is bubbling on the stove though Jimmy is nowhere to be seen. He must be at the office. "You're mad at me, aren't you?"

"Furious."

"I promise, I didn't know."

"Stop right now," she says. I've never seen this side to her personality. "I'm not angry about Elijah, just you."

"Me?"

"We're supposed to be family, and the first sign of trouble, what do you do, cut us off?"

"I never—"

"Yes, you did," she argues. "How many times have I tried to call you in the last few days?"

I'm filled with shame as she takes a seat, crosses her arms which tells me she's closed off, and kicks another chair out. "What could I possibly say?"

"Something, anything is better than being ignored."

"I just needed time."

"Why?"

"Why do you think?"

"Is it his fault?"

I know she's referring to Elijah. "No."

"Whose fault is it then?"

"The transplant service," I reply, seeing where she is trying to lead me.

"Exactly, so why disappear, knowing we'll all be frantic with worry."

"Did you tell Helena and Ben?"

"They know everything." I shouldn't have expected anything else. "Both were shocked but see it for what it is."

"And what is it exactly?" I hear pain woven through my words.

"Fate, Serena."

"I'm sick of hearing that word."

"Tough. Sometimes, unexplained things happen."

"You're telling me…"

"Did Elijah know?"

"He told me he'd been the recipient of a man's heart, but nothing else. I didn't want to pry though he did say he knew very little anyway."

"While you believed Jamie's heart went to a young woman, as did I, correct?"

"Yes."

"Talk to the boy, Serena, he'll be suffering, yet did nothing wrong."

"Why do you care so much about him?" It's a low blow I'll live to regret.

She takes it better than I would have done. "He's lost so much, just like we all have, and now, through no fault of his own, somebody he might have seen a future with has walked away."

"Who said I walked away?"

"Tell me, how is Elijah feeling today?"

"We've not spoken."

"Funny that!" She's wasted as a housewife and should be a chief negotiator for the United Nations. "Before this, I'd wager you spoke to him every day, and to go from that to nothing, how do you think he feels?"

"It's not his fault," I admit.

"Finally." She leans across the table. I'm too late to move my hands away, not wanting her sympathy. "Life is hard, people die and for those who remain behind it can be unbearable. But sometimes, we're given second chances… Elijah could be that person for you."

"I barely know him."

"You know his heart, is that not enough?"

"Oh, Miriam, what am I going to do?"

She pushes herself away from the table and walks around it. She stands behind me, resting her hands on my shoulders. "First of all, we're going to have a slice of cake washed down with as much tea as you can handle, then you're going to call him and make plans to meet, if only to hash out your feelings."

"That's a tall order."

"Never go to sleep with things unsaid because you don't know if it's going to be the last night you'll spend together."

"Elijah and I have never been intimate."

"That's your business, Serena, but what I'm saying is, look back to the night Jamie died, you got to have that last conversation with him. He told you he loved you, nothing was left unsaid, can you say the same for Elijah, that if something were to happen, there would be no regrets?"

She's right, and I've been unfair only thinking of my own feelings. "Forgive me."

"If you promise never to just vanish again, you have it."

"Cross my heart…"

She bends down to kiss the top of my head. "You're forgiven, but don't think Jimmy is going to just let you off the hook like I have."

If she thinks that is letting me off the hook, I dread to think what Jimmy is going to say to me. "I'll go into the office on the way home and see him."

"Good idea. Now, would you like chocolate, or lemon sponge?"

"Erm…"

"Perhaps a slice of both."

"That might work."

"That's my girl." She chuckles. "Some things never change."

Chapter Twenty-Nine

Two Become One

Leaving the office, I feel much better than when I arrived.

Jimmy didn't give me a hard time, not really, but basically echoed Miriam's sentiments. With another promise to stay in touch, my mind is free to focus on Elijah.

"Come on, Serena, you're a big girl now." There's no time like the present. I find his number and hit the call button.

He picks up after the first ring. "Are you okay?" are his first words.

"Getting there," I reply, feeling calmer after hearing his voice.

"I'm so sorry."

"Elijah, stop!" I say. "Doing this over the phone isn't the right way."

"Okay. Then what do you suggest?"

"Are you free to come over to my place?"

"When?"

"Give me an hour to get home and settled."

"If that's what you want?"

"It is."

"Fine, I'll see you then." I end the call then admonish myself for not having the common decency to ask how he was.

Once home and with only twenty minutes to spare, I race inside and change. The house is tidy. I prepare a fresh pot of coffee, or perhaps he might prefer something stronger. But I'll cross that bridge when I come to it.

I'm hopping about like it's a first date scenario, but it's not. We're friends. I know him, he's a good man and won't hurt me.

The doorbell sounds and my pulse races.

"Coming," I call out, though he can see me through the glass panels in the door. Pulling it open, I see worry etched across his face.

"I didn't think I'd ever hear from you again."

Stepping aside, I invite him in. "Living room okay for you?"

"Wherever."

He follows me but not too closely.

I take a seat and to my surprise he sits next to me. "Do you want me to move?"

"No, it's fine." The coffee pot is on a tray on the table. I pour us both a cup and hand his to him.

"How are you?" he asks.

"Better," I reply. "What about you?"

"Still in a state of shock I think."

"Me too," I admit.

"I really had no idea."

"I know."

"Eleanor has been on the phone again this morning. They're still looking into how it happened. The shit really has hit the fan."

"Does it really matter now?"

"I guess not, but I suppose it happening once is enough to scare them into thinking there are more letters that have gone to the wrong people."

He's right. I'd hate for it to happen to anyone else. "It doesn't bear thinking about." Suddenly, he reaches for my hand. I jump back. "What are you doing?"

"I don't know," he replies. "Sorry, I just thought..."

"What?"

"That if you could feel my heart beating, you'd know I'd never hurt you."

"In my mind, it's still Jamie's, not yours."

"No, Serena, it was his, but not any longer."

His words hurt but there is no malice behind them, only fact. "You're right but it's hard to get my head around that."

"I don't want to sound cruel, but it's one of the first things Louise told me to remember, that it belongs to me now."

"She's right and I'm sorry for not seeing it that way."

"And though it's mine now, I still guard it because I know somebody died so I could live."

"I'm glad it's you."

"You are?"

"Mostly, yes, though I can't help thinking how strange it is we met."

"I'm not going to bore you with the same old cliches, but Louise said sometimes things are just meant to be."

"Do you think that's what we are, meant to be?"

"I don't know, but what I can say is, there are seven billion other people on this planet, and we found one another."

"You've got the plotline for your next book." I try to lighten the mood.

"It'd be a bestseller, that's for sure."

"Write it," I say, surprising myself.

"Are you serious?"

"I think I am, yes."

"You know, I hated seeing you upset like that but lost my cool when the hospital wouldn't allow me to stay until you woke up. Security basically threw me out."

"I'm not the fainting type, I hope you know that."

"I felt like I'd been hit by an invisible force."

"That's just what it was like for me. I couldn't control anything."

"I won't ever hurt you, Serena, I hope you realise that."

"As men go, you're up there with the best."

"High praise indeed. Now we know the truth, I hope I'm worthy of the compliment?"

"Always."

"My life feels like a rollercoaster but looking back, I was such a horrible person that even now I have to remind myself everyone deserves a second chance."

"Were you really such a nightmare?" He doesn't seem the type to step out of line, but appearances can be misleading.

"I thought I was invincible and almost paid the ultimate price." His hand hovers over the centre of his chest.

"Tell me everything." Now, I feel I have the right to ask for the whole truth.

"After Kara died, I was a mess and took anything I could get my hands on, coke, marijuana, molly, you name it, I tried it."

"Heroin?"

"Yes."

Though I'd pushed him to talk, he hit me right between the eyes with this particular revelation. No pause, no indecision. Wallop, and there it is. "Jesus Christ, Elijah." As a nurse I know how serious that would have been. "You're lucky to be sitting here talking to me."

"I know. But I took the doctor's words to mean it wasn't my addiction that caused the problem, but a run of bad luck. I thought I could walk on water, that I was untouchable."

"We're human beings, Elijah, it doesn't quite work like that."

"Oh, I know, trust me, I found out the hard way."

"Yes, it seems you did, but you recovered, and turned your life around, that's the main thing."

"Not right away, I didn't."

"Oh?" I sense another wallop coming.

"Like I said, I thought I was invincible, that I'd been through it once and it wouldn't happen again, so I carried on snorting that shit and sticking needles in my arms, and when those veins collapsed, I found other places to inject." He looks down at his arms and I notice old scars and track marks I'd never spotted before. "My addiction intensified until I spent most of the time blitzed out of my own mind."

I'm shocked by the extent of his addiction, but it makes me admire him more for beating it. "And then you had more cardiovascular issues?"

"The second heart attack was far more serious than the first and damaged my heart so severely, the only option for me was a transplant, or death." He unbuttoned his shirt slowly, then pulled it open to reveal his scar.

In my profession, I knew of the procedure—a midline sternotomy extends from the substernal notch to the xiphoid process. It is the most common cardiothoracic incision performed.

"That's a neat scar." *Touch it*, my inner voice cajoles. Reaching forward, I trace the scar line from top to bottom. "Does it hurt?"

He shakes his head but shudders to my touch. "It itches at times but it's nothing compared to the alternative. I brought everything on myself, so I try never to sound ungrateful."

"None of us are perfect, Elijah, I'm certainly not."

"I'm walking around with a stranger's heart, and all because I didn't listen to those who knew better."

"People donate organs, not to judge the recipients, but to help."

"Without it, I wouldn't be sitting here baring my soul to you."

"I'm glad you told me everything, and I hope you know it'll go no further."

"The whole truth doesn't make you think badly of me?"

"Are you clean now, Elijah, really and truly?"

"What?" It takes a few seconds for him to cotton on to what I'm asking. "Erm, yes, absolutely."

"Do you promise me?"

"I haven't touched drugs since and don't intend to do so ever again." He seems resolute and defiant not to slip back into the dark world of addiction. "The old Elijah is gone which is why I come to the group. Being part of this helps me deal with losing Kara and keeps me on the straight and narrow."

"Then you have my absolute admiration." I wasn't lying and though it hurt to have this conversation with him, he deserved the praise.

"I thought you'd hate me, and that was before what happened the other day."

"Why would I hate you?"

"Because of what I was."

"It means so much that you're able to confide in me. I won't lie though, it's still painful for me to think about so until I get it straight in my own mind..."

"Serena, there is no need to explain. I'm here whenever..."

"Thank you."

"Shall we go out for coffee, or do you need to be somewhere?" It's his attempt to lighten the mood. "Fresh air would be nice."

"I'd like that too."

"The funny thing is, I hated coffee until I had my transplant. I'm not sure I ever told you that but now I can't get through a day without it."

"Jamie was a big coffee drinker, and like you, he couldn't manage without it."

"The man obviously had taste."

"Oh, he was quite the oddity and hated anything other than the type of food his grandma used to give him. A cappuccino was probably the most exotic thing to pass his lips."

"Good old-fashioned grub, eh?"

"Oh, yes! And Stew, what some would call a poor man's meal, was his favourite thing of all."

"He was a good guy."

"The best." I feel a wave of guilt when speaking of him whilst sitting with the man who has his heart, but our relationship was never based on jealousy, and I felt sure Jamie wouldn't hold it against me. "We don't have to talk about him though."

"I'd like to hear more about him and your life together, and if you don't mind me saying so again, your face still lights up when you speak of him."

"Thinking about him makes me happy."

"Then that's what we should do, talk about him, think of him, and without feeling guilty for it."

"Is that okay for you?"

"I'd like to talk about Kara too. She was everything to me."

"Yes of course it is. Jamie was everything to me, so I know how you feel."

"He was a very lucky man."

"I was the lucky one."

"Made for one another, huh?"

"Many people thought so." Dark clouds of misery suddenly appear. "But he died and that was the end of that."

Elijah reaches for my hand. "No, Serena, that's not the end of it at all." Searching to meet my eyes, he continues, his melodic tone soothing my charred soul. "Memories belong to you, and no matter what happened, nothing can take them away."

"That's a nice way to look at it."

"I was given the gift of life by a stranger, your husband, and it means more than I could ever say so hearing about him is healing for me too."

"I still can't quite believe it."

"Do you know, for some relatives who have lost loved ones, hearing the heartbeat brings them a sense of peace?"

"Is that true?"

"I've seen it on documentaries." He touches his scar. "Is that something you could ever see yourself doing?"

"Right now, no, but maybe one day."

"Without people like Jamie, I'd be dead and forgotten, just another casualty of drugs."

"Deep down, I know our connection is special, but there is resentment lurking inside me that somebody, even you, has his heart."

"How could you not feel like that?"

"I don't want to offend you by saying it, that's the thing."

"I wake every morning and feel guilty for being alive, that a person better than I died and gave me something I should never have needed if I'd taken better care of myself."

"Don't feel guilty for living, Elijah. We all have that right."

He reaches to caress my cheek. "Can I kiss you?"

I'm taken aback by his request, and while our lips have met in the past, it's been fleeting. "Do you really want to?"

"It's what I've wanted to do since I first met you."

"Okay." I close my eyes and wait. His lips touch mine and for a moment, I force myself to remember it's Elijah I'm kissing and not Jamie. It's not a long, drawn-out kiss, but something new alongside the acceptance that I care for him. I know his heart is pure, that he won't hurt me. He buries his fingers in my hair and with his free hand gently holds the back of my neck. This time, I take the lead and lose myself in him.

I have the sudden urge to reach out and touch the scar but pull back.

He sees it and guides my hand where it needs to be. "Place your hand over my heart, feel its rhythm, and tell me it doesn't beat only for you." His words are poetic, and truthful.

I felt its gentle rhythm as tears fall.

Chapter Thirty

Past Meets Present

A few weeks ago, I officially stepped away from Tate Technology so Jimmy could take over without my interference.

Days later, I started back at The Royal in my old position.

The welcome from old friends and colleagues brought about a wave of happiness because I'd come to realise nursing was and is still a big part of my life. I'd never take it for granted. Looking after the sick and dying is where I belong, and the reception from staff and patients alike solidifies that fact.

Betty was the first person to greet me upon my return. She accepted my apology for disappearing out of her life.

Louise is home and safe from her trip, thankfully putting the kibosh on my prophecies of doom. She's doing well. Living with cancer is how she sees it, with the emphasis firmly on living.

As expected, the group is safely back in her hands. I'm pleased to hand back the reins, and although Elijah and I still attend, we've passed that crossroads in our lives but gladly offer our support even if we take less from it.

To my surprise, Betty and Louise met and forged a bond I couldn't have foreseen.

The hippy-dippy lady who believes in everything fantastical versus the nurse whose beliefs are rooted in science and anatomy—conversations are interesting, and exchanges are heated, but both thrive with the stimulation of respectful disagreement. It's a joyous thing to behold.

My relationship with Elijah has moved forward, and though there is intimacy, something stops me from taking the final step.

He's endlessly patient and reassures me that it will happen when it's meant to.

I worry he will get bored of me, but I'm assured that's my insecurity playing a mind game.

Six months down the line there are no secrets between me, Jimmy, Miriam, Helena, and Ben. They're happy and accepting of Elijah and while I hadn't pushed the issue of a meeting between us all, today is the day

"Are you nervous?" I ask as he focuses on the winding country roads.

"Scared stiff to be honest." He puts his foot down but never exceeds the speed limit.

Still, it's too fast for my liking. "They're all lovely but I'd like to get there in one piece."

He slows down a touch. "I know, you've told me many times but I'm in quite a unique situation or have you forgotten already?"

"Yes, you are, but they're gonna love you just like I do." It still feels strange loving another man, but I learned not to deny my own feelings if they became detrimental to my happiness.

"I hope so." He's quiet which means he's worried.

"Take a left here, then it's just around the corner."

"Shit..."

"What's wrong?"

"My stomach is in knots."

"Stop worrying... left here." He almost overshoots the turn.

"See, I'm going to end up in a hedge at this rate."

"Calm down, you're going to be fine, I promise.

"If you say so." He pulls into the driveway.

"Park over there." I direct him to my usual parking space. "Here is fine." Miriam looks out of the window as the car drives over the gravel. "Right, brace yourself."

"Why?"

"Look right." He does as Miriam walks toward the car. She must have dashed from the living room to the front door. I jump out to intercept her first. "Hiya."

"You made it?" She kisses my cheek and gives me a quick squeeze.

"Of course." Elijah climbs out of the car. I feel his nerves. "Miriam, this is Elijah."

She stares at him for a moment, obviously overwhelmed. There's a weird silence.

Elijah takes the lead. "It's lovely to finally meet you, Miriam." He steps forward and extends his hand.

Miriam gasps and I know instantly why. She'd expected him to sound like Jamie, but he's very much his own man.

"May I?" She finally speaks then opens her arms.

He's a good foot taller than her. She steps into his arms. He hugs her. She seems settled with her ear pressed against his chest, though the position is entirely accidental. "You're very welcome here, Elijah." She looks up, then holds his face in her hands. He bends to accommodate her height. "Handsome, you've done very well, Serena."

"Thank you," we both reply.

She returns to hug me again. "Come on, the rest are inside and waiting."

Elijah blows out a breath.

"He's been worried about today."

"Please, don't be, we're all very excited to meet you."

He nods but says nothing.

"Who is here?"

"Jimmy, Helena and Ben."

"No Keegan or the kids?"

"Not today."

I know why–they don't want to overwhelm him. "That's a shame."

"There will be plenty of occasions going forward for us all to get together. Today is just about the immediate family."

"It's lovely of you to invite us."

We walk under the rose covered archway and rather than head for the kitchen, we veer left into the living room with the attached conservatory where Jimmy, Helena and Ben are stood waiting.

I expected Helena to cry, and she doesn't disappoint.

Ben and Jimmy look at him and appear wonderstruck.

"This is Elijah," Miriam announces.

I hang back and let things progress naturally.

Ben steps forward first but seems tentative. "It's nice to meet you, mate. I'm Ben."

"And you, Ben. So good to finally meet you too."

Helena is next but is too overcome to speak. He reaches out for her, but she falls into his arms. Elijah seems surprised but goes with it and hugs her. "It's a pleasure to meet you too, Helena."

"I'm so sorry for crying, but seeing you walk in, it suddenly hit me…"

"That Jamie's heart is in my chest, I know what you mean."

She too is shorter than him and cranes her neck to look into his eyes. "A part of him is still alive because of you."

Her assessment caught me unaware. It's not something I've given much thought to before. But there are no truer words spoken. Elijah might be alive because of it, but a part of Jamie still lives for the same reason. It's a powerful moment.

She steps aside but can't take her eyes off him.

"I can't take any credit because Jamie saved my life." Jimmy hasn't moved yet so Elijah steps forward. "It is a pleasure to meet you, Mr Tate."

"Jimmy, please." He finally moves and offers his hand. "You don't know what this means to us all to have you here."

"I think I do."

"Shall we all have a drink?" It's Miriam's attempt to hurry things along. "Let's go into the garden and relax. The poor boy must feel like a zoo attraction."

I notice them all watching as Elijah is guided away by Miriam.

They're looking for things that remind them of Jamie. If they look closely enough, they'll see it. I know I do, but I take it for what it is. People often do the same things, and yes, he might have similarities, but he's very much Elijah Hart.

When we're all seated around the rectangular table on the patio, Helena is the first to ask the question I expected to crop up. "So, you're the real Grace Hart?"

He laughs. "Well, she's me really. I just hid behind her for a while."

"I'm a huge fan, but Serena probably told you."

"That's very kind of you to say, Helena."

"Mum is too, aren't you?"

"You are very talented, Elijah."

"Thank you."

"Oh, for heaven's sake leave the boy alone," Jimmy adds. "At least let him have a few drinks before you start harassing him for signed photos."

"We won't ask for them until the second meeting," Helena teases.

"You'll have to excuse my sister," Ben adds. "She always did go overboard for good-looking guys."

I see he's taken with Elijah.

"Shut it, arsehole, he's more your type than mine."

I chuckle, having already warned Elijah they bicker like children.

"Language, Helena, we have guests," Miriam warns as Jimmy rolls his eyes.

"Oh, it's fine really. I have a bit of a potty mouth sometimes."

"That's all well and good, Helena was raised to have better manners."

"You'd never think I was a mum with two kids, the way she tells me off, would you?"

And just like that, it's like Elijah has always been part of my crazy family.

Hours later, the sun is on the brink of setting, and the garden is bathed in a golden hue.

Elijah rubs his stomach. "That meal was delicious, thank you, Miriam."

"I told you she was a great cook, didn't I?"

"Yes, and I agree."

"Oh, hush, you'll give me a big head."

"A bigger head," Helena teases.

She shoots her daughter a medusa-like stare. "Don't you and Benjamin have a dishwasher to stack?"

Ben groans at the use of his full name.

"I'll do the dishes," Jimmy adds.

"No, you can sit and relax," Miriam orders. "Let them do it for once."

"Before anybody goes anywhere, I wonder if I could steal a few moments?"

I feel everyone's eyes fixed on me, but I don't know why.

"Take your time," Jimmy says, placing his arm around Miriam's shoulder.

Elijah turns to me, and though I hadn't noticed where it came from, he's holding a red velvet box in his hand. The lid is open and the biggest yellow diamond I've ever seen glints in what is left of the sunlight. "Serena…"

"Erm…" I gasp at the realisation he's about to propose. Frantic I turn to look at my family and see nothing but delight in their eyes. Without words, they're acknowledging my new love, though they know Jamie will never be far from my thoughts.

"… from the moment I set eyes on you, I knew you were the one…"

Helena is making the strangest grunting sounds and dabs at her eyes with a handkerchief while Jimmy, Ben and Miriam look on in awe.

"…Call it divine intervention or a certain someone giving us a nudge in the right direction, but since that day, only one person in my life made sense, and that person is you."

"Oh, Elijah…" I'm overcome but feel a little shy with an audience.

He drops to his knee and takes my left hand. Looking up I see nothing but love radiating back at me. "So, all being said, if those present would give their blessing, I'd like to ask you to be my wife."

Helena jumps up and down on the spot clapping her hands.

I haven't said yes, yet.

This time it's Miriam who wipes her eyes.

Jimmy is beaming from ear to ear while I know it's bittersweet for Ben.

Despite how they all feel, I watch as each nod their head.

"Say something," Elijah adds.

"Yeah, go on," Helena interrupts, too excited to hold her tongue.

Miriam shushes her then waits for me to speak.

I'm genuinely overwhelmed and know what I want to say even though words fail me. Instead, I nod my head hoping that is enough.

"So, will you marry me?" Elijah asks again.

"Yes." My reply is a quiet but absolute one.

Weirdly, I touch the wedding ring I've never taken off. Now it feels like the right time, but he stops me before I can. "No," he says. "Leave it—"

"But..."

"I had the ring designed to fit around Jamie's."

"You did?" He never fails to surprise me.

"Don't ever take his ring off. It's part of your past, and in a weird way, mine too."

He slips his ring onto my finger. It fits perfectly and I can't stop looking at it. "It's beautiful, thank you."

"Just because you're marrying me doesn't mean you forget what Jamie was and is to you, okay, and that goes for all of you."

Helena and Miriam are sobbing noisily behind me. I'm close to joining them.

I see Ben fighting to retain his composure and want to hug him.

Jimmy looks on with pride. "I couldn't have said it better myself," he says. "Well done to you both."

As the sun goes down, my family congregates around us offering congratulations.

It's a Disney moment for me, and I can't wait to tell Louise. I'm just sorry she wasn't here to witness his proposal.

Chapter Thirty-One

Moving On

Life whizzes by, and while I can't forget the past, I've finally made peace with it.

I'm packing freshly laundered clothes into the new set of Louis Vuitton luggage set Elijah originally purchased for our honeymoon.

"Are you sure you have to go?" Elijah removes his glasses and curls his lip, pretending to sulk over my upcoming trip to America but is probably relieved at the idea of quiet time to work on his new book without constant wedding-themed interruptions.

His latest release, The Last Kiss, a semi-autobiographical piece was an international bestseller and knocked Julia Quinn off the top spot. It still sits in the top ten of The New York Times Best Sellers List after four months on sale. Readers devoured the love story between Sarah and Jason, and along with his publishers, who offered a huge advance, demanded a sequel. Adamant as he was not to be dictated to, eventually he was forced to concede. Pre-orders for The First Kiss have smashed records worldwide. My fiancé is truly at the top of his game.

"If you want me to marry you looking like a bride, then yes."

"I'd be more than happy to get married in ripped jeans at this year's Glastonbury Festival."

"It's a good job you're marrying me then and not Elly May Clampett from The Beverly Hillbillies. Muddy fields and wellies aren't my thing."

"You know what I mean."

"Is it all too much for you?" I've gone overboard on this wedding under the guise of celebration. But is there more to his dithering of late, I wonder?

"Not really, but you know I don't like all this fuss, let alone the idea of making a speech."

"Now you're an international celebrity, you should be used to being the centre of attention."

"All I want to do is write, the other crap I have zero interest in."

"I can see it bothers you, and as a simple nurse going about her day in a hospital, witnessing that level of fame up close is strange."

"You, my gorgeous girl, are more than just a simple nurse, and don't ever forget that."

"We're eerily similar in personality but worlds apart career wise." It's another aspect I like about our relationship. "That juxtaposition between us is interesting though."

"There's never a shortage of conversation, that's for sure, and though I get satisfaction from what I do, a part of me regrets outing myself."

"Really?" It's the first time he's expressed it so clearly. "You've never said so before."

"I think it's more to do with losing my privacy than telling the truth about who I was."

"That's understandable, Elijah."

"Seeing news reports of Kara's death played out in the media is no fun especially as she's not here to defend herself."

It was one of the most difficult days for him but there was nothing I could have done to shield him from that pain. He had to go on record and defend her to a judgemental society. "It wasn't fair on Kara, or you, but it'll die down when the press finds something more interesting to write about."

"You have more faith than I do, Serena. You saw those reporters last week, they practically stalked us from the house to the restaurant."

"The group of girls that followed us around Lakeland were more worrying to me than the gutter press."

"Weird," is all he says. "I'll never understand people like that."

"I found it quite amusing when I thought about it later on. After all I get to go home and share my bed with the hottie that is Elijah Hart."

"That's your bonus, what's mine?" His lips curl at either end.

"I'd rephrase that if I were you." He pulls me onto his knee and holds me tight. "Oi, I have packing to finish, there's no time for hanky panky."

"Leave it for now." He wraps his arms around my waist. "We have time, don't we?" His grin is that of a mischievous child and one I know so well. Elijah has a voracious appetite for all things between the sheets.

I could fight him off, but revel in these intimate moments. "So, go on, what were you going to say?"

"You keep me grounded."

"What do you mean?"

A more serious expression replaces the playful one. "The party we attended at the museum a few weeks ago, I didn't tell you at the time, but some dickhead offered me a bag of coke."

My blood boils and feels like molten lava surging through my veins. "What the hell? Why would anyone do that?"

"Dealers are everywhere and make a fortune from gullible idiots like I used to be. He cornered me in the toilet, right shady bastard he was. I've never met him before, but it made me more adamant than ever not to engage with that world. In fact, as soon as we got home, I emailed Penny and told her to decline any future invites to celebrity parties, no matter who sends them."

"Were you tempted to take it?"

"Absolutely not, but no matter how many years sit between now and my last hit, I'll always be a recovering addict and that's always at the forefront of my mind."

His confession bothers me. I've always seen him as a former addict, but he's right and recovery is his status quo until the day he dies. "You said no, I'm proud of you, baby."

"I left that world behind, Serena, and have no desire to lose control again. Besides that, I've got so much more to live for."

"I know." I wrap my arms around his neck and plant a lingering kiss on his cheek, wanting to offer comfort and reassurance. "You've changed so much in the time we've been together that I can't fathom the person you were before we met."

"The difference now is I feel loved and valued. That brings no end of confidence. But in a relationship when both are addicts and co-dependent, the next hit is the only thing that matters."

"I do love you, very much, I hope you know that, Elijah."

"You don't have to reinforce that, I feel it, I see it, every morning when I open my eyes and before I close them at night."

"Will you be okay if I go away?"

"Yeah, I'm just kidding with you. Besides, I would never stand between you and your dream gown."

"I can't wait for you to see it, but no sneaking a peek once I get it home, do you hear."

"You must know many hiding places after living here for so many years." We decided to stay in my house. It made sense and because Elijah has no hang ups over Jamie, it was also easier than finding somewhere else when this place has everything we need. The only thing we installed were security gates, a camera, and an intercom. Fans are wily creatures and on occasion have wandered up the driveway and rang our doorbell, wanting an audience with the man himself. It's a gross invasion of privacy that is part and parcel of his world, but having the gates installed stops them from coming closer to the house.

Following the move, Elijah put his swanky apartment up for sale. The following day he received an offer way above the asking price which was quickly accepted.

"Probably, but I trust you." That's not a lie, but there is no way I'll leave it in an unlocked room. Just in case he's tempted to look. I know I would be.

"With your custom-made Vera Wang wedding dress at stake and your fear of superstition of us seeing one another before the ceremony, don't tell fibs."

"I do." I kiss his soft lips.

"Hmm. Don't think distracting me will force a change in the subject."

"Okay, okay, I really do trust you, but just to make sure the dress is kept as safe as possible, she will be locked up."

"She?"

"Yes!"

"So, this magical dress might get up and walk away unless she's under lock and key, is that what you're telling me?"

"Yes, let's go for that, sounds reasonable enough to me." I'm trying to keep a straight face.

"You're crazy." He nibbles at my neck. "But I happen to love crazy."

I'm reduced to giggles "Then kiss me, you big strong brute."

"I wanna do so much more than that."

"You're the boss after all." I play the submissive role well, but outside of the bedroom, we're equals.

It took us a while to get to where we are mainly due to lack of confidence on my part, but our sex life is dynamic and exciting. He's everything I want and need in a lover and don't mention what's lurking below the belt line–wow.

"So, you keep telling me, but you misbehave quite often." He lifts me into his arms and walks toward the door.

"Only because I know you'll whisk me off to bed and reassert your masculinity."

"Crafty–I like it."

"Where are you taking me, Mr Hart?"

"Did I hear you say you fancied a soak in the jacuzzi?"

"No."

"I'm sure that's what you said."

"Well, if I did, you better hurry up because I don't want to miss my flight."

"Your wish is my command."

Two hours later he carries my luggage down the stairs. "Two cases, you're only going for four days."

"I need to be prepared." The limousine has arrived to take me, Miriam, Helena, and Louise to the airport. They're waiting for me in the car, so I can't be too long. I hold onto my man as long as I can. "I'm going to miss you, Elijah."

He strokes the back of my neck with his index finger. "Just enjoy yourself, it'll fly by."

"Yes, I know, but it's the longest we'll have been apart in ages."

"The girls will keep you entertained."

"We'll probably get deported knowing Helena."

"I've never known anyone to drink as much as her, aside from me way back then."

"She's never been any different." I thought motherhood would tame her but she's as wild as ever.

"Do you think she has a problem?" He asks because he genuinely cares for her, as she does him.

"Helena is the perennial party girl, and that's the only thing she has a problem with, realising she has to grow up and act responsibly."

"Keegan must never know what's coming next where she is concerned."

"The kids are her everything, but I think she enjoys cutting loose every now and again, whereas he is more the stay at home type."

"She seems to love working at Tate Technology with Jimmy."

"When I gave her the shares, I assumed she'd take the money and that would be that, but all credit to her, she wants to know every facet of the business, and as a shareholder, has every right to. Mother, and professional by day, party girl by night, that's her."

"Just be careful, I don't want to see my fiancé on the news being escorted out of some shithole bar in the big apple by the cops."

"She did mention something about that place featured in that movie Coyote Ugly."

"Is it even a real place?"

"No idea, but if it's there, Helena will find it."

"God help New York City."

"Hurricane Helena is about to blow in and they don't know she's coming."

Chapter Thirty-Two

Wedding Fever

I'm gripped by wedding fever, and thankfully I have Miriam, Helena, and Louise to accompany me on these trips, though this time we're a little farther from home.

Currently, we're walking down Fifth Avenue in New York City.

Organising the wedding has become an albatross around my neck, but the finish line is in sight. "Over the last few weeks, I've eaten enough cake to sink a battleship and really don't think I want dried fruit after all."

"Then have whatever you like," Louise urges, marvelling at the city that never sleeps. "It's your day after all." Her being with us means the world to me, and despite a spell in hospital, she's doing well, and life is good again. We're both aware it isn't forever but choose to focus on the here and now.

"Elijah loves dried fruit though."

"Then have as many tiers as you like but a different flavour for each one."

I'm in agreement with Louise and her words tip the decision in my favour. "Is it wrong to have four tiers—dried fruit, lemon, chocolate and red velvet?"

"Not at all," Miriam adds.

"It's done then, four tiers it is."

"I'll call the bakery later and confirm. It won't take too much effort to add the extra tier."

"What about this store?" Helena points at a huge sign that says Saks Fifth Avenue. "You might find something you like in there, Mum."

"It's a bit above my price range, darling."

"Nonsense," I say knowing she's being too careful. I know how much Jimmy earns and what their shares in the company are worth and what dividends are paid out on a monthly basis too. "You can afford it."

"Go on then." She admits defeat.

We enter the enormous building, marvelling at its interior and find the right floor.

Miriam tries on an assortment of hats. The one she is currently modelling looks like it's been designed by Big Bird from Sesame Street. It's saucer shaped with yellow feathers of every shade sticking out at every angle. "What do you think of this, girls?"

"You look like a muppet." Helena is as subtle as a sledgehammer but says what we're all thinking though we would have been a little kinder in our delivery of the criticism.

The assistant smirks then bows her head.

"Oh, that's a lovely way to speak about your mother," Miriam replies, slamming it back onto the mannequin's head.

"Too many feathers, Mum, and you know dad has allergies. Nobody wants to hear him coughing his spleen up during the vows."

I've saddled myself with a crazy lot, but it's been so much fun. "If you like it, Miriam, you wear it," I say.

"No, Helena is right. I'm not sitting next to Jimmy while he's having a sneezing fit."

"You'll find something, Mum."

"What about this?" Louise adds, picking up something classic with a small veil.

"Oooh, I like that," She takes it and plonks it atop her head. "But can I get away with a veil?"

"Pull it down a bit and it might hide those bags under your eyes," Helena says, still not missing a beat.

I'm dying to laugh, as are the rest of our group, but that's the nature of their relationship.

"I'll throttle you in a minute, my girl."

Louise is bent double while the assistant makes a snorting noise. "You ladies should be on Broadway."

"Just kidding, Mum. That is a lovely hat."

"It is." We all nod and agree. "Plus, it matches the dress you bought earlier."

"It suits you," the assistant adds, totting up her commission.

"That's it then. Sold. I'm having it."

"What time is it?" Louise suddenly asks, squinting at her watch. "Hells bells. Forty-five minutes and Serena has her final dress fitting. We can't be late, girls."

I'm nervous. What if they hate it? Does it really matter when I love it so much? It's definitely me and I know Elijah will love it too. A few months back I flew stateside with him and looked at some raw designs though he has no idea what the finished dress will look like. "Come on, let's pay for this hat, then head over to Vera Wang's. If we're lucky, they have the champers chilling already."

"Sounds good to me." Helena leads the pack and drags us toward the cashier.

Once the hat is paid for, we trek across the city to Vera Wang's Bridal House Ltd. It's the swankiest and no expense has been spared–we want it to be a celebration and not about budget.

"I can't wait to see you in the dress." Miriam has been a Godsend during this process. Nothing has been too much trouble for her. "You'll have to forgive me if I cry."

"Me too." Louise says.

"And me." It's a given Helena will cry.

The day itself is destined to be magical, not least because Louise and Helena will act as my joint Maids of Honour while Jimmy has kindly agreed to give me away.

"Can we try our dresses on today too?"

"I imagine so, yes."

"Fan-friggin'-tastic."

Miriam's eyes narrow. "Helena, we didn't fly thousands of miles for you to start speaking like a trucker."

"Elijah swears and you never tell him off."

"It's not ladylike."

"Whatever." She chunners away under her breath about Saint Elijah but is only joking.

"Did you say something, darling?"

"No, Mother, I did not."

"Keep it that way."

She looks to me for help. I wave my hands in front of myself, not wanting to get involved.

It's a miracle Elijah slots in so well with us all but we're an unconventional mix.

We walk along the sidewalk arm in arm, and I'm reminded of Sex and the City, one of my favourite shows.

Louise suddenly stops dead. "By the way, I've been meaning to ask. What's the deal with the transplant business? Are you going to tell the guests because I don't want to put my foot in it?"

"We don't want to cause any fuss, so we've agreed as a family to keep it to ourselves."

"Got ya." She drags a finger across her lips.

The subject was a bone of contention at first. But for Elijah's sake it made the most sense.

I'm dragged along the sidewalk listening to their chatter and soon enough we're standing outside Vera's Bridal House. I feel the fluttering of butterflies in my tummy.

It's been a year since Elijah proposed. We hadn't intended on waiting so long, but another round of book signings and promotional tours of the UK pushed us back somewhat. I look on it as something that was meant to be. Plus, it allowed me time to find the dress of my dreams.

We're invited into the inner sanctum—I feel like I've entered a holy space.

"It's out of this world." I look at the dresses hanging perfectly on the mannequins.

"This way." Naomi, my assistant for the day is friendly and inviting. Walking through the double doors I see bottles chilling in ice buckets. "Please help yourself to Champagne." Then, I'm whisked away into a separate room and helped into my dress.

A team of dress fitters help fix the Medieval-style bridal crown—known as the Safran Headpiece—with oversized pearls, in place. "Are you ready to see yourself, Serena?"

"Should I be this scared?" I close my eyes, terrified I won't look as I imagined.

"Most brides feel the same way, but you look sensational." She helps me up onto the small platform. "Open your eyes."

I've chosen a Princess Mikado wedding dress with long sleeves. It's an unorthodox ballroom gown in off-white mikado and has sparkly Chantilly lace inserts and row buttons on the illusion back and sleeves. "Now?"

"Whenever you're ready."

I open my eyes, dazzled by the dress and how well it fits. Mirrors surround me so I can see this magnificent creation and how it clings to my body at every angle. "Oh, my..." *Don't cry*, I tell myself. *Don't cry.* I turn slowly, taking in every shimmer and flow of material. "It's the most beautiful dress I've ever seen." Completely forgetting I'm not alone until I hear sniffing sounds from behind me, I turn to look at Miriam,

Helena, and Louise as they blow their noses in unison, too overwhelmed to speak. "Do you like it?"

They all nod. "I think that's a resounding yes," Naomi says.

"It-it's just…" Louise blows her nose again. "…you are flawless."

"Do you like the crown?"

"I love it," Helena adds in between sobs. "You look like a Princess."

"Simply breath-taking," Miriam finally speaks while trying to contain herself. "I didn't think it would affect me this much, but–"

"Don't upset yourself, Mum." She links her arm through Miriam's.

"This isn't about your brother by the way…it's just I never thought I'd find my smile again."

"You're not smiling, you're crying and making a right mess of yourself."

"I know, I'm being silly, but this is a moment to celebrate."

"Serena is a lucky lady," Louise adds. "Some people never get to find love once, never mind twice, embrace it."

I twirl again, slowly, mesmerised by the dress. "I couldn't have picked anything more perfect for me."

"Except for Elijah," Miriam reminds me.

"Aside from him I mean." Now, my wedding day can't come soon enough.

Later that evening we sit down for our last meal before flying home tomorrow morning.

We are on our second Cosmopolitan of the evening. It's well deserved. From my point of view, the trip has been a successful one. "Do you like your dresses?"

"It's so pretty, and I love the colour," Helena adds, happy with her cassis V-Neck Halter Gown with the slit up the side I knew she would love. "What about you, Lou?"

"It's gorgeous."

"What about the colour?"

"Amethyst is my favourite," Louise adds.

"I remembered you telling me." One is a greyish-purple while the other is reddish-purple. Both compliment the other perfectly. "Are you both sure because there is still time to change them when we get home."

"I'm keeping mine," Helena says.

"Me too," Louise agrees though hers is a different cut without the halter neck. "It's totally my style and doesn't reveal too much of my skin."

"You both looked sensational, in fact you all did." I don't want to leave Miriam out. "It all feels so real now," I admit. "Before this trip, everything seemed so far away, and I pushed it to the back of mind. Now it's right around the corner."

"From what you've told us." Louise has asked but I've only shared so much. "It's going to be a day to remember."

"Jimmy agreeing to give me away is the pinnacle—aside from Ben, there is nobody else that could have done it."

"He wouldn't let you down on such a special occasion."

"It must be hard for him."

"I don't think hard is the right word." Miriam knows him better than any of us. "Jimmy's happy for you, but for all of us that knew Jamie, it brings it all back somewhat."

"I've cried a lot lately." I hadn't intended saying anything, but it feels right to be open about it. "Jamie was my entire world so it's odd now that I'm marrying somebody else."

"Till death us do part," Miriam adds. "You honoured your vows and so did Jamie, nothing more could have been asked of either of you."

Her words are poignant and hit me hard. "Nothing else would have torn us apart." The mood has taken a downward turn. "Come on, finish your drink, Helena wants to find this Coyote Ugly place."

"I'm not dancing on any bars at my age," Miriam adds before downing the last of her cocktail.

"Oh, I am," Louise confirms, though that isn't a surprise. "Flames and all."

"Me too," Helena decides.

I shake my head at this motley crew before me and realise how lucky I am. "You're all bloody mad!"

Chapter Thirty-Three

In Dreams

Standing at the altar, before God, we'd spoken our vows to one another.

Finally, Elijah and I are on the cusp of marriage.

Father Lawton draws the service to a close but there is one last line the congregation waits with bated breath for. "…You may kiss the bride."

For the first time as man and wife, our lips meet, as applause rings out in the packed church.

Our kiss is full of passion though a respect for the church is observed.

We turn to face our friends and family to rousing cheers then make our way down the aisle.

"I don't know about you, but I need a drink," Elijah whispers in my ear.

"Make mine a double." So far, it's been a day I'll never forget, but now it's done, the stress melts away.

"You're on."

Well-wishers congratulate us as we pass them.

At the doors to the church, Francois, the wedding photographer, is poised to capture us for posterity.

"I hate having my picture taken."

"You look like a movie star," Elijah encourages.

"Look at me," Francois instructs. "Now this way…and smile, Elijah. Yes, yes, yes, the camera loves you."

I think it's more a case of Francois having a thing for my husband. I don't mind because he's mine.

"Serena, this way, yes, and one, two, three, big smile."

Elijah and I follow direction well and pose like never before. We move from one end of the church gardens to the other. Another pose, click, smile, then a final pose.

We climb into the white Rolls Royce where we share another kiss, though this is less chaste than before.

"I love you, Mrs Hart."

Hearing my new name catches me by surprise. "Oh, wow, that will take some getting used to."

"I suppose it will."

There was never any question of me not taking his name. "Are you ready for the next part?"

"Can we skip the rest and head straight to Portofino?" It's a fishing village on the Italian Riviera coastline, southeast of Genoa city, and my surprise wedding gift from Elijah.

"Don't tempt me."

"It will be over soon, but it will be nice to celebrate with our friends and family."

"Yeah, you're right though my side is a little thin on the ground."

"The important people turned up and that's all that matters."

"True."

The chauffeur drives slowly. I turn and see a fleet of cars following behind and pray it won't alert the media to the venue. We've done everything to throw them off the scent. There's no magazine deal in place because the day is sacred to us.

As we arrive at the stately home where our reception is to be held, I see helicopters flying overhead. Luckily for us, the wedding planners anticipated the intrusion and erected tents so cars can drive right up to the door without the paparazzi snapping them. It also means they won't get a picture of my dress.

We asked all guests to leave their mobile phones in their car just in case something was posted to social media in error.

An hour later, we've finished the wedding breakfast and it's time for the speeches.

 Elijah and I are seated at the top table, with Jimmy and Miriam to my right. To his left is best man Tony, an old school friend, and one of the only people he speaks to from his past.

Tony stands and brings order to the room. "Invited guests, welcome, now please give a big cheer for Jimmy."

The room erupts into applause as Miriam ushers Jimmy to his feet.

He clears his throat.

Memories of the speech he made when I married Jamie march back into my mind. It's not lost on me how special a moment this is, that he's agreed to speak for me.

There is silence as he begins. "I'm not one to dwell on the past, but everyone here knows why I wanted to be the one to give Serena away..." He takes a cleansing breath.

I think of my make-up as emotions swell within because never in my wildest dreams would I ever have imagined my former father-in-law taking on such a monumental task.

"Serena was married to my son Jamie for nearly twenty years, but their own happily ever after wasn't to be."

I can see how hard it is for him and look to Miriam as her eyes are proudly focused on her husband.

"Now, when I met this young man, it was easy to see the love he feels for her. It was almost palpable..." His voice cracks and I see the frustration in his eyes because I know he will have rehearsed what he wants to say. Understandably, the moment is overwhelming for him. "...like it was meant to be." He waves his hand, defeated by the swelling tide of emotion.

Miriam stands to offer the support he needs and links her arm through his. But it's too hard and he cannot continue.

With a small cough she takes the reins. "My son meant the world to his family and many others here, he still does…" She pauses for a few seconds. "In Serena we found the most amazing daughter-in-law and though today is a special one, it is tinged with sadness for me, but none of that negates the joy I feel for her, that we all feel for her, and Elijah of course…" She takes another breath and lifts her glass. "So, please raise your glasses and join me in wishing them all the happiness they deserve." She raises her glass. "To happiness."

A cheer rings out. "To happiness."

Applause follows as Elijah leans over. "Thank you both," he says, nodding their way.

Miriam hasn't quite finished. "May I just add that Serena and Elijah will always be a part of our family and we couldn't be happier they have found true love in one another."

"Thank you, both," I add, deeply moved.

Jimmy finds his voice again. "It's all we ever wanted for her, and what they both deserve." He lifts his glass too. "To Elijah and Serena."

Elijah and I raise our glasses as Tony stands again. Once more, he gently taps the crystal flute he's holding, allowing its chimes to bring order to the hullabaloo.

Then, he speaks the words I know Elijah's been dreading for months. "And now it's time to hear from the groom."

As the room breaks out in applause and support, he kisses my cheek, then forces himself to his feet, hating tradition and all it stands for.

There is absolute silence as all eyes focus on him. This is a far cry from the many book signings Elijah's attended but I can see he wants to run and hide. He won't because it's important that he does this, despite me telling him we can dispense with the formality of speeches.

I look up at him, proud that he's my husband.

"I'd like to thank you all for being here today to celebrate what is the happiest day of my life." He speaks slowly and with confidence, choosing his words carefully. "Serena is everything to me, my life, my present and my future. She's also my past and I can't let this moment go by without paying tribute to an amazing man that can't be here today."

I've no idea where he's going with his speech. "Elijah...?" I gently tap his arm.

"It's okay, I want to do this."

I look to Miriam and Jimmy to my left. They shrug their shoulders.

"The man I speak of, I wasn't fortunate to meet, though many here were lucky enough to."

Now I know what's coming, I feel a flutter of panic. "Elijah, what on Earth are you doing?"

"I'm sorry, Serena, but I have to do this." He looks to Miriam and Jimmy. They nod their heads, giving him what he needs, while our guests look on in confusion. "Please, it's important to me."

"Okay."

"To him, I have this to say; I am alive, and have a future with this beautiful woman because of your generosity, and while I hadn't planned on revealing this now, he deserves to be honoured."

"You don't have to do this, Elijah."

"As a family, blended or otherwise, it was agreed what I am about to say would remain private, and yes, there may be a few gathered here that may find it odd, but it's fitting he plays a part in this, our, special day." He looks into my eyes for approval to carry on. It's not my decision any longer, but what he feels he has to do.

"Do it," I say.

"So…" I hear the tremor in his voice. He's determined to speak his truth and while the assembled guests look at one another in a confused state, Elijah tries to carry on. "I-I…"

"Take a deep breath, honey, it will be fine. They will all understand."

He closes his eyes and takes a moment to himself.

A smattering of applause rings out and pushes him forward.

"The truth is, I used to be a very different person to the one most of you know now and as a result of my poor choices, I suffered heart failure and required an urgent transplant."

He not only holds the room in the palm of his hands, but me too.

"The fact is, I was ashamed of my past and didn't believe I was good enough…"

A few guests' applause.

He holds his hand up because he's not finished. "…I felt like the luckiest man alive, that I'd been sprinkled with a kind of magic, that I'd finally found my soulmate, but more importantly, in Serena I felt a kindred spirit, like we were, are, meant to be. It felt like we'd met before, somewhere, somehow."

I reach out for his trembling hand and stand at his side. "You're doing fine," I encourage.

He kisses me quickly but tenderly.

"As it turns out, fate seems to have played its role because a part of me had indeed known her before our initial meeting." He kisses the top of my hand. "You see, with

Jamie's passing, I was offered another chance at life." He allows his words to sink in.

Looking about the room, their expressions tell me most understand what he's hoping to convey.

"Neither Serena, nor I had any idea, but Jamie was my donor." He places his hand where the scar is and takes another deep breath.

Gasps ring out around the room, and even the serving staff abandon their duties to look our way.

Emotion finally takes over and renders him unable to speak.

Ben and Helena are suddenly on their feet. They're protective of him.

Serena, help him, Helena mouths.

He leans on me for support and somehow, I find the strength to speak when he no longer can. Confidently I address the room. "When I lost Jamie, I fell into a pit of despair, but through the pain and agony of existing without him, I could hear his voice in my mind, urging me to move on and find a purpose." I turn to look at Miriam and Jimmy.

They flash smiles my way.

"That voice told me I still had so much to give and slowly, I picked myself up, dusted myself off and found a wonderful group and a treasured friend sitting just there called Louise…"

She stands and blows me a kiss.

"…who gently pushed me to rejoin the world. Then, and when I least expected it, I met Elijah and felt an instant connection." I look about the room. "You all know how practical I am, but some things can't ever be explained, and even though I still can't tell you how, I knew Elijah was the one."

Another burst of applause.

"I felt safe with him, certain he'd always look after me. But the strangest part of it all…" I pause for a moment. "…I never told anyone this but from the day Jamie died, I dreamed of him every night, and in those dreams, he would be standing at our gate, beckoning me toward him." I'm struggling to get through this. "And as hard as I tried, I could never reach him. But that first night with Elijah was the last time I saw Jamie and the difference was, I did reach him that time."

I hear a few ah's from the guests.

"There were no words spoken between us. He kissed the palm of my hand then turned and faded away."

I hear a few people crying.

"I didn't know what to think but now I know it was him giving his blessing, that he could move on, that he didn't need to stay behind and protect me anymore."

"I love you," Elijah whispers into my ear.

"But it turned out to be something more because with Elijah comes a part of Jamie which means he is still with me." I can feel my legs shaking. "Against all the odds, Jamie knew his heart had found its way back to me."

Miriam looks at us wide-eyed. She clings to Jimmy while Helena and Ben have made their way to the top table. They stand behind us, their support unwavering.

Elijah is ready to speak again. "I had vivid dreams of a woman, so far out of reach that I couldn't see her face, then I met Serena and I knew she was the one who came to me when I dreamed. We were destined to meet and fall in love, and not just because of Jamie or his amazing gift of life, but because she is a kind, gracious and beautiful soul who deserves to be happy."

"Thank you, my darling."

"And while I can never thank Jamie personally, I promise to guard this heart beating inside my chest and protect the woman it loves with every fibre of my being."

I watch as many of our friends and family pull out their handkerchiefs. It's a touching moment for us all, but the truth is finally told.

"So, without further ado, I'd like to ask you all to raise your glasses."

I pick mine up and the rest of the guests swiftly follow suit.

"To Jamie," he says.

A loud chorus of 'TO JAMIE,' rings out, and most of the guests are visible wrecks.

Jimmy leans in. "I'm so proud of you both."

Elijah holds me in his arms, but I'm not quite done. "To Elijah, my wonderful husband."

"To Elijah," our chorus of guests' roar.

I'm unbelievably moved by the unexpected moment. It means Elijah isn't standing in Jamie's shadow on our special day. He embraces who Jamie was and is to so many. It's a testament to the man he has become.

I fall back into Elijah's arms, blissfully happy.

Tony takes over again. "And now the bride and groom will share their first dance as Mr and Mrs Hart."

Elijah walks me to the edge of the dancefloor.

This is another moment he's terrified of, but I'll do all I can to help him.

"This way, my love." He leads me to the centre of the dancefloor. It's my turn in the spotlight though I'd happily forfeit it too. "It's time for me to show you what a horrible dancer I am."

"Just follow my lead," I whisper.

"Okay."

I know the idea of dancing in front of an audience horrifies him, but I try to calm his nerves. "You'll be fine, just look into my eyes and it'll be over soon."

He chose the song for our first dance.

I have no idea what it is.

"Are you ready for this?"

I'm too worried for him and take little notice as the song begins. "Not really," I whisper.

"It's fast become one of my favourite songs," he says as we sway.

Realisation suddenly hits me. "This is..." Words sit on the tip of my tongue. It can't be coincidental.

"I'd never heard it until about two weeks ago, then I knew it was perfect for us."

"*In Dreams* was Jamie's favourite song."

"Why doesn't that surprise me?" He's beaming from ear to ear.

I look over to the head table where my family are. They all nod their approval. "Shall we dance?" I ask.

"We better had," he replies, "or the song will be over."

"Let's do this."

In the blink of an eye, he transforms from the guy with two left feet into Fred Astaire and spins me around the floor. "Surprise," he says sporting a huge grin.

A thunder of approval spurs me on. I can't hide my joy as it feels like we're soaring through the clouds, weightless, dancing like nobody else is watching.

The cheers from family and friends tell me he's done good, but his smile is all I need to bolster me.

"You learned to dance?"

"I didn't want to show you up on our wedding day."

"I'm so proud of you, Elijah."

He pulls me close to him.

I allow myself a quick journey back to the past, to the damaged soul believing her life was over. Now looking up into his eyes, no words are needed to convey what is true love everlasting. Not only am I lost to the dance but the poignant lyrics to a song that now belongs to the three of us.

Syncopated, we move to the gentle rhythm of the music as our guests take to the floor to join us.

As I gaze into his eyes, the final words of the song usher in our new beginning as husband and wife.

THE END

A Note from the Author

Not everyone gets a second chance. If you do get one, take advantage of it because it's a gift, and it may be something better than you had before!
(Quote: Nishan Panwar)

Thank you for reading 'THIS HEART WILL LOVE AGAIN.'

I am extremely proud of this book. I truly hope you enjoyed it.

It belongs to you now...

DHANI

X

More from the Author

"True Love Is Written in the Stars... At least, that's how it appears."

For Raven, only child of ruling President, Phillipe Andre, and his wife, Adriana Andre, First Lady of the Republic of the United Kingdom, losing her beloved husband, Dalton, in a tragic accident robbed her of her happy ever after.

Whispers speak of a way; a chance for her to gaze into his eyes one final time, but this route remains forbidden to all.

Those who rule guard the secret, but there are always those who will talk and others only too willing to listen.

Confronting her father, Raven must convince him to break the laws of the land and send her to a place no other has ever journeyed to before.

LOCKDOWN LOVE

"Nothing has to change. It's not as though it's the first time I've kissed a guy."

As the world is held in the grips of a global pandemic, straight, handsome, athletic builder, Damon Boyd, is forced into lockdown.

His only company is gay, primary school teacher and housemate, Joey Reynolds.

Bonding over their love of superhero movies and buoyed by their shared love of good food, drink and company, harmony exists between the pair.

As time passes, growing anxieties force Damon permanently behind closed doors, leaving Joey to take care of everyday chores outside of the house.

But while sequestered, their friendship grows, and a spark is soon ignited between them.

Only Joey has the courage to fully acknowledge the change in dynamics, yet stealing a drunken kiss pushes them further into friend zone.

Damon refuses to admit what he is truly feeling, and believing the best way to re-assert his sexuality, he takes a risk that could have devastating consequences for them both.

ALONE

"I shoulda been there—ride or die, Rox, ride or die."

With his marriage in tatters and the country struggling to emerge from the grips of the pandemic, ex-army mechanic Dallas McCall makes the biggest mistake of his life, resulting in many of his crew serving prison time.

Abandoned, he's left out in the cold—alone, with no wife or loyal brothers to fall back on.
With only one friend left in town, Dallas knows he lives on borrowed time, but scrambles to get enough cash together to leave Billings, Montana when a blast from the past re-enters his life begging for another chance.

Steadfast in his refusal to cast aside his own heartbreak, sending her into the night opens an opportunity for his unforgiving ex-crew members to exact revenge for what they view as the ultimate act of betrayal.

Acknowledgements

Angel Nevaeh – thank you for riding this wave with me and supporting me while writing this book.

Raven Canely & Cheryl Blackburn – your guidance continues to be appreciated. Thank you!

Lara Luck – thank you for coordinating my Street Team. You are a busy lady but totally kick ass with it!

Dhani's Dharlings. These wonderful women stepped in to help me out of the kindness of their hearts. I knew nothing and still have a lot to learn, but I appreciate everyone for taking me under the protective wings and helping me to fly.

To all who come to play in Dhani's Devilish Tongue –thank you for taking a chance on a new author.

And to the many authors and PA's who reached out to support me and invite me into your wonderful groups – your kindness is appreciated, and I hope one day I can be there when you need me.

My editing and formatting team. Thank you for shaping my work so I can present it as beautifully as possible.

Harsha – Thank you for taking my design idea and bringing it to life. The cover fits the story perfectly.

With love and gratitude

DHANI

X

About the Author

Dhani Ewing is a Best-Selling Author who was born and raised in Liverpool.

As an only child, he grew up with his single mother in a warm and loving environment. To this day, she remains his best friend.

Recently completing a medical degree, he travelled to America during his gap year, but was forced to return to England due to the global pandemic.

Once home, he set his mind to conquering a life-long dream of writing.

Finding immediate success with his debut novella, 'THE STRANGER', writing has now become a full-time hobby with many planned releases to follow.

As well as a burgeoning writing career, Dhani has started a three year core training course in psychiatry.

Life is busy but stay tuned... there is so much more to come!